THE SURVIVALIST 15
OVERLORD

There was a whooshing sound, then a whistling, then a roar as a grenade from the multi-barrelled grenade launcher exploded into the Russian position. Bodies sailed into the cold night sky.

Rourke found cover behind a wide ice ridge that signalled a crevasse below, touched his finger to the trigger of the M-16, burning through ten rounds, shifting the muzzle and doing it again. Bodies fell as Russians died.

Then Rourke was on his feet, changing sticks, ramming the fresh thirty-round magazine up the well. He started forward around the edge of the crevasse.

And then his footing was suddenly gone, and he was plummeting downward into the dark emptiness of the bottomless chasm . . .

The Survivalist series by Jerry Ahern published by New English Library:

The Survivalist 15 Overlord

Jerry Ahern

NEW ENGLISH LIBRARY
Hodder and Stoughton

Copyright © 1987 by Jerry
Ahern

First published in the USA in
1987 by Kensington Publishing
Corporation

NEL Paperback 1987

Printed and bound in Great Britain
for Hodder and Stoughton
Paperbacks, a division of Hodder
and Stoughton Ltd., Mill Road,
Dunton Green, Sevenoaks, Kent.
TN13 2YA.
(Editorial Office: 47 Bedford
Square, London WC1B 3DP) by
Cox & Wyman Ltd., Reading.

British Library C.I.P.
Ahern, Jerry
    Overland. —
    (The Survivalist: 15).
    I. Title   II. Series
    813'.54 [F]   PS3557.H4/

ISBN 0-450-41348-9

For George's friends Mike, Annette and Rick — keep fighting those slimy tentacles, guys —

Chapter One

Predictably the leader of the reconnaissance patrol had sent one man ahead. John Rourke waited for him in the rocks as the man entered the gorge, the man's assault rifle at the ready. Rourke imagined the man's knuckles would have been white if they could have been seen beneath the heavy winter gloves the man wore.

Rourke's own knuckles were white — of his right hand only, the hand which gripped the hollow handled Crain Life Support System X, hand-made for him five centuries ago by the Weatherford, Texas knifemaker, a knife John Rourke had saved for his son but which his son no longer would need. But John Rourke needed it.

It was a special knife, longer in both blade and handle than Jack Crain's usual fighting/survival knives, almost the dimensions of a short sword, the blade an even foot in length, saw-toothed along the spine, the recurving Bowie-like false edge as sharp as the primary edge.

Rourke waited where the gorge narrowed. It was the logical place. The man coming through the gorge ahead of his patrol, if he were any good at all, would anticipate this as the most logical place to be attacked and be doubly vigilant.

John Rourke waited, slowly moving his left hand upward and cross body to meet with his right, his right hand held high, above shoulder height, the System X pointing upward, Rourke's back flat against the cold of the rock wall of the narrow waist of the gorge.

The gorge was only eight feet across here and, logic again dictated, the Soviet trooper would make the wise decision and walk along the precise center, thereby keeping a safe distance from either wall. The gorge walls were pockmarked with indentations, some large enough to hide a man from plain view. It was in one of these where Rourke himself hid.

But the angle of the indentation was such that Rourke could, by keeping his face at its very edge, easily observe. The man was some eight feet back along the gorge, entering into this narrowest part, his pace slowing, the rifle moving into a better semblance of a hard assault position than it had been earlier. Rourke could see the man's gloved right first finger edged just outside the trigger guard. Rourke heard a telltale click over the shifting and scratching sounds of loose gravel. It would be the safety of the man's rifle, being moved to the burst fire position.

John Rourke waited, his left fist closing over the base of the System X's handle, his right hand edging slightly upward and tighter against the massive matte stainless steel guard.

Rourke took a deep breath and held it, edging back slightly as the man he was about to kill drew closer.

Both Rourke's hands tightened their interlaced grip. He could hear the man's slightly labored breathing, the rattle of some item of equipment or another.

Beneath the man's chin was a metallic framework, the framework holding a microphone just below the level of the man's lips. The microphone would be on, someone with the main body of the man's unit monitoring the fact that the man kept breathing, listening for some untoward sound that would betray an encounter with foul play which would then alert the unit. It was for this reason, its almost total soundlessness, that John Rourke had chosen the method for the advance man's death.

The Soviet soldier was even with Rourke now—it crossed Rourke's mind that the soldier was "dead even" with him. Rourke stepped from the rock indentation with his left foot, his left leg extending outward, his right leg sweeping after it. Rourke's body weight pivoted on the ball of his left foot as his right foot came down, both fists, the arms following, snapping outward to maximum extension, arcing the primary edge of the Crain knife toward the throat of the Soviet scout.

The man was young, his eyes were brown, a startled look coming to them as he started to shout.

The primary edge of the System X connected, Rourke's full body weight behind it now, torquing the blade through muscle, flesh and bone, the expression of surprise in the brown eyes freezing there as the head severed from the body. Rourke, without his customary aviator style sunglasses, squinted, averting his eyes as the blood spurted from the stump atop the now headless torso . . .

John Thomas Rourke had always felt it erroneous to label character traits as good or evil—it was, instead, how such traits manifested themselves that was subject to moral judgment. Vladmir Karamatsov was consistent, consistent in his practice of evil, which was an evil, but consistent in other things as well. It was another manifestation of Karamatsov's consistency for which John Rourke found himself now quite pleased—the predictability of the man. Habitually, as Karamatsov's troops moved eastward, Karamatsov, or more likely one of his underlings, with Karamatsov's full acquiescence, dispatched recon patrols in tandem, going off at oblique angles to the column's line of march (as best terrain allowed) and ahead of the slow-moving army. A solitary Soviet gunship would move directly over the line of march and ahead, back and forth, covering the immediate ground over which the column would move.

It was one of the twin reconnaissance patrols which

Rourke, Natalia Anastasia Tiemerovna beside him, now observed, the patrol's point man the soldier whom Rourke had just killed.

Rourke looked up from their line of march and across the gorge which the patrol now entered. He could not see Paul Rubenstein, nor any of the commandos of New Germany. And that was very good.

Rourke glanced at Natalia, their eyes meeting, his eyes rivetting to the almost surreal blueness of hers. He thought for an instant of the brown eyes of the dead soldier, perhaps the newest soul to join the ranks of those who died for ideologies they did not comprehend, simply to serve the ego of a dictator. He let his eyes drift past Natalia. A half dozen German commandos, armed, ready.

It was a risky operation, but a reconnaissance patrol would perforce possess maps potentially useful as intelligence data; and the officer leading the patrol and perhaps his senior non-com would have valuable data in their heads, to be sure.

Sixteen persons attacking twenty-three men from ambush — the dead soldier with the brown eyes had been the twenty-fourth — with the element of surprise in their favor was not the risky part. The risky part was attempting to take as many live prisoners as possible. Corpses provided little knowledge except to the budding anatomist or the pathologist, but neither of these disciplines was a concern at the moment.

But he had hedged against the risk. Immediately after killing the point man, Rourke had plugged his own microphone unit — earlier liberated from another hapless Russian — into the belt pack of the dead man's radio, maintaining the regular breathing, murmuring the Russian equivalent for "shit" into the unit and then indicating he had slipped and fallen. And now the faked radio transmission was kept up by a soldier of New Germany in Argentina who marched on a respectable distance ahead of the Russians he

10

was trying to deceive, marched on in Soviet battle dress utilities lest Karamatsov's roving helicopter should for some reason diverge from its customary path and observe him, marching on to keep the distance right on the radio transmission, keep up the sound of labored breathing from exertion in the cold, thin mountain air.

John Rourke settled the Steyr-Mannlicher SSG on his shoulder, the bolt already worked, a boat-tail 7.62mm already up the spout. Silently, he worked off the SSG's safety, settling the crosshairs of the 3x9 variable over the backpack radio being carried by the second man on the far side. Each individual soldier had his helmet radio, the power unit attached to his belt, the range of the individual units less than a mile in terrain as mountainous as this.

It was the patrol radio which could reach the column and summon help. The distance to the column was too great for the sound of gunfire to carry. Rourke eased his breathing, the first finger of his right hand snapping off the set trigger at the rear of the trigger guard, then moving to where it nearly touched the forward trigger, this now set to trip when barely nudged.

Rourke licked his lips, taking a deep breath, holding it a moment, then letting almost all of it go, locking the rest inside his throat.

His right first finger twitched, the Steyr Special Rifle bucking against his right shoulder, the image in the scope blurring, the crack — and then a shout from the gorge as the Soviet trooper fell forward, his radio backpack shattering, pieces flying everywhere. Rourke was up, handing off the SSG to one of the German commandos, moving, clambering over the rocks behind which they had hidden, shouting, "Follow me!", running.

Suppressive fire was coming from the rocks on the other side of the gorge, the Russians turning their attention away from Rourke and Natalia and the men with them for a precious instant. Rourke threw the M-16 forward on its sling, his thumb finding the safety tumbler, levering it to auto, the assault rifle at his hip now. The reconnaissance patrol started into defensive positions.

Two troopers with portable missile launchers strapped to their backs were starting to run further along the course of the gorge. Rourke swung the muzzle of the M-16 toward them, firing. The first man went down, a line of wounds stitched across the small of his back beneath his equipment, the second man turning to fire, Rourke cutting him down with a burst across the upper arm and across the chest and into the throat, the body still spinning as it fell.

Natalia shouted from behind him. Rourke sidestepped as he wheeled, gunfire plowing the ground where Rourke had just stood, Natalia's assault rifle opening up, a tall, burly Soviet soldier on the opposite side of the gorge going down. Rourke looked right—the Soviet officer and his non-com, the officer with a small submachinegun and the non-com with an assault rifle, were shooting their way out of the trap, running back the way they had come.

"Natalia!" Rourke started after them, at the far left edge of his peripheral vision seeing Natalia do the same.

As the two men crossed through the narrowest portion of the waist of the gorge, there was a single blur, then another just after it. Paul jumped from the high rocks, tackling the officer, one of the German commandos doing the same, sacking the non-com.

Rourke, Natalia beside him, closed quickly with them. Rourke stepped in between Paul and the Russian as the Soviet officer pulled away and started to his feet. The M-16's flash deflector tipped the officer at the base of the jaw, the head snapping back, Paul grabbing the man by the front of his parka, the partially stunned Russian reaching for the pistol at his belt, Paul's right fist crossing the already bloodied mouth, putting the man down.

Rourke wheeled right, the German commando on his knees, both fists balled as though they held some invisible baseball bat, the fists lacing the Soviet non-com across the mouth as the man tried to get up. The commando sagged forward over the man. Rourke could see Natalia rifle-butting another Soviet trooper in the crotch, then knee smashing to the side of his head. The others from Paul's original position on the far side of the gorge had closed with the Russians now, the two elements of the German commando unit having all but subdued the ambushed Russians. It would now be a job for the German truth drugs . . .

John Rourke watched the movement of the Hero Marshal's column, comparing it in his mind to a giant snake, slow moving but with the potential for incalculable deadliness. He swept the armored 8x30s along the course of the ridgeline over which the tanks, armored personnel carriers and armored truck transports moved. It was a snake of considerable length, and with the naturally undulating pattern of the ridge, the snake almost seemed to move like some grandiosely proportioned sidewinder.

He shifted his gaze from the snake.

Moving along a steep defile toward the ridgeline was a single file of men, two dozen of them the precise count when he had last looked. And he counted them again as they trudged slowly upward to intersect the snake's line of travel. the snake still at least a mile-and-a-quarter away.

No men had joined the file or broken away from it.

It was the second reconnaissance patrol, the men of the first patrol dead or captured, those captured being interrogated by intelligence specialists. Rourke would have felt more confident if Natalia had been supervising it.

It was one of many reconnaissance patrols Rourke had observed in the weeks since Karamatsov's abortive attempt to conquer the Soviet Underground City, in the weeks since Karamatsov had begun the movement of his vast army to the east.

The forces of the Underground City seemed to be still recovering from the effects of the gas attack and ground assault, by means of which Karamatsov had nearly overthrown his own Soviet Communist leaders. What the leadership of the Soviet Underground City would decide upon as their ultimate course of future action was as yet uncertain. Because of this, considerable numbers of the forces of New Germany with whom John Rourke, the Icelandics and, at least in name, the leadership of Eden Base had allied, remained in the low ridges and high valleys encamped near the principal entrance to the Underground City. Should the Soviet forces there commit to the field, the Germans would be hard pressed to contain them.

With a still smaller force, the Germans monitored the movements of Karamatsov's army. Had there been only one force of Russians, it would have been difficult to attack, the odds perilously high in favor of the enemy. But with two enemy forces and those friendly forces divided, the possibility of attack was non-existent.

Observe, occasionally harass, try to outguess—it was the only strategy allowed them now. That, and learning their destination.

The Icelandics had no army, no weapons of war except those provided by the Germans since the recently inaugurated alliance, no fighting men except the men of their largely ceremonial police force.

At Eden Base, there were teachers, construction specialists, medical and biological sciences personnel, agriculturalists, astronauts all, almost the last survivors from before the Night of The War. The Eden Project itself was a last ditch survival scenario for the best and brightest of humanity when the unthinkable occurred. Some indeed were among the best and brightest, Rourke mused. Akiro Kurinami, Dr. Elaine Halversen, some others. But some had no more to offer the desolated earth than did the Karamatsovs or the short-sighted, hard-headed men who had allowed the Karamatsovs to thrive, to grasp power and run with it.

John Rourke had not stayed with the German army which doggedly pursued Karamatsov. There had been no imperative. He had flown, instead, directly to the Hekla Community in Iceland where Sarah, his wife, had remained.

John Rourke had held Sarah in his arms as they stood in the snow and stared at the all but obscured cross which marked the grave of Michael's murdered wife, Madison, and of the unborn child she had carried. Once, as Rourke had held his wife, his hand had touched at her already slightly swelling abdomen and he pondered the fate of their unborn child. His grown son, Michael, his grown daughter, Annie, and her husband, Rourke's best friend Paul Rubenstein, had stood with him there. And beside Michael, a look of not belonging but wanting desperately to belong in her eyes, had been the German archeologist Fraulein Doctor Maria Leuden.

Natalia too had been there. The look Rourke had seen in Māria Leuden's eyes was one with which John Rourke had considerable familiarity. He had seen it so often in Natalia's eyes.

Madison Rourke and her unborn child had been casualties in the growing war for the future of mankind, a war which had begun five centuries earlier when the super powers had launched against each other, a war that had nearly claimed all life on earth, when the very atmosphere had ionized and the sky had turned to flame, the flames rolling across the skies of earth with the rising sun.

Then five centuries had passed, Rourke and his wife and his son and daughter and his friend Paul and—and Natalia—having survived in cryogenic sleep, awakening to await the return of the Eden Project Fleet to bring life again to earth.

But there had been life within the earth—the Germans in their mountain redoubt in Argentina, a people stifling under a resurgent Nazism and literally gasping for the breath of democracy; the survival communities of Iceland, the always peaceful island spared from the Great Conflagration by a freak of nature within the Van Allen belts, dedicating themselves to peace and learning; the Soviets in their Underground City in the Ural Mountains, preparing to return to the surface of the earth after five centuries of readying for conquest, their leader one who had survived the intervening five centuries by cryogenic sleep, as had Rourke and his family, their leader Vladmir Karamatsov, and with him a few selected members of his KGB Elite Corps.

There was other life as well—the community called "The Place" from which Michael, Rourke and Paul and Natalia aiding him, had rescued the girl Madison, unknowingly rescued her for an early grave in a land which she had never heard of, the victim of a war which had begun five centuries before her birth.

Madison's birthplace had been a survival community as well, but ill-prepared physically or emotionally for survival. Rourke at times wondered what mass graves archeologists of some future epoch would uncover, mass graves that were to have been mass shelters, survival redoubts. And there was, at least, one survival experiment which had gone equally as wrong but through totally different means. The result was what were called by the Soviets "The Wild Tribes of Europe," their bodies malformed, malnutritioned, their intellectual development all but arrested, the last remnants of a French survival community which had left its shelter and returned to the surface too soon, the background radiation from the Night of The War still too high. They had resorted to primitivism, the kind earliest man had arisen from.

Rourke had found himself thinking often now that perhaps these men and women of The Wild Tribes were the incarnate destiny of all mankind.

Rourke had wanted to stay with Sarah, but could not, and because of her pregnancy, she could not accompany him. He had first returned to the Retreat in the mountains of northeastern Georgia, taking Michael with him, Paul and Annie staying behind in Hekla with Sarah, Maria Leuden staying with them.

There had been no desire to visit the site of Eden Base—there was bad feeling still there which had not healed. But soon he would have to return, for the forthcoming wedding of Kurinami and Halversen, friends he valued.

At the Retreat—he could only spare two days and a night—he had resupplied, both the Retreat and himself, bringing to it cases of the German manufactured ammunition for his handguns and long guns, the ammunition manufactured to be the duplicate of the Federal ammunition he had trusted and used and with which he had originally stocked the Retreat. Thousands of rounds now—the Germans made for him as much as he wished—he secreted with Michael's help. New food supplies, new tires for his vehicles which the Germans had manufactured to the tolerances he had specified, new belts, new gaskets, everything that in five centuries could have become damaged or potentially unusable he now replaced, the Germans willing to meet his every need with their manufacturing expertise. As their leader Deiter Bern had said, a small reward to be given to a man who had almost single-handedly brought New Germany democracy. And, most sought after of all the fresh supplies, fresh meat, bombarded with radiation to kill bacteria and then frozen for storage.

Michael had asked, "Why are you doing this? Re-stocking the Retreat?"

And, John Rourke had told his son, "It pays to plan ahead."

Michael had asked nothing more.

Rourke had taken some necessities from the Retreat as well—more of the cigars Annie had faithfully made for him. They somehow tasted better than the non-carcinogenic types the Germans produced, several thousand of which were now stored in the Retreat in his freezers. A new lensatic compass,

17

his broken during the fighting at the Soviet Underground City, an occurrence he had only realized long after it had taken place.

And a new knife.

They had flown back from the Retreat to Iceland, then with Paul and Natalia as well, Rourke and his son had returned to the icy wastelands of Europe, Rourke first briefing Sarah and Annie as to the new supplies he had laid in at the Retreat.

And then Michael, Maria Leuden, and a team of German commandos, had gone on ahead.

Rourke's head ached from staring through the binoculars, as he had almost without stop for more than an hour, with no sleep in the last thirty hours, with the fatigue of combat so recently endured.

Rourke looked at Natalia beside him as he set the binoculars down on the snow-covered rocks in which they crouched. "You watch that recon patrol for a while."

"Why don't you take something for your headache, John?"

Rourke only nodded. He carried painkillers with his medical kit, but the kit, his musette bag with its spare magazines and other necessities and his assault rifle were at the base of the rocks with the Germans who waited there out of sight of the Karamatsov army or the slow moving reconnaissance patrol which was attempting to rejoin it.

Instead, Rourke unsheathed the knife he had taken from storage at the Retreat from the heavy, black leather scabbard on the belt of his Levis. He had saved this knife for Michael, but with the knife given Michael by old Jon at the Hekla Community, Michael would have no need of it. He began to unscrew the knife's buttcap.

He felt Natalia's eyes for an instant and he looked over to her, but she had already looked away, peering through the German field glasses she had adopted. But she spoke. "It's curious."

"What's curious?"

"That knife the old gentleman at Hekla gave Michael—a copy of the knife that you had saved for Michael, only smaller. But a copy of the same maker's work. I mean, it is a strange coincidence."

"Quality endures," Rourke nodded, slipping the transparent plastic tube from inside the knife's hollow handle, uncorking one end, the end nearest the painkillers, the water purification tablets and the antibiotic tablets.

Inside the knife's hollow handle, he had placed other items of possible necessity: a spare extractor that would fit either of the twin stainless Detonics pistols he carried, or for that matter, fit the Scoremasters now frequently carried in his belt; hooks and sinkers (an old survival habit) in the event somewhere on earth fish still remained, the nylon cord which wrapped the machined steel tube that formed the handle the necessary line; a sealed plastic capsule of lubricant; waterproof and windproof matches; an emergency suture.

A pouch on the outside of the sheath body accommodated a small sharpening stick and a still smaller magnesium ingot, a few shavings of the magnesium sufficient to ignite a fire even in conditions of extreme dampness.

The painkillers were essentially the modern equivalent of extra strength acetaminophen tablets.

Medicine had made great strides through the research of the scientists of New Germany in the five centuries since the Great Conflagration. But headaches, along with the common cold, athletes foot and warts still eluded comprehensive cure.

The technology for delivery of medication to the system had also advanced. The painkiller tablets were as small in size as the water purification tablets.

He needed no water to swallow the pills.

"Satisfied?" Rourke asked Natalia, smiling.

"Yes," she murmured. "How much longer?"

John Rourke glanced at the black-faced Rolex Submariner on his left wrist. It was twelve past the hour. "Three

19

minutes."

Natalia nodded, her eyes still seemingly glued to the binoculars.

It was a psychological victory which they hoped for, and a tactical victory in that however much Vladmir Karamatsov's march could be slowed was that much more time in which to anticipate his final objective and somehow take steps to counter it. Time for Michael to perhaps locate Karamatsov's objective.

Rourke eyed the Rolex again. A minute and a few seconds remained. He turned his body around, crouching now to peer over the rocks, but not using the binoculars. It was too early in the medication's cycle for the headache to even begin to subside.

With the naked eye, the snake of Karamatsov's column appeared more wormlike, and the twenty-four men of the second reconnaissance patrol seemed little more than stick figures as they struggled upward to reach the ridgeline. He was almost glad the time had nearly arrived. The exertions of the stick figures, in vain, would soon be ended.

Rourke looked still again to his watch — the sweep second hand was moving inexorably toward the twelve.

Faintly, perceptible to him perhaps only because he listened for the sound, came the whining roar of German fighter aicraft, the entire squadron of six which had been sent from Argentina to aid their efforts against the Russians. Rourke had not yet flown one. And six were all the Germans could spare, attempting to defend their own homeland in what had been Argentina, Eden Base in Georgia in what had been the United States and the people of Iceland, all from possible attack from Karamatsov's as yet unaccounted for forces in the Western Hemisphere.

Rourke craned his neck toward the sound, not bothering with binoculars, seeing the gradually growing dark shapes coming in low over the horizon, like streaks of black smoke, growing disproportionately large as they passed overhead,

Rourke's eyes following them. "Duck!" Rourke commanded, pulling Natalia down, his right arm coiling around her shoulders, drawing her head against his chest. But he kept his own face just by the lip of the rocks, so he could see.

The six fighter aircraft fired their machineguns, strafing the twenty-four man patrol, the stick figures scattering like leaves before a strong wind, the bodies tumbling along the defile, battering against the rocks below, all but one of the six aircraft flying on, the sixth fighter breaking off, half-barrel rolling, banking steeply, flying back. Rourke held Natalia tighter. The fighter swept low, a contrail from one of the missile pods beneath the portside wing, and suddenly the defile seemed almost to vaporize, the fighter streaking over it as the black and orange fireball belched upward, the fighter vanishing in the direction of the five other fighters, toward Karamatsov's column.

John Rourke swept the binoculars up, peering through them, Natalia fully erect beside him now, Rourke standing as well, explosions starting in the distance. It would be hit and run, a single pass along the length of the column, then a return pass and then gone. But it would slow the inexorably advancing snake as it made its way—toward what, Rourke wondered?

Chapter Two

Michael Rourke stepped down from the German jeep-like vehicle almost before it had stopped, the gravel still crunching beneath its wheels as it settled, crunching beneath his combat boots as he stepped away, his left hand coming to rest on the butt of the four-inch Model 629 Smith & Wesson .44 Magnum. He moved his hand away. It was becoming a habit and somehow he had always found himself resisting the formation of habit.

The granite spires and upswept walls of the Greater Khingan Range rose before him, an offset spinal column separating Inner Mongolia from Manchuria, separating one near subarctic expanse of nothingness from another. They had rolled the jeep-like vehicle from its carry position inside the largest of the three helicopters that morning and decided to examine the terrain from the ground as opposed to the method, the search pattern, which had been used since they had first set out.

Hammerschmidt's musical baritone habitually ill-concealed amusement, as it ill-concealed it now. "A wild duck chase, hmm?"

"Goose," Michael automatically corrected. "But you're

probably right, Otto."

"Then where are the Communists going?" It was Maria Leuden who spoke now, her voice musical as well, deeper than a woman's voice often was, a throaty alto. Michael turned and looked at her. Her gray-green eyes were barely visible above the scarf which swathed the lower portion of her lovely face against the cold, the hood of the parka all but obscuring the dark brown hair except for the few stray wisps which fell across her forehead and caught in an errant gust of wind now as she continued to speak. "Karamatsov cannot be taking his army just nowhere. That would be irrational."

"Most likely, yes," Michael agreed. "If he is moving without a definite geographic goal, we'll all have been operating under a misapprehension, a potentially dangerous one."

They were near what, five centuries ago, had been the city of Harbin, northeastern China's most important industrial base. But he doubted any of it would remain now, no gutted ruins.

But Harbin had drawn him. From his readings in the endless nights of the long years during which his father had returned to the Sleep, he had learned that Harbin had been a "Russian" city in the China of old, the Russians and the industry drawn there by Harbin's uniqueness as a railhead. He had wondered, when Karamatsov's line of march had seemed to indicate the direction of China, if somehow Harbin or its environs still possessed something Russian, or Russian lusted.

Karamatsov—the name still filled Michael Rourke with hatred. It was on Karamatsov's orders, whether directly given or merely established as policy that the suicide raid on the Hekla Community in Iceland had taken place. And as a result of the raid, Michael's wife, Madison, and their unborn child had died.

His father had spoken little of the desire for vengeance which Michael attempted not at all to conceal. His father, almost more than he, wished vengeance as well. Karamatsov was Natalia's husband and tormentor. Karamatsov was a relic of the five centuries ago war which had nearly destroyed all of humanity and which was still being fought. Karamatsov was incarnate evil.

To Michael, Karamatsov was all of these things, but they mattered not at all. Karamatsov was the man responsible for the death of Madison and their baby. For this reason alone—none of the others really mattering—Karamatsov would die. Michael did not desire conflict with his father over the ultimate fate of Vladmir Karamatsov, the Hero Marshal of the reborn Soviet Union, but it would not be his father, John Thomas Rourke, who would kill Vladmir Karamatsov. It would be him. And the desire so consumed him that he was prepared to fight his father for the right.

Maria Leuden's voice interrupted his ruminating. "He must have a purpose."

Michael looked at her again. She was obvious about her feelings for him. Love, perhaps, Michael thought. But the memory of Madison Rourke mitigated against that now, perhaps always. There was always sex without love, and he did not dismiss the idea out of morality. There was, though, in sex, the risk of love. And he would not be so destroyed within himself again until he had eradicated the cause of this destruction—forever.

"Otto," Michael told the captain of commandos from New Germany in Argentina, "signal the gunships that we're going up into those mountains." It would have helped, Michael Rourke mused, if he had known what he was looking for.

He looked into the eyes of Fraulein Doctor Maria Leuden, archeologist. What he saw in her eyes—love for him—was not what he was looking for at all. Not now . . .

Bjorn Rolvaag stroked Hrothgar behind the ears and the massive animal seemed almost to purr, although purring was

24

not something a dog could really do.

He sat in the back of the vehicle, watching, slightly nervous as he always was in one of these modern contrivances, but less so in this one which bumped and jostled over the rocky ground than in those which flew like great ugly birds in the sky. There were birds in Hekla, in aviaries. He understood that they had once flown freely in the skies of the entire earth. A pleasant thing to see, he thought.

He watched the young man who successfully ignored him, the young man an identical duplicate of his father, the great John Rourke, who seemed at once to ignore everything yet notice everything. The boy and the man — both men, though Rolvaag understood not at all truly how father and son could be well less than a decade apart in ages — were as alike as snowflakes falling from the gray winter sky when viewed at great distance. But he wondered, if like snowflakes when viewed very closely, would differences emerge.

Bjorn Rolvaag watched Maria Leuden as well. The German was very beautiful, though he considered the trousers she wore, trousers like a man might wear only tighter fitting, to be immodest. And it was evident, when she looked at Michael Rourke, that she loved him. Bjorn Rolvaag somehow felt pity for her because of that. She spoke to him — Rolvaag — in dulcet tones, the words something of which he could understand precious little. But she seemed kind, and her voice was like the sound of melting ice welling up as cool water and breaking free in the spring. She would stroke his dog, Hrothgar, beneath the chin, behind the ears, the careless attention of her fingers something the animal seemed to adore. There was great love in her.

And for this, he felt all the more the sorry for her. Bjorn Rolvaag closed his eyes, sleeping something that would be required when soon this contraption would no longer be able to go on and they would walk as men were meant to do . . .

Maria Leuden huddled inside the coat, but the cold came from within her. She glanced beside her as her gloveless left hand stroked the fur of the mighty animal, wolf-like but so much like a child, eager for affection. Hrothgar showed no sign of sleeping, though his master was apparently of a different mind. The green clad man of Iceland's lids masked his eyes and his breathing was regular, even. Despite the jerky movements of the vehicle over the roadless rockstrewn terrain, he seemingly slept. She wished she could.

Her eyes drifted forward, settling for a moment on Captain Otto Hammerschmidt, his massive shoulders, his gloved hands smothering the steering wheel. But her gaze shifted. Michael Rourke. His head was obscured by the hood of his parka. His shoulders were equally as massive as those of Hammerschmidt, both men together seeming to be dwarfed by the massiveness of Bjorn Rolvaag who, along with his dog, occupied the rear seat. But unlike Rolvaag, Michael showed no signs of being asleep. And unlike Hammerschmidt, there was a tenseness which seemed to radiate from him even when he sat unmoving, an energy waiting to change from its kinetic state at the slightest provocation.

She had not said to him, "Michael—please make love to me." But she had let him know in other ways that she wished that he would, would beg that he would if she thought that her entreaties would make him do so. And she felt terribly brazen for this, and at once terribly embarrassed. She had never been what some of the older novels in English which she had read—underground books—called "loose." There had been plenty of men who had tried to make her their own. She had not wanted them. She wondered if it were somehow poetic justice or divine retribution that the man she desired with all of her being was intentionally cold to her.

But his coldness did not alter her desire.

She closed her eyes. She could see Michael Rourke. Tall. Straight. Dark brown hair, full. The eyes—penetrating.

Dark. His muscles rippled beneath his shirt and he moved with the grace of an animal rather than a mere man. His hands—when he touched her for whatever the reason she felt inside herself something she had never felt before.

If she kept her eyes closed, the image of Michael might remain. And perhaps it would carry her into sleep.

Chapter Three

There was an advantage to the dresses worn by the women of Iceland, Annie Rourke noted. Though her mother's pregnancy was showing, the high waisted dresses Sarah Rourke wore effectively camouflaged her condition. Annie longed for the same condition, but had agreed with Paul that they would not have their first child until the thing with Karamatsov was over.

She felt cheated, having to stay behind while Natalia and even the German girl Maria Leuden went into the field. In part it was to keep her mother company. In part that was the reason that she stayed. But in part it was to keep a Rourke presence in Iceland among the peaceful people who were its inhabitants and the New Germany allies who were its guardians.

Madame Jokli had come to rely on her, in fact, in her dealings with the German commander, Major Volkmer, asking her — Annie — to accompany her when necessity demanded going to the German base just outside the cone of the volcano that walled Hekla against the ice and storm of the arctic environment in which it was an island of warmth and flowers and beauty.

And Annie Rourke looked forward to it as she did now, because the meetings allowed her the opportunity to meet with Dr. Munchen, Munchen always arranging his appointments so they could talk without interruption, disregarding the occasional emergency.

Annie Rourke had boarded the German helicopter following closely at Madame Jokli's heels, the President of Lydveldid Island swathed in a woolen shawl which covered the tiny woman from the tip of her head nearly to her ankles and could have wrapped around her at least twice.

Annie sat beside Madame Jokli, fixing her dress, slipping her own shawl down from her shoulders. It was equally as heavy as that of the Icelandic President but Annie, rather than cocooning herself inside it, had felt its warmth repressively heavy here inside the cone. But when she disembarked the German gunship, there would be a few moments of bitter arctic cold between the helipad and the heat lights which blanketed as much of the base exterior with warmth as could be arranged. And for that Annie knew from experience, she would need every calorie of warmth.

It was a routine to which Annie Rourke was well used now. As the helicopter rose over the Hekla cone, she surveyed the landscape below through the swirling snow, her throat catching slightly as she spied the patch of ground which was the common cemetery, where Madison Rourke and Madison's and Michael's unborn child rested for all eternity. The cross could no longer be seen and she consciously lied to herself that it was merely the altitude at which the German gunship flew and the swirling snow around it which obscured the gravemarker. But it was none of these. She shivered and drew the shawl up about her shoulders and tightened her knees more closely together beneath her navy blue woolen ankle length skirt. For a moment, she had pictured herself lying cold and dead beneath ground that was forever still colder than death itself. It was not a psychic flash—she recognized those when she had them. It was no premonition of her own death. Instead, it was, she realized, her empathy with the dead girl, her "little sister," her sister-in-law, her girlfriend, really the only one she could ever remember having.

They had shared their wedding day, worn identical dresses, arranged their hair identically, carried identical bouquets, married two of the three finest men in the world together. And now Madison was dead.

Annie Rourke drew herself deeper into the folds of her shawl, the helicopter starting the downward leg of its arc, the swirling snow parting sufficiently around them that she could see the helipad and the warm yellow of the lights beyond it.

Habit took over. Methodically, her eyes rivetted to the helipad for a moment, then to the movements of the pilot at the gunship's controls, then alternating back and forth between them. She began to cocoon herself within the shawl, draping it over her hair, swathing it across her chest and folding it back over her left shoulder so it all but completely covered her face.

The helicopter began to hover, then seemed to skid downward—she imagined an unexpected gust of wind—and then settled just over the helipad, touching down. German soldiers in arctic gear ran from the heat lamps and toward the helicopter's hatchway, wrenching it open, profferring hands to assist Annie and Madame Jokli down from the machine. Annie, though she needed no assistance, took it, waiting despite the cold on the snow-slicked tarmac for Madame Jokli to disembark. Then, together, huddled in their shawls, they walked on the arms of German soldiers from the icy blast into the yellow warmth.

She lifted the double fold of wool from her head and arranged the shawl about her shoulders.

Madame Jokli remained as she was, still apparently cold, Annie passing through the open airlock-like door after the Icelandic President, then stepping over the second flange and at last inside.

In here, she was warm and she slipped the shawl completely down, beginning to neatly fold it, one of the enlisted men saying in poor but sincere sounding English, "May I take Frau Rubenstein's coat?" It was not a coat and the temperature in some portions of the base structure was at times at considerable variance from the warmth of the entrance foyer.

Annie Rourke Rubenstein smiled. "No—but thank you, soldier."

He smiled at her.

She followed Madame Jokli along the corridor, an officer—a lieutenant—joining them and ushering them along.

The matters of diplomacy were none of Annie's concern unless requested by Madame Jokli to assist. There had been no such whispered remark aboard the helicopter this day and so, Annie volunteered, "If it is all right, Madame, I'll visit with Doctor Munchen while you confer with Major Volkmer."

"Yes child," she smiled, her blond hair, her blue eyes, all in concert with the smile somehow.

Annie entered the medical laboratory section off the main corridor and started across it. There were ranks of test tubes, retorts and burners and lab coated men and women, German military and civilian, working here. A few, whose faces she recognized, nodded, smiled, then returned to their work. She returned their greetings, stopping before Doctor Munchen's office and knocking.

After a moment, the door opened, Munchen tall, rapier thin, his face beaming as it always seemed to when he saw her. "Frau Rubenstein—I anticipated you."

"Herr Doctor Munchen—may I?"

"Of course, my dear," and he ushered her inside. The door closed behind her and he took her shawl. "You'll find it if anything a bit over warm today. They are still balancing the system."

Doctor Munchen held a chair out for her on the side of the desk opposite his and she sat, folding her hands into her lap, waiting. He would offer refreshment.

"Coffee, my dear?"

"Yes, thank you."

He began to pour from an insulated coffee pot at the side of his desk. It had thermal sensitive heating coils, she knew, subtly rewarming the contents when the coffee dropped below a certain temperature. She had never decided at exactly what temperature she would set such a thing. She took the cup and saucer, holding it like she had learned to hold a tea cup, as though it were fragile. But indeed these were not, made of something that was apparently plastic but felt like china. She had seen a similar cup dropped once to the floor here and it had merely bounced.

"More discussions, then. Is there word of your father, my dear?"

"Not unless you have heard anything. My father and my husband were still with the main body of troops when the last regular report was relayed to us. And Michael was still substantially ahead of them. I wish I were there with them."

"Ahh—but you cannot be."

"When we talk like this, Herr Doctor, are you psychoanalyzing me?" And she smiled, then sipped at the black coffee. It was very good and warm as it reached her stomach.

"What would you prefer that I say?"

"The truth?"

"The truth—you are so remarkably well-adjusted that you amaze me. And, without being rude I hope," and he smiled at her across his coffee cup, "I suppose I am more than curious."

"Women have to be well-adjusted. They can't afford the same luxuries as men."

Munchen laughed, asking as he always did as he withdrew a cigarette from his case, "May I smoke, Frau Rubenstein?"

"Certainly—but one day I'll have to try it."

"As you wish." He made the case disappear inside his uniform jacket. Men were lucky to have so many pockets, she had always thought. He set the lighter down on his desk top, exhaling smoke as again he spoke. "You were little more than an infant when what you call the Night of The War took place. You were shunted from one place to another by truck, by horseback, saw incredible violence, then slept for almost five centuries and all but raised yourself, all but educated yourself—"

"My brother, Michael—he did the same thing," she interrupted.

"But perhaps my own sex prejudices me—but a man will adjust more to violence."

"Men expect it more, that's all. And anyway, after Daddy found us at the farm where we were hiding out with the Resistance, there wasn't really that much more violence. I was too short to see the video monitors that showed what was going on when the sun rose. And I don't remember too much of the other, before I mean."

"But subconsciously, you do—don't you see?"

"I don't see."

"Your subconscious of course affects your conscious actions and decisions, colors your choices, as it were."

Annie Rourke sipped at her coffee again, then set cup and saucer on the edge of the desk, returning her hands to her lap, palms up, one inside the other.

"You exude tranquility."

"Isn't it," she began, "that which men so need in women— islands of tranquility amid the storm of life?"

"Is that a quotation, Annie?"

"No— I think I made it up. But I read so much, perhaps it is. Don't snitch on me."

"Snitch?"

There was a knock at the door. It was a man's knock, she could tell.

"I think it's time for me to go," she told Doctor Munchen, rising, Munchen rising with her, Annie arranging her clothes. She wondered if she were becoming manipulative.

"I shall look forward to our next meeting."

"As will I, Herr Doctor Munchen."

He called for whoever was at the door to enter and a male lab assistant half-entered the office, saying in German which Annie could understand by now quite well enough, that Madame Jokli awaited her near the entrance foyer.

Annie allowed Munchen to press her offered hand and left on the heels of the lab assistant, passed along the work area and through the doorway into the corridor, seeing Madame Jokli and the same young German lieutenant at the end of the corridor.

Annie quickened her pace. She could see it in the set of Madame Jokli's mouth. There was something wrong . . .

The flight aboard the helicopter had been quiet, fast, uneventful, Annie lost in thought — considering one's own nature was difficult.

When the helicopter returned to the grassy parkway near the presidential residence which also served as the meeting place of the Althing, Madame Jokli quietly asked, "Annie, would you come with me please?"

Annie merely nodded, having expected the request.

As she followed beside Madame Jokli, the quite pretty older woman began to speak. "Major Volkmer relayed to me some rather alarming news."

Annie usually trusted her abilities to differentiate between a psychic flash and natural apprehension. But she asked anyway: "Is it something with Paul or my father or Michael — or Natalia?"

"No — but it is related directly to their actions — not those of Michael, I understand. But your father, Doctor Rourke. He and the others apprehended several prisoners from among the Russians whom they have been pursuing. I was given to understand that intelligence data found among the prisoners or extricated from them by means of drugs —

Major Volkmer was not specific in that area—suggests a major attack on our community. And very soon. I fear great loss of life on all sides. I fear it greatly."

She fell silent.

Madame Jokli stopped before the low steps of the presidential residence, turned, faced Annie, Madame Jokli drawing her shawl tighter about her shoulders, the purplish aura of the growlights to which Annie had so well adjusted as an artificial sun now something of which she was suddenly acutely aware.

"I was asked to leave my residence here and take refuge with our German friends at their base. I told them I could not, while one of the people of Lydveldid Island was unable to do the same. Major Volkmer commended me. He will spare as many troops as possible to assist in our defense but sees the base as being the most desirable strategic objective. Therefore, it must be defended. I would consider it a personal favor, Annie, if you and your fine mother would take refuge at the German base. Major Volkmer asked that I offer his hospitality to you both. He mentioned that you or your mother would be the ultimate strategic prize for a Soviet offensive. Logic dictated that no argument could be given in that regard."

"I'm sure that I speak for both my mother and myself," Annie began, looking down at her feet, trying to find the toes of her slippers beyond the hem of her skirt. "We will stay unless you directly order us to leave. We can help with the defense. And if the Russians are able to take over Hekla, we wouldn't be much safer at the German base, I don't think." She finally found the toes of her shoes and then looked up into Madame Jokli's face.

"All right, Annie. As you wish. I will summon the head of our police and then make a general announcement to the community and see to it that word is spread among the other communities as well, that they should be prepared, should the Russians attack them as well."

"I don't think," Annie interjected, "that they'll do that, divide their forces I mean."

"Then you'll have work to do, Annie. I won't detain you."

"Yes ma'am," Annie smiled. She always felt as if she should curtsy or something when she left Madame Jokli's presence.

But she turned now, walking back along the path — there was a great deal to do . . .

Annie Rourke shifted the lighter weight, crocheted shawl from her shoulders to the crooks of her elbows as she picked up the German assault rifle, a German non-com and a German private moving about the twelve seated Icelandic police who were dubbed by Annie and her mother the SWAT Team.

She worked the rifle's action to hold open the bolt and began to speak. "In real combat with a firearm you'll learn one thing. Count your shots, be ready for a swift magazine interchange — or there's a substantial chance you'll die. The sergeant has been training you to function as a unit." Old Jon, the swordmaker interpreted as Annie paused. He finished, nodded and she continued. "My father has an expression that he got from his father. It sums it up best. As John Rourke puts it, 'Plan ahead.'"

Chapter Four

John Rourke had finally slept, for seven hours, angry that Natalia or Paul had not awakened him sooner, but forgiving of their motives.

He sat now, beneath a rocky overhang around a German military portable heater unit, eating from a bag of German field rations and listening as Captain Hartman discoursed on the intelligence data gleaned so far from the Soviet prisoners. "The attack against Hekla seemed, of course, inevitable. In addition to alerting Major Volkmer, I have also alerted our forces with the Eden Project Base in Georgia. I believe that Marshal Karamatsov plans to attack at several locations using those forces not already joined with him in the possible hope of drawing us away from the main body of his force."

"What about the possibility of an attack on New Germany itself," Natalia suggested.

"Colonel Mann has been alerted as well. He has placed our forces on alert."

"I doubt Karamatsov would attack in Argentina, Iceland and Georgia simultaneously," Paul Rubenstein noted.

John Rourke looked at the younger man and nodded. "I'm in full agreement. It won't take much to cause grief for Eden Base. Likely, Karamatsov's forces will send in as few people as they can get away with to go against Eden, because they'll need substantial forces to go against Hekla. Hekla and the German base outside Hekla are considerably more defensible. There's been no sign of Karamatsov bleeding off forces from his main body of troops and if that pattern holds, that means he'll be relying on the forces he already has in the field under his commanders. And there's no telling what the loyalty situation is among Karamatsov's people now, after his attack on the Soviet Underground City. He's not going to want to dissipate his forces while the possibility exists for defection.

"And," Rourke continued, setting down the food packet and plucking one of the long, thin, dark tobacco cigars from the right pocket of his shirt, "he hasn't been able to hand his people a victory. The attacks we've been running, although militarily ineffectual, have to have been demoralizing." Rourke flicked back the cowl of the battered Zippo with the thumb of his right hand, then rolled the striking wheel, thrusting the tip of the cigar just above the lighter's blue-yellow flame, drawing the flame up into the cigar. It was one of the non-carcinogenic German cigars, physically identical to the cigars he had always smoked and to the ones Annie had rolled for him, but somehow just slightly less satisfying.

"What would you propose, Herr Doctor," Hartman asked, lighting a cigarette.

"I'm becoming more convinced that Karamatsov has some definite goal which he's drawing closer to and that he sees it as some sort of panacea for his current situation. It can only be one thing."

"The Chinese," Natalia supplied.

"Yes," Rourke nodded. "Obviously, he has additional intelligence data from before the Night of The War which has led him to believe that some substantial advantage lies to the east. He still has the gas, but without a base from which he can manufacture more of the substance, the scope of its use is rather limited. I think we're talking nuclear weapons."

Paul Rubenstein visibly shuddered. Natalia made to light a cigarette, Rourke lighting it for her instead with the Zippo.

"That would be insanity, Herr Doctor Rourke," Hartman said softly.

"Vladmir is insane," Natalia murmured.

"If a stockpile of Chinese nuclear weapons exists, and since the Chinese, as far as everything I've learned of the aftermath of the Night of The War seems to attest, utilized only tactical nuclear weapons in their land war against the Soviet Union, the rest of their nuclear arsenal was unused when the Great Conflagration took place. If some of it could be made usable, as I'm sure it could, he'd be master of the earth. Which is what he wants anyway," Rourke concluded.

"But the Soviet Underground City would be insusceptible to nuclear attack, as would—"

"Your mountain in Argentina, Captain?"

"Yes, Herr Doctor."

"Structurally, yes," Paul interjected. "But if you could never go outside again, never—it wouldn't be like before. There was always the hope—"

"Of seeing the sunlight, feeling the wind again," Natalia interrupted, her voice seeming possessed of a distant quality, a sadness.

"Yes," Paul nodded. "That."

"But such a rash act—another nuclear war—it might well destroy all life, making the planet forever uninhabitable." Hartman stubbed out his cigarette.

John Rourke, exhaling a cloud of gray smoke as he spoke, almost whispered, "There's a line from *Paradise Lost*—"

Natalia said it. "Better to reign in hell than serve in heaven."

Chapter Five

The darkness was something John Rourke could almost feel against his skin as he walked, silently, Paul and Natalia flanking him, toward the waiting German gunship, its main rotor tossing almost lazily, almost totally silent.

In his left fist, Rourke carried his pack by the shoulder straps. In his right fist, the Steyr-Mannlicher SSG, an M-16 slung cross body, diagonally, muzzle down, across his back.

Natalia boarded the aircraft first, Paul following after her, John Rourke tossing his backpack inside, staring around him for a moment, studying the night. The rotor speed was increasing, Rourke squinting against the downdraft, feeling his hair caught in it, running his left hand back across his high forehead, the fingers splaying in his hair, pushing it back from his face.

He jumped aboard, the German pilot looking back toward him as Rourke slid the fuselage door closed. Rourke gave a thumbs-up signal, the rotor speed increased drastically now; then Rourke felt the rise, the change of main rotor pitch, the helicopter sweeping across the snowsplotched rocky landscape, upward, Rourke settling into the bench seat at Natalia's right, Paul Rubenstein sitting at her left.

Rourke shrugged out of the arctic parka, the double Alessi shoulder rig with the twin stainless Detonics .45s worn over a gray, crew-necked sweater. The temperature inside the German helicopter was quite tolerable and to keep the heavy outer gear in place when it was not necessary was to defeat its purpose when it was necessary.

Paul was helping Natalia with her parka as well.

Paul Rubenstein spoke. "I'm worried about Annie. And Sarah too. Ever since — ever since — "

"Madison," Natalia supplied.

"Yeah — ahh — "

Rourke leaned forward and looked into the younger man's eyes. "We'll be there in time. And Major Volkmer seems to be a competent commander. The Russians won't have any easy victory out of him. And Annie and Sarah are very good at taking care of themselves."

"Ever since Madison died," Natalia almost whispered, her voice barely audible despite the subdued rotor noise, "I've realized that all of us — I suppose I should have realized it before. But we are living on borrowed time."

"We always have been," Rourke told her, told both of them, reaching out and folding his left hand over both of hers. "We survived World War III, we survived the burning of the atmosphere. We've survived more battles than I would have ever thought possible."

"Then why, John — why are we still alive — and Madison is dead? There is no justice."

Rourke held her hands more tightly. "Did you ever wonder, Natalia, Paul — did you guys ever wonder why we did survive — I mean all of that?"

"What do you mean?" Paul asked. "You mean — is there some kind of — ahh — some kind of — "

"Purpose? I don't know. We did what we did because we had to, didn't we. And because we wanted to. Maybe that was the most important part — wanting it. I mean, we never wanted the killing, the fighting. But we all sort of wanted what came afterward."

"Do you think we'll ever find what comes afterward, John,"

Natalia asked him. "Do you think we'll still recognize it if we ever do find it?

"I mean," and she cleared her throat. "Sometimes it is very hard. Would we still recognize it?" And she looked at each of them.

John Rourke had no answer for her, let alone for himself.

Chapter Six

Captain Dmitri Pavornin considered it a challenge. A small force against heavily entrenched enemy forces, small in number but well equipped. It was the least important of the two prongs of attack ordered by the Hero Marshal Karamatsov. But it could be important for him, Pavornin knew. If he could distinguish himself here—if only—

The sun had long ago set. He glanced at the chronometer on his wrist.

It was nearly time for the attack to begin.

Pavornin walked across the open expanse of the staging area. It was desert here, inhospitable dunes of coarse sand, shifting and blowing in the wind, a wind pummelling his face now with grains of sand which stung like sleet. His survival training had been in the Urals. He knew discomfort. His men moved busily at the last of their preparatory tasks, the gunships ready, their rotors in all-but-silent motion, their downdrafts adding to the wind which blew the sand. He wore goggles to protect his eyes, thin gloves to protect his hands. It was cool here, nearly what one could call cold. But after the Ural Mountains survival training, he rarely called anything cold anymore.

He checked the timepiece again, starting toward his command helicopter. He would use it to join those elements of his forces already moving up on foot for the ground attack against Eden Base.

Eden — Pavornin was aware of the Judeo-Christian creation myths, the Garden of Eden a paradise on earth from which man was forever exiled. He scoffed at such superstition, both openly and privately.

And he wondered, privately, if the men and women who had journeyed to the edge of the solar system and back during five centuries of sleep had thought they would awaken to paradise somehow renewed.

Pavornin smiled. If they had, they would learn very quickly that they were mistaken.

Akiro Kurinami had been attempting to see Commander Dodd since word had first been disseminated to expect a Soviet attack. And Dodd, Kurinami had determined several hours ago, had been trying equally as hard to avoid him.

Kurinami looked at his wristwatch. Elaine would be worried that he had not returned, but Kurinami felt that if he abandoned his vigil outside Dodd's command tent, all chance of seeing Dodd before the attack began would probably be lost.

And so he waited, trying to fill his thoughts with Elaine Halversen rather than the growing disgust and distrust he felt for Commander Dodd.

Elaine was older. She was, of course, black, while he was Japanese.

But he had never felt this for any other woman except his wife, now five centuries dead, as was the rest of his family, every friend he had ever made, every cadet with whom he had trained, every man he had ever flown with. Someday, he promised himself, there would be time. He would take a gunship and fly to Japan, taking Elaine with him. He promised himself that, though he had never told Elaine this, she should see the land that had been so rich in history. And somehow, he felt that he owed it to the land itself, to go there and shout to the emptiness that there was one who lived who had not forgotten.

He would shout it until he could no longer speak.

Commander Dodd exited his tent, with him one of the German officers. Akiro Kurinami started forward. "Commander. I must speak with you, Commander Dodd."

"I'm really very busy, Lieutenant Kurinami. With this impending attack and all. Tomorrow?"

Dodd, his brow furrowing the way he always furrowed it to show intensity, thoughtfulness, and concern, smiled. Kurinami ignored the man's words. They were empty at any event.

"This can't wait, Commander."

Kurinami stood his ground. Dodd seemed to weigh his words, then waved the young German officer on with a salute. The German returned it and moved off, Dodd's smile fading as he spoke. "Now, Lieutenant, what is so important that it takes precedence over the defense of Eden Base at a moment of crisis such as this?"

"Two dozen assault rifles and three thousand rounds of ammunition. Two lots of botanical samples and about fifteen per cent of available emergency rations. Add lighting, medical supplies—we have a problem, sir."

"I don't understand, Akiro," Dodd began. "I mean—what are you trying to say?"

"Missing, sir—all of what I mentioned and more. No accounting of its whereabouts. And the master onboard computer was used and the file which contained the locations of all the supply caches was blanked. The computers on all the other shuttles were similarly altered."

"What are you saying, man?"

"I made back-up files."

Dodd was silent for a moment. "Thank God for that," he said, exhaling loudly. It seemed like a stage gesture, Kurinami thought, but dismissed the idea since he didn't like

Dodd and looked for such things in the man. "These back-up files," Dodd began again. "What prompted you to make them?"

"I felt the locations of the supply caches were so important and that if something should happen to the Shuttles with a set of back-up files we could always get the Germans to modify one of their computers to bring up the data."

"Good thinking, Lieutenant. Thank God you were on the ball. Where are these files?"

Akiro Kurinami licked his lips. "I don't know if I want to let that information out, sir."

Dodd cleared his throat, looked at his feet for a moment, then looked up. Sand was swirling in the heightening wind, and the temperature was dropping with the night. Dodd said, his voice low, "That could make you a very powerful man, Akiro."

"It could make someone very powerful, Commander, someone who wanted to be very powerful."

"Yes—exactly. Don't get yourself killed when the attack comes, Akiro. Should the files be lost, well, I shudder to think what Eden Base might do without them."

"The Germans would help us," Kurinami blurted out.

"Oh, I'm sure they would."

"But the weapons, Commander."

"You're sure it wasn't a miscount then, something wrong in the inventory?"

"I'm sure."

Dodd seemed to consider his words again. Then, "Perhaps we have a saboteur among us."

Akiro Kurinami thought of Elaine's counsel to speak prudently. But he said it anyway. "Or a revolutionary."

Kurinami turned and walked away, the blowing sand stinging his eyes despite the hand he held before his face.

Chapter Seven

Sarah Rourke started to cry. "Damnit!"

The zipper on her faded blue Levis would not close no matter how she tried to suck in. It was the baby. She had almost forgotten about the swelling of her abdomen with the high waisted skirts and dresses which were the fashion here, the baby merely giving a certain roundness to her abdomen.

But the jeans were hopeless.

And she felt stupid going into battle wearing a dress. But it was either that or wear nothing but panties.

She backed toward the bed, plopped down and started skinning the blue jeans off her legs. And you couldn't wear a T-shirt with a long skirt without looking stupid. "Shit," she snarled through her tears.

Sarah Rourke had discovered that the web pistol belt which she used to carry the beat up old .45 automatic that she had taken from the bureau drawer on the very Night of The War, one of the last things remaining which survived from their house, which had burned to the ground the next morning — the belt just didn't fit either and extra minutes had been needed to expand the belt.

She'd broken a nail on the fasteners which interlocked to

determine the size of the belt. Chipped a nail anyway.

As she walked down the stairs of the dormitory and toward the greenway which dominated the center of the Hekla community, she realized she had never cried so much in — not since —

John was away, with Natalia and Paul.

And Michael was away. And she was pregnant and chronologically, though she was only a few years older than her twenty-eight-year-old daughter, she was old enough — too old? She didn't think she was too old. But why did she cry all the time?

It was deathly quiet, and she could hear the rustling of the fabric of her skirt, feeling stupid all the more with the gunbelt — enlarged — worn with it. The skirt was navy blue, the blouse she wore a pale blue, the shawl a medium blue. She could see Annie ahead with the Icelandic police unit that they laughingly called the SWAT Team. But Annie dressed this way by preference and didn't feel stupid, she thought, feeling her cheeks flush. Her cheeks flushed more these days. But Doctor Munchen, who had personally taken charge of the medical aspects of her pregnancy, had told her that her blood pressure was normal and her nurse's instincts had told her that too.

Sarah Rourke stopped at the edge of the knot of Icelandic police, the two Germans who assisted Annie with the training and the SWAT Team. Annie turned and looked at her, sensing her presence again perhaps, or perhaps just hearing her coming.

"Hi, momma."

"A symphony in blue reporting for duty, ma'am," Sarah grinned.

Annie laughed.

Beyond Annie, others of the German advisors were marshalling more of the Icelandic constabulary, while some of the actual German units sent to assist in the defense of Hekla were disappearing in the distance toward the rim of the volcanic cone. "German or American?" Annie asked, gesturing toward the stacked assault rifles near her.

"I'm a traditionalist — American," Sarah answered, starting to walk now toward the nearest stack of M-16s. And Sarah Rourke laughed at herself — she did that a lot these days too. She had never gone into combat before dressed for a Gay '90s lawn party.

Annie Rourke Rubenstein had determined that the more experienced of the Icelandic personnel, counting herself and her mother and the two Germans who had aided in the training, could best serve the defensive needs of Hekla by guarding the President, Madame Jokli having finally, after much urging, consented to taking shelter in the cellar of the presidential palace with her maid and some medical personnel who had set up a field hospital there.

Annie cradled the M-16 in her left arm as she walked along the porch at the height of the main entrance steps. So far, there had been no sounds of gunfire. But soon there would be. She wondered if the Russians would attempt to infiltrate first or merely attack in strength. If they tried a repeat of their earlier gambit to take Madame Jokli and perhaps some others as hostages, the battle would be here before it began near the rim. But she was ready for it. The German sergeant and herself had taken six of the twelve men of the SWAT Team, the SWAT Team personnel looking nearly as incongruous as did she and her mother. Like the typical Icelandic police officer, they wore their green tunics and carried their swords. Her mother and the German corporal had taken the remaining six to guard the rear of the building, the more difficult of the two posts if there were trouble, but the least likely to be first attacked.

At her waist was her pistol belt, the Detonics Scoremaster .45 in one holster, the Beretta 92F military pistol in the other. The Detonics had been a present from her father, the

Beretta a "trophy," if that were the correct term, from Forrest Blackburn, the Soviet infiltrator who had first brought her to Iceland by kidnapping her from Eden Base during an attack.

She had come to like the 9mm as much as the .45. Michael carried two of them himself. Slung crossbody from right shoulder to left hip was a musette bag, in it spare magazines for the M-16 and a few spares for the Beretta and the Scoremaster. An identical musette bag — her father called them Swedish Army Engineers Bags — was slung from left shoulder to right hip, identically loaded. The weight was all she could carry, but she told herself it kept her thin.

She suddenly thought of her mother. For Sarah Rourke to have shown up for battle dressed as she was, meant that blue jeans no longer fit. Annie wondered if she would soon have a little brother or little sister. And she wondered how her mother felt about the whole thing, because her mother never really talked about it and Annie felt she shouldn't ask. She decided, on the spot as she turned and started back across the porch in the direction from which she had come, that when she next saw her husband Paul, she would ask him if he felt she should try to talk with her mother about the pregnancy or just wait to be invited to talk about it. Paul was sensitive to this sort of thing, and gave her good counsel. He always gave good counsel. And he was cute. Sometimes she missed the glasses he used to need to wear. Once she had even asked him to put them on for her because she knew he always carried them with him just in case somehow the regenerative effect of the cryogenic sleep instantly wore off and he found himself needing the glasses again to see.

He had put them on and she had laughed and he had taken them off and she had made a big thing out of begging him to put them on again. And then she had laughed again and he hadn't taken them off but instead just laughed with her and at her and at himself and they had made love. She thought about this. It was the last time they had made love before they had left Iceland to search for her father, just before Karamatsov had tried to use his madness-inducing poison gas to launch a revolution against his government at the Soviet Underground City.

Annie Rourke Rubenstein thought of her mother again, of her mother being pregnant. Annie wanted Paul's baby but they had agreed, not until the world was rid of Karamatsov and it would be safe to have a child, to bring a new life into the world. If anything had made their resolve more, more — she tried to think of a word — more resolved, she almost verbalized. If anything, it had been the death of pretty Madison and the baby.

She shifted the M-16, carrying it at the pistol grip in her right fist.

She thought she heard a sound from the greenway at the center of the community, just beyond the last step. She didn't change her pattern of movement. To do so, if an enemy were present, would be to invite a shot. She kept walking, forcing herself not to increase her pace as she crossed the expanse along the height of the steps, perfectly in the open, an easy shot for even an indifferent marksman.

The German sergeant, Ludwig Peiffel, had heard the sound too, and with his eyes he telegraphed it to her.

If it were Russians out there — and some of their commando units were good at infiltration, very good — it might somewhat disarm them to think that Lydveldid Island was guarded by women, that the situation were so desperate that just defenseless women — and she smiled despite the danger she knew she was exposed to as she walked on, in the open. She had never felt herself to be particularly undangerous because of her sex, or that sex automatically made someone more or less of a danger. Maybe, if it were Russians who had caused the all but undetectable noise, they would learn about dangerous women this night. She was nearly to the edge of the open space, nearly to where she could duck beneath the comparative shelter of the porch railing.

Sergeant Peiffel cleared his throat and she didn't move her

51

head but let her eyes follow his out toward the greenway.

Had it been movement?

There was still no gunfire from the rim of the volcano.

"Ludwig — awful quiet, isn't it?" she said in a not overly loud stagey voice.

"Yes, Frau Rubenstein, it is very quiet," Sergeant Peiffel agreed, his eyes shifting toward the greenway again.

Annie stopped beside the vertical where the porch rail began and looked deliberately down into the greenway. She saw nothing. She felt something. She closed her eyes, trying to focus her concentration. What she could do with her mind sometimes was starting to scare her. It wasn't something she could see, but she could feel it just as surely as she had felt the presence of the man who had knocked at the door of Doctor Munchen, known his purpose. It was a combination of logical interpretation of fragmentary available data and some power she didn't understand at all. She had talked about it with her father. He had told her that she shouldn't push it, but rather let it develop naturally as it already had. She had read about such things, in women seemingly coming on at the outset of the menstrual cycle, but sometimes vanishing when the metabolism changed during and after pregnancy. Logic dictated that it was some delicate chemical balance.

She felt the men out there. Her gift, if indeed it was that, was not so well-honed as for her to be able to tell numbers, even see them. But she felt their presence. Many men. And she felt a mixture of anger, hatred, and fear.

Sergeant Peiffel had a radio set with which he could contact the defenders at the rim of the volcano, the two German counter snipers in place — precariously — on the roof of the presidential residence. She whispered to him without moving her lips, "I want you to alert the snipers on the roof, and then the forces at the rim. We have company."

Peiffel raised his eyebrow and smiled for an instant and then moved to reach the radio at his belt.

The smile froze on his face.

Annie saw that before she heard the burst of automatic weapons fire and threw herself down to the floor of the porch, but inside herself she had felt it a split second before and that, more than his death, more than her immediate danger, terrified her. It was hard crawling in an ankle length skirt without falling flat on your face, but she made it behind the rail, automatic weapons fire tearing into the porch itself, into the railings, shattering glass despite the protective shutters that had been installed when the building was sealed with Madame Jokli inside. Annie stabbed the M-16 through an opening in the porch rail and opened fire, razor edge chips and granite dust so heavy around her that she had to squint to protect her eyes.

"Get 'em," she screamed, returning fire now general from the porch, the heavier cracks of the counter-sniper fire from the roof coming too now. Annie shifted the M-16 to her left hand, outstretching her right arm, balling her tiny fist into the uniform tunic of Sergeant Peiffel — but she knew already that he was dead and the wide open stare that she had seen too often before confirmed that. She released the grip on his uniform and moved her hand down toward his utility belt, going for the radio. Automatic weapons fire from the greenway laced across his chest and abdomen as she drew her hand back.

They'd hear the gunfire at the rim, she told herself. But they wouldn't hear it if there were a battle in progress at the rim. "Shit," she snapped. She screamed up toward the roof, drawing herself deeper into cover, the M-16 in both hands now again. "On the roof — call for help! Use your radios!"

There was another volley of the heavier rifle fire from the snipers, but now in an arc all along the greenway facing the presidential residence there was heavy automatic weapons fire and Annie recoiled as the body of one of the counter-snipers plummeted past her from the roof above, catching for an instant in the bushes which fronted the high porch, then tumbling away.

There was no more of the heavier sounding gunfire of the sniper rifles. Had a radio transmission gotten through? In an instant, the Russians would charge the porch . . .

Captain Pavornin had given the attack signal and the gunship which would transport him forward to join the ground assault team was airborne now, some of the German mini-tanks already in motion, Pavornin's gunships firing their rockets. The German armor was tough.

"This is Pavornin—Lieutenant Askonikov—bring up the left flank—quickly and get your grenadiers and missilemen into position—heavy concentration of the German mini-tanks coming right at you!" He was beginning to reconsider joining Sergeant Borov with the right flank. A trio of German gunships was coming at him now, Pavornin elbowing the pilot opposite him. "There!"

He had heard about this strategy from those who had fought against the Germans before, seen it himself during the attack on the German stronghold in Argentina. Rumors circulated that the strategy had been taught the German military by the American John Rourke. Cut a wedge through the battle lines at all costs and attack the field commander and thereby so disrupt the chain of command that the battle was broken off.

Pavornin suddenly felt very naked in his gunship. "Take me away from here now!"

His pilot nodded rather than replying through the headset radios they both wore. He glanced back. The door gunner was strafing the German counter-attack below. The pilot wasn't using his missiles—not yet. The helicopter rose, then fell, then rose again, the streak of a missile contrail just passing beneath their chin bubble. Pavornin felt it—fear.

* * *

Akiro Kurinami spoke almost softly into his headset radio. "The Russian pilot is trying to avoid us—I wonder why. Ed—go high. Walter, stay on me!" Kurinami dodged the chopper down and to starboard, now giving the German gunship maximum acceleration, feeling himself pushed back into the pilot's seat as he climbed the machine, the G force pressing against his chest. The Soviet gunship rotated one hundred eighty degrees on its axis, hesitating for a split second, then started back toward the advancing Soviet lines. Kurinami worked the safety release for his starboard missiles, punching the button as he levelled off, firing his machineguns as well, the gunship vibrating with the missile launch. The contrail—the missile streaked toward the Soviet command gunship, the tail rotor, the entire tail section vaporizing in a fireball of black and orange and yellow. Kurinami still fired his machineguns as he made the pass across the dorsal side of the Soviet gunship. There was an explosion, even more violent than before, the chin bubble of Kurinami's helicopter smudged suddenly black with it, Kurinami banking his machine hard to starboard, glancing back over his shoulder. The Soviet gunship had vanished.

He spoke into his headset mouthpiece. "All right—let's help our people on the ground," and he started the chopper down at almost maximum pitch, near maximum speed . . .

Annie Rubenstein had no way of knowing if a radio message had gotten out to the rest of the defenders and, even if it had, whether or not reinforcements could be expected to arrive on time. Five of the Icelandic police remained alive with her there on the front porch of the presidential residence, though one of them was wounded and bleeding badly from a shoulder wound, another's face cut from a spray of rock chips.

She asked herself what her father would do in the same situation, and she knew what he would do instinctively. "All right—you and you—cover us—you three—with me—now!" She was up, firing a burst from her M-16, the assault rifle in her right fist along with a handful of her skirt as she vaulted the railing and dropped toward the ground. Her body caught up in the bushes for an instant, then rolled free, tearing her clothes, feeling the branches as they swatted against her face and tugged at her hair. She hit the ground in an undignified roll, firing the M-16 again as she got to her feet. The three Icelandic police were just behind her, one of them on the steps as she looked back, the man taking a burst across the chest and going down. Annie shouted to the other two, "Stick close!" hoping that they understood enough to do it. She dodged left, into a zigzagging run at a tangent toward the arc of Soviet gunfire, throwing herself down just inside the borderline of the greenway, gunfire plowing the grass near her head as she rolled onto her back, then over again onto her stomach, the assault rifle at her shoulder now, on full auto, firing, spraying into the Soviet cover.

One of the Icelandic police was beside her, firing out his assault rifle, the second—as she stopped to change magazines she could see him—a few feet to her left behind the trunk of a tree, up on one knee, still firing.

The Soviet attackers broke from cover and stormed forward, laying down such a heavy volume of automatic weapons fire she couldn't raise her head long enough to return fire.

Suddenly, the pattern of gunfire changed, a heavy concentration from behind her and she looked back. Her mother and three more of the Icelandic police and German corporal were coming in two units from both sides of the presidential palace. Her mother led two of the Icelandics and the German corporal led the other, Sarah Rourke's M-16 on full auto. Some of the Soviet attackers started to go down, their attacking wedge broken; others dodged for cover.

Annie shouted to her two men, "Now!" She was up, running, firing, the M-16 in her right fist, the Beretta from

56

the Bianchi holster at her left hip, firing in her left hand. She emptied the assault rifle into two of the Russians, then slapped the muzzle into the face of a third, took a half step back and fired into his left eye with the Beretta. The rifle fell on its sling, empty, to her left hip; no time to reload. Her right hand snatched the Scoremaster from the identical holster on her right side as she turned half to her left, discharging both pistols simultaneously into the chest of one of the Russians. She looked behind her, her mother gut-shooting a Russian officer as he turned toward her to fire.

Sarah Rourke snapped the rifle up and left and fired it out, shouting across the din of battle, "Not bad for a pregnant lady who's busting out of her blue jeans, huh!"

Chapter Eight

There were flashes in the darkness, the sweep of search-lights, the brilliant bursts of light from explosions. John Rourke was ready by the open gunship door, holding to one of the safety straps with his left hand, his M-16 in his right fist, the hood of his parka up against the cold. The German base loomed ahead; the German gunship banked, Rourke feeling it, skirting the edge of the aerial battlefield, well beyond the furthest edge of the German base which fronted the Hekla Community, aiming as Rourke had ordered toward the interior of Hekla itself, which had to be the ultimate Soviet objective in the attack.

Natalia's voice drew him back to the moment. "When they let us out, you and Paul cover me — I'll take the grenade launcher."

"Agreed," Rourke shouted back over the icy roar of the gunship's slipstream. He glanced back into the subdued green light of the cabin. Paul was readying himself, an M-16 slung on each side, bags of grenades slung cross-body on each side along with bags of spare magazines for their weapons.

There were explosions behind them now, and explosions and pinpoint lights of small arms fire in the distance ahead by the crater rim. Rourke's plan was a simple one — insert behind the main body of the attacking Soviet force and counter-attack from the rear, the gunship going airborne again and strafing the Soviet line, attempting for radio contact with the German and Icelandic defenders at the rim of the volcano to start a second wave counter-attack. If it worked — but if it didn't, Rourke considered. But there was no other option. He had counted on arriving before the Soviet attack began, but fate and Soviet battle plans had mitigated against that.

The helicopter was steadily dropping, the land beneath it steadily rising, the effect unnerving slightly as Rourke's eyes surveyed the battlefield they fast approached at the rim of the cone. The main body of Soviet forces and hence the main thrust of the Soviet attack against the Hekla Community seemed concentrated against the face of the cone nearest the German base — a poor move, Rourke felt subjectively, but if the Soviets had been better tacticians and strategists, they would have been that much more difficult an enemy.

Rourke shouted to the pilot, Rourke's radio set already stripped away before he had entered the open doorway. "Bring her down now!" It was convenient that the German officer corps spoke English, but for himself and Natalia, though her accent was better and her vocabulary broader, German was not a problem at any event.

The pilot made a hand signal showing recognition, Natalia joining John Rourke at the fuselage door, holding to the same safety strap that he did. Paul Rubenstein wedged himself just inside the door as he pulled up his parka hood then regripped the M-16s. The German MP-40 submachinegun was strapped to and snugged tight against his chest.

The rotor pitch shifted abruptly and Natalia was thrown slightly off balance, Rourke feeling her impact against him. "Be careful," she shouted over the slipstream.

"I love you too," he told her.

"I know that," she nodded, leaning up quickly, tugging away the scarf which protected the lower portion of her face against the wind and the cold, kissing him full on the lips, but briefly, then pulling away and raising the scarf again. Rourke glanced at his friend Paul. Paul nodded.

The helicopter was nearly down, but attracting no noticable attention from the rear of the Soviet lines as it swept in. The chopper skimmed the glacier crusted surface now, stopping abruptly to hover in mid-air, then seemed to skid into touchdown.

Rourke loosened the security strap and jumped, nearly losing his balance on the glacial ice, breaking into a dead run as he regained it. Paul and Natalia jumped out side by side as Rourke glanced back, Rourke diving for cover behind a wide ice ridge which signalled a crevasse below, looking back again. Paul and Natalia had taken up positions nearer the landing, side by side behind the protection of a massive upthrust boulder. Rourke worked the safety tumbler of the M-16 to full auto, shouldering the rifle, waiting. He glanced right, across the snowfield, the light nearly bright enough to read now that the clouds above which had darkened the sky during most of their journey from Europe had broken to reveal a three-quarters full moon. Natalia nodded and Paul loosed one of his M-16s, gave a handsignal and then shouldered the other assault rifle. Rourke moved his right first finger inside the trigger guard.

There was a whooshing sound, then a whistling sound and then a roar, the first grenade from the multi-barreled German grenade launcher impacting, exploding, into the core of the Russian rear. Bodies sailed into the night sky, plummeting downward, in whole or in fragments, a puff of orange tinged white smoke belching upward. The whoosh, the whistle, the roar again, another grenade detonated; some of the Russians dodged to take cover, others turned to fire. Rourke touched his finger to the trigger, spraying, burning through at least ten rounds, shifting the muzzle, doing it again, confident against burning out the barrel with the sub-zero temperatures. He blew out the entire magazine, bodies falling as the Russians rushed their position.

The grenade launcher again, assault rifle fire from Paul's position as Rourke changed sticks, ramming the fresh thirty-round magazine up the well, continuing firing. The whoosh, the whistle, the roar, more Russians down. Rourke was up on his feet, spraying out the entire magazine, then dropping as enemy soldiers fell and others rushed toward him to take their place. Paul was up, an M-16—one his and one of them one of the two Natalia carried—blazing from each hand, the guns on full auto, Russians going down. Paul ducked down, Rourke up to his knees, the M-16 to his right shoulder, spraying death again. The whoosh, the whistle, the roar, then the whoosh, the whistle, the roar again—then again and again.

Rourke changed sticks and was on his feet. He glanced toward Paul, the younger man doing the same now, but an M-16 in each hand, Rourke and Rubenstein firing simultaneously into the attacking Russians.

Bodies fell and men died. The whoosh, the whistle, the roar, then again and again.

Rourke changed sticks for the M-16 again and started forward around the edge of the crevasse. He felt it, shouted over the roar of gunfire, "Paul!"

His footing was suddenly gone and he was plummeting downward, into the crevasse . . .

Annie Rourke felt something stabbing her, dropping to her knees, loosening her rifle from her grasp, her hands going to her temples as she screamed.

They had been moving across the greenway searching for what remained of the Soviet infiltration team, her mother near enough to her that she was beside her the next instant. "What is it, Annie?"

"Daddy—oh my God, Momma!"

Chapter Nine

John Rourke let go of the M-16 the instant he realized what was happening, before he even shouted. The impact of the explosions had forced apart the crevasse and the ice-bridge had disintegrated beneath his feet. His right hand had grasped upward for the surface, his gloved fingers slipping across it, his body hurtling downward, his left hand reaching to the butt of the Crain System X knife he had just recently added to his gear from his supplies at the Retreat. And he silently thanked God that he had. There was no time to verbalize. As his body skidded downward, the space surrounding him narrowed dramatically with each foot, the light ebbing even faster. His left hand tore steel from leather and as his left fist balled over the tubular haft, he stabbed, his right hand splaying outward, his feet twisting outward, his legs spreading. The Crain knife bit deep into the ice, his shoulders and neck taking the shockwave as it engulfed his body, his full weight with its acceleration abruptly stopping, Rourke's body swinging by his left fist from the haft of the Crain survival knife.

Rourke's eyes closed and he breathed.

He opened his eyes. The darkness was near total. He couldn't shout, could barely breathe. Rourke's right foot was wedged into the crevasse and he realized that had he fallen any further he would have broken the foot, or dislocated his hip. He flexed the toes of his right foot inside his combat boots. They were numb with cold and pain but moved. His left shoulder was screaming at him to let go of the knife as he pried his boot free, struggling for a new, less punishing purchase against the glass-smooth wall of glacial ice which could at any moment close above and around him, entombing him.

Rourke's right hand moved slowly along the ice, toward the bottom edge of his arctic parka, then raising it, his gloved hand searching against the small of his back, near his right kidney. He found the vastly smaller knife he always carried, had always carried even before the Night of The War. The Sting IA Black Chrome. He tugged it free of the inside-the-pants sheath, balling his right fist over the skeletonized handle, then drawing his right arm up and back and stabbing forward, gouging the A.G. Russell knife into the ice, his body weight suspended from both hands now, swinging free as his foot lost its purchase.

Rourke tested his weight against both knives. Both knives held.

Both knives were at approximately the same level. He began to pull himself up, his shoulders seeming to burn with the pain. There were times he wished he were still Michael's age.

If Natalia and Paul had seen him fall, if Paul had heard his shout — but the distractions of battle. They had just begun their advance. The ice groaned around him, shifting, Rourke feeling it push against him. The crevasse was closing.

He had his shoulders to the level of both knives, holding on with his left hand to the larger handle of the Crain knife, shifting his right hand for a terrifying instant to get his forearm above the Russell knife. The little knife held. Rourke inhaled, shifting his grip on the Crain knife, his body thrusting upward, above the level of the knives. He pushed himself upward, to maximum extension of his arms, nearly locking his elbows.

John Rourke closed his eyes for an instant, trying to ignore the groaning of the narrowing walls of ice in front and in back of him, then ripping the little Russell knife free of the ice with his right hand and, as his left elbow locked, his grip started to go, stabbing the smaller knife into the ice above him, clinging there, taking some of the weight off his left hand and arm and shoulder.

John Rourke breathed. He could not see the opening in the ice above him, but he ignored the possibility that it had already closed and encased him here forever. But forever wouldn't be very long. He would freeze to death quickly enough.

Already, his limbs were numbing from something else than pain.

But there was no time and each second he hung suspended here the ice would close that much more. He started pulling himself up on the little Sting IA Black Chrome, getting his left foot up, onto the hollow handle of the Crain Life Support System X. He stood, catching his breath, the knife not shifting beneath him.

To climb this way would be too time consuming, deadly. There was no way to gauge the exact distance remaining to the top, but he judged he had fallen some thirty feet, perhaps more than that. Rourke's mind raced. The little Sting IA had a ring through its butt for attaching a lanyard. Rourke shifted slightly on his purchase, with his left hand grasping at the sling of the M-16. The sling was not made to be removed one handed. But he started working at it, prying, the sling of the clip type rather than one which threaded through the swivels and was bound by the buckle. He had one clip all but free — free now, the rifle starting to slip away. He caught the end of the sling in his teeth.

With his left hand, Rourke caught up the rifle and loosed the sling from his teeth. It was the waste of a perfectly serviceable M-16, but there was nothing else for it. He held the M-16 between his legs, working loose the other clip which was at the buttstock. He had it, as the rifle slipped away into the darkness of the abyss below, Rourke nearly losing his balance, catching himself. He reached up his left hand, snapping the sling into the hole at the base of the skeletonized handle of the Sting IA.

Rourke breathed.

He was starting to grow numb all over from the cramped position, from the cold, from the—he had never seen any logic in self-deception—fear. Rourke started feeding the slack in the sling through the buckle to give himself as much length as possible with the sling.

If the sling held and if the short blade of the Sting IA bit deeply enough into the ice—Rourke was shivering. The darkness seemed to be increasing—was it the ice closing over him or simply a cloud passing in front of the three-quarter full moon?

He told himself the latter. Sometimes, self-deception was necessary, however illogical.

He worked the method through his mind several times.

Using the massive Crain Life Support System X, he would gouge into the ice surface while hanging by one hand from the sling attached to the little Sting IA, then get a foothold and raise himself up, then regrasp the sling and free the Crain knife, then repeat the process all over again. A third knife would have made it easier, pitons made it almost a practical means of traverse.

John Rourke reached to maximum extension, his booted feet balanced on the handle of the Crain knife, his right hand wrenching out the Sting IA, then his right arm extending upward, driving the knife into the ice like a stake into the heart of a vampire. He wrapped the sling around his right fist and tugged. The knife moved slightly, then held, locked in the ice—he hoped at least. Holding to the sling, he eased himself down to where his knees could bend, searching for a toehold against the ice, finding none but wedging his legs against the narrowing walls which were glass slick. He used his left hand and fought at the Crain knife, ripping the Life Support System X free, swinging crazily for a moment as the force of his exertion freed his body from the wedged position he had taken.

Instantly, he modified his plan of attack against the sheer ice face. Instead of driving the Crain knife into the same wall, he would drive it into the opposite wall, using a modified rock chimney technique.

Rourke balled his gloved left fist more tightly still over the handle of the Crain knife and drove it into the ice almost at chest height, pulling himself up against the sling's tension, getting his left foot into the handle of the Crain knife, raising himself up, the walls closer together here, an advantage for what he had determined as his means of locomotion, but a growing danger. Rourke ripped the smaller Russell knife free, then stabbed it into the ice at the maximum extension of his right arm's upward reach.

Again, he half swung, was half wedged—and he wrenched the Crain knife free, then drove it in again at nearly chest height, raising his left leg, getting a foothold, starting to drag himself up—his boot slipped. Rourke started to lose his hold on the sling, but caught himself as his left hand grasped for the haft of the Crain knife.

He swung there, knowing that at any moment one of the knives might lose its bite into the ice and he could fall.

The ice groaned around him again, a sound like tortured metal under great strain.

Again, he brought his left foot up, getting it as firmly as he could into position on the haft of the Crain knife, then pushing himself up. There was no time to rest. He tore the smaller knife free, then hammered it into the ice with all the force he could summon, at maximum reach above him. Again, he grasped the sling/lifeline, again he tugged the Crain knife free of the ice, each time the task more difficult, his strength ebbing, he knew.

He drove the Crain knife home, again rising to stand on its handle. His shoulders were touching the walls of ice which confined him and the crevasse seemed even narrower in the gray light above him.

John Rourke repeated the process—drive the smaller knife into the ice, swing from the sling, wrench out the larger knife and then drive it into the ice, then climb up to stand upon it, then begin again—he didn't know how many times, realizing at one level of consciousness that he was moving automaton-like, marveling at still another level of consciousness that he was moving at all. His arms ached with weariness; his legs cramped.

As he rose to perch precariously again on the handle of the Crain knife, his head impacted something above him—ice.

"Jesus," Rourke cried into the darkness.

He was trapped.

Annie Rourke—Sarah Rourke watched her, praying for the child. The gift the girl had was also a curse, perhaps more a curse than a gift at all.

"I can feel him, Momma—he's trapped—he's in darkness. He's never been so tired. I can feel him thinking—about us and never seeing us again—Momma!"

Sarah Rourke held her daughter tightly in her arms. They were trapped under enemy fire; had no radio, were still at least a quarter mile from the rim of the volcano. And Annie Rourke had said a word which said it all, moaned the word like pain—ice.

"John!" Sara screamed her husband's name until her throat ached with it . . .

Natalia Anastasia Tiemerovna felt something—Annie? She looked at Paul Rubenstein beside her, crouched near the height of the cone, Russians in front of them, some still behind them, the defenders of Hekla counter-attacking now, Natalia and Paul pinned down. Natalia closed her eyes.

"Where's John," she asked.

In her self-imposed darkness, she heard Paul Rubenstein saying, "Where the hell is he?"

Annie . . .

Annie Rourke focused her concentration. If her father were in danger Natalia and Paul might be near by. Natalia . . . She whispered the word, "Natalia . . . Natalia . . . please, Natalia . . ."

Chapter Ten

He was sealed in the crevasse. The ice could have been
feet thick or only inches thick. He didn't know which.
Rourke stood, balanced on the handle of the Crain knife, his
legs cramping because he couldn't move them, his feet falling
asleep, losing all sensation. He tried wiggling his toes inside
his boots but with the added numbing effect of the cold, they
could barely respond. With the A.G. Russell Sting IA he
chiselled at the ice over his head, hammering at the butt of
the knife with the Pachmayr gripped butt of the Metalifed
and Mag-na-Ported Colt Python from the holster at his right
hip. The ice was chipping away, but piteously slowly.

The walls of ice groaned again. The last time they had
made it such that he could not keep both shoulders level and
still be able to move freely; this time it confined him still
more.

He stopped hammering, his strength, his very ability to
raise his hands all but ebbed away. The next time the walls
closed, he would be crushed or forced to drop downward,
abandoning any hope of survival. But his will had not ebbed
away.

John Rourke could barely see, the darkness all but abso-
lute now.

He had never cared to gamble at cards or dice — life was

too much of a gamble as it was, no matter how one planned ahead. And it was time again to gamble, the stakes all or nothing. If the ice were too thick —

He blotted thoughts of defeat from his mind. Again, his thoughts focused on Sarah, Michael, Annie, Paul — and Natalia. He loved two women. He might never see either of them again.

John Rourke wrapped the sling carefully around the blade of the Sting IA and pocketed it. Clinically, his years of firearms expertise summoned up, as though he were punching up a file in a computer. The .357 Magnum over the .45 ACP had the greatest hydrostatic shock value. It would be the Python then. He wasn't looking to knock down the ice, but rather burst through it.

He drew himself downward; ironically, it was easier now with the walls having closed in around him, the ice making him shiver with the cold.

Rourke took his dark-lensed aviator style sunglasses from an interior pocket, placed them over his eyes. He was totally blinded. He removed the glasses, could barely see the section of ice he had chipped away at, memorized the range of motion needed and then replaced the glasses. As he clung to the ice wall, wedged there over the Crain knife which still supported his feet, John Rourke thrust the Python upward, the muzzle pointed by feel, the six-inch rocking gently in his fist as he fired, his ears ringing with it. He fired a double tap, chunks of ice toppling down around him. He fired another single round, then the last double tap, the cylinder empty.

Rourke could no longer hear even his own breathing. His ears were filled with hollow roars.

He removed the sunglasses, looking up. He could barely detect that some larger chunks of ice were shot away. Still no opening into the arctic night above him.

Rourke worked the cylinder release catch, thumbing it rearward, with his trigger finger pushing out the cylinder, shaking the revolver over the abyss, the empty brass falling away. He felt in one of the musette bags, finding one of the Safariland speedloaders, ramming it by feel into the cylinder, against the ejector star, the cartridges dumping as he awkwardly held the revolver between his knees. He pocketed the speedloader. If he survived, it would be needed.

He told himself he would survive.

He closed the cylinder, taking the revolver again in his right fist. The ice walls shuddered, closing around him again. Rourke turned sideways, the walls against his chest and back. The pistol overhead, he worked the trigger as fast as it could be double-actioned, the howling roar in his ears intensifying, the pelting of chunks of ice intensifying, his glasses pocketed, his eyes averted, closed.

The Python was empty.

John Rourke looked up.

Moonlight.

Rourke rammed the Python into the full flap holster at his right hip, closing the flap so he wouldn't lose the revolver. The Crain knife — he must get it. The walls of ice started to shudder, closing, faster now, Rourke pushing himself up, finding the Sting IA in his right pocket, gouging it into the ice overhead, holding to the sling.

He let his feet slip from the handle of the Crain knife, using almost the last of his strength to pry it free of the ice, then throw his arms up sideways in a ragged arc and thrust the knife into the ice overhead. He pulled himself up, still holding to the sling with his right hand.

He pulled — his head pushed through the crack in the ice. The crevasse was shuddering closed.

John Rourke wrenched the Crain knife free of the ice as he thrust his upper body into the sub-zero night, a strange warmth rushing over him. He rolled his body free, his legs barely responding, jerking at the sling which was still attached to the Russell knife, the smaller knife arcing up and out of the crevasse as the crevasse sealed, the ice beneath

Rourke's body shuddering violently, Rourke sagging to his back, his left fist still clutching the Crain knife.

"American!"

The English was bad, but it was heavily accented with Russian and Rourke couldn't hold that against the speaker.

He saw the man, one of the Soviet assault rifles in both the man's fists, the man less than six feet away, levelling the rifle to fire.

The Life Support System X was not made for throwing, was not balanced for throwing. A good man, Rourke's father had once told him, could underhand anything from a kitchen knife to a shortsword at small distances. Rourke snapped his left hand and arm forward as he rolled toward the man, his left hand loosing the haft of the Crain System X, the foot long blade snapping into the moonlight between them, burying itself in the Soviet soldier's chest as the assault rifle sprayed into the ice. John Rourke tried to stand, but couldn't. His eyes started to close.

Chapter Eleven

Paul Rubenstein had elected to go, Natalia providing covering fire for him with two of the M-16s, friendly forces to close for use of the grenade launcher. "Ready?"

"Ready," Rubenstein answered, swinging the M-16 forward on its sling.

"Now!" Natalia shouted, Paul Rubenstein pushing up from the crouch and sprinting away from the rocks behind which they had taken cover, heavy light machinegun fire coming at him as he dodged and ran, the sound of Natalia with an M-16 behind him.

He was making toward the sparsest portion of enemy resistance behind them, going back to look for John Rourke. Natalia told him that somehow she sensed Annie and somehow she sensed that something was wrong about John. She didn't know how or why.

And Paul Rubenstein ran. The Soviet forces were nearly finished, but fighting to the last man as Rubenstein had anticipated they would, as John Rourke had soberly predicted, bitterly predicted. It seemed ingrained in the Soviet military mentality to fight until resistance was no longer possible, then to continue to fight. He wondered if it were a subconscious racial memory of the Sege of Stalingrad, or just indoctrination, or perhaps both. He kept running, two

Soviet troopers opening up from behind an ice ridge to his left. Rubenstein threw himself down, firing, spraying into the ice ridge, huge chunks of ice flying; Rubenstein found one of the German grenades, baseball shaped and copied after American grenades he had seen in movies—how long ago. He pulled the pin, hurtling the grenade toward the ice ridge, then pushing up to his feet and running again as it exploded, knowing the damage it would do.

He kept running, nearly clear of enemy fire now, a few straggling Soviet soldiers still to be seen, some fewer of them wounded. Rubenstein started shouting. "John! John Rourke! Where are you?" It seemed inconceivable to him that something could have happened—he realized subconsciously that he thought of John Rourke as being like an immortal, somehow impervious to death. "John!" The thought chilled him more than the bone chilling cold of the night.

He saw something—far to his right, farther away from the volcanic cone. Paul Rubenstein threw himself into the run. The clothing color was wrong for the Soviet troopers or even the Germans—white snow smock, but part of it pulled up, black winter gear revealed beneath it in the moonlight, the body tall, even fully reclined as it was—a man well over six feet in height, long limbed.

"Shit! John!"

Paul Rubenstein let the assault rifle fall to his right side on its sling, grasping the Schmeisser from where it was suspended at his left side, throwing back the bolt, ready for close range work, whatever came. "John!"

He skidded to his knees on the ice, half calculated, half miscalculated, slipping. He fell face forward, his face inches from the unconscious visage of the tall, lean man. The face was gray, seeming lifeless. John Rourke's face.

"John!"

Paul Rubenstein crawled toward his friend, his left glove coming off, ripping it away with his teeth. His hands

74

touched at Rourke's face — cold as death. "John! Answer me! John!"

Behind him, he heard movement. Rubenstein wheeled there on his knees beside the best friend he had ever had, the man he loved more than a brother — There was a dead Russian, a knife impaling him through the chest, the knife John Rourke had started carrying since the last quick trip John and Michael had made to the Retreat.

Beyond the knife-dead soldier was a figure, moving, then another. Two Russian soldiers, advancing out of the shadow beyond a rising ice ridge.

Paul Rubenstein threw his body over that of his friend to protect him, throwing the Schmeisser on line with the enemy soldiers, inside himself screaming at the senselessness of this, all of it, killing men who were total strangers. "Die! Fuck you!" Rubenstein triggered a burst from the subgun, then another and another, the two bodies going down, then still rocking with the hits as he kept firing until the Schmeisser was empty and still. Rubenstein drew the battered Browning High Power from the tanker holster beneath his parka as he almost ripped it open, setting the pistol on John Rourke's chest, shrugging out of the jacket, then folding it around John Rourke as he raised his friend's lifeless seeming form into a sitting position, the body cold, stiff — rigid? "John! Damnit, answer me! John!" Rubenstein gripped the High Power in his right fist, hugging his friend's body to his, trying to give John Rourke the warmth of his own body.

"Natalia! Help me! It's John!" He kept screaming for her, praying inside himself that John Rourke would say to stop the noise, would at least stir. But there was no movement. "John! Damnit, don't die!" And he rocked his friend's body against his to give him warmth.

Chapter Twelve

It was stupid to move in the darkness, but the light they had seen, like a fire but where a fire should not have been, had been impossible to ignore. There were fires of course, a lightning strike. But this fire—something different about it, Michael Rourke had felt, resisting the thought that he had felt it intuitively. He left the mysticism to his sister, Annie.

The fire—it had to be investigated.

Michael Rourke glanced behind him, the thin line of pale yellow along the horizon almost imperceptibly wider than it had been a moment earlier; nearly dawn. His eyes shifted to Bjorn Rolvaag and Rolvaag's dog in the valley below them, placidly sitting beside the German vehicle.

Then Michael's eyes shifted to Maria Leuden. She clambered along the rock face beside him, her pale cheeks flushed red with the cold and with exertion in the thin atmosphère. Her gray-green eyes met his. Michael looked away. He had no desire for the eyes of a beautiful woman now, half hidden behind glasses.

Ahead of them by a few yards was Otto Hammerschmidt, the German commando captain, holding his rifle in a hard assault position when the terrain allowed, Hammerschmidt hatless as was Michael Rourke, despite the cold, Hammerschmidt's blond hair moving with the vagaries of the icy

76

wind.

Maria Leuden started to speak, Michael putting his right index finger to her lips in a gesture for silence. As he glanced at her she nodded comprehension and they continued moving.

Hammerschmidt disappeared over a large, breadloaf-shaped rock, the granite surface splotched with snow, Michael quickening his pace, Maria Leuden keeping pace with him. He admired her tenacity.

Michael reached the breadloaf-shaped rock and started searching for toeholds for his boots, clambering up then, but slowly, peering over the top of the rock surface. A gust of wind from the high plateau, which now spread almost endlessly before him assaulting his exposed skin with tiny specks of ice. He squinted against them, his eyes averted from the wind, turning his head to follow the vast expanse of the plateau with his eyes.

And then he saw what he knew Otto must have seen. He closed his eyes, tight — but not against the ice and wind. He opened his eyes. What he had seen was still there, though it shouldn't have been there.

And there was no sign of Otto Hammerschmidt . . .

Otto Hammerschmidt had always enjoyed watching the videotapes from the twentieth century, especially the ones which were proscribed for viewing — it was like innocent sinning. In one such tape he had seen persons such as these. They were called barbarians. But, though the fur trimmed robes, the fur trimmed high boots, the long, curved bladed swords and the unnaturally small Asian horses were all much the same, in the videotaped film the barbarians had not carried guns. But these men did, unless the lone sentry who drowsed beside a snowswept rock a few feet from the remains of the massive fire which had drawn their attention during the night, had the only one.

He had always been a student of arms, and he recognized the general profile of the weapon held limply in the crook of the guard's left elbow. It looked for all the world like a 7.62mm Type 68, which would have made it the Chinese counterpart of the antiquated but deadly efficient rifles the Rourke family still favored, the M-16.

There were six horses, and five sleeping men huddled near the fire wrapped in robes and blankets, plus the sixth man, the sentry.

The look of these men bespoke a dearth of technology, certainly such as would have been needed to survive the Night of The War and the Great Conflagration.

Their existence, then, was impossible, but here they were.

He had learned much recently about accepting the impossible as fact and then setting out to investigate what made it possible.

Hammerschmidt pushed himself up from the cluster of rocks behind which he had hidden, to peer more intently at the gear of the semi-sleeping guard. There was a belt pack radio.

"Fascinating," Hammerschmidt murmured, exhaling, watching the steam of his breath cross his line of sight.

The guard turned around.

The man started to his feet, shouting something in a guttural language that sounded like it could have been Chinese but was spoken badly.

Hammerschmidt had no real knowledge of languages beyond German and the mandatory English demanded of the officer corps — he was just guessing. But he didn't have to guess that he had been detected.

The sentry swept his rifle up toward his shoulder. Hammerschmidt noticed a holster for a pistol on the man's belt.

"Wait! I come in friendship!" He tried English first considering it more likely that a Chinese would speak English than German.

The sentry shouted again, some of the sleepers near the

fire starting to rise, grabbing up rifles from the ground beside them and pistols from beside their saddles where they had slept.

Hammerschmidt tried German—the same words had the same apparent lack of effect.

"Scheiss!"

His mind raced. To kill one of these men could so damage the potential for contact as to—

One of the men coming up from a night's sleep on the cold rocky ground fired a pistol, the pistol too, in the brief instant in which Hammerschmidt saw it, appearing for all the world like something belonging in a museum.

Hammerschmidt swung his assault rifle on line and sprayed, firing low, into the dirt about two meters in front of the sentry, the apparently sleepiest man of the bunch.

The pistol shot had missed by a wide margin, impacting one of the rocks about a hand's breadth from Hammerschmidt's left shoulder, Hammerschmidt dodging down and right.

He heard gunfire from behind him, starting to wheel toward it, realizing it had to be Michael Rourke and Maria Leuden, then keeping down . . .

Michael Rourke shouted to Maria Leuden, "Stay down," as he swung the German assault rifle to his shoulder and fired, aiming for the partially burnt logs of the fire at the center of the—the Mongol camp. Great chunks of the logs—thick pine trunks—split and cracked and sparks flared, the five men nearest the fire starting to take cover, the sixth man, some sort of sentry dressed for all the world like someone from the army of Genghis Khan but armed with a Chinese Communist assault rifle, was still firing, either too brave to care or too dumb to understand. Michael somehow assumed the latter.

Maria Leuden was suddenly beside him, screaming and

Michael took his eyes from the German assault rifle's sights and looked toward her, then followed her eyes toward the far left edge of his peripheral vision, then wheeled, turning toward the north, toward what she was staring at.

A cloud of snow, and perhaps dust too, rose in the distance, still diminutive figures of men and horses at its front, riding, now rifles firing into the air, what had to be war cries screeched into the wind.

"Holy shit — come on!"

Michael Rourke realized, as he grabbed Maria Leuden, shoving her along beside him, then finally the woman breaking into a run — the men around the campfire hadn't hidden from his gunfire, but from seeing the same thing she had seen.

And none of it — none of it at all should have existed.

Maria Leuden beside him, he ran, toward Hammerschmidt — but after that . . . "Run!"

Chapter Thirteen

John Rourke opened his eyes. He almost whispered, his throat parched as he spoke, "I must be in heaven—I'm surrounded by angels."

His wife started to laugh, his daughter hugged him and Natalia Anastasia Tiemerovna closed her eyes and audibly sighed.

"What the hell's that make me?"

He turned his head to track the voice—his ears were still ringing—and that was a mistake because when he moved his head began to ache maddeningly, his neck stiff, every muscle in his body seeming to come alive at one moment and scream at him to cease whatever idiocy he was attempting. He found the voice, already knowing its owner. It was Paul Rubenstein. "Don't ask," he smiled, closing his eyes with the pain . . .

Paul Rubenstein walked from the room at the Hekla base German military hospital and into the corridor where Dr. Munchen was waiting, after having summoned them from his office that John Rourke was reviving.

Munchen's usually cosmopolitan look of reserve cracked into a smile. "Your marvelously lucky friend will be impossible to hold down here in the hospital in another few hours. I'd like to keep him for observation, but it probably isn't necessary. Let him go home this evening—"

"Where's home," Paul Rubenstein smiled.

"A point well taken, Herr Rubenstein. But between all of you see if you can get him to drop by tomorrow—at his convenience of course. But my best medical opinion and my instinctive reaction is that he will be unimpaired by his ordeal except for some minor stiffness for a few days and some minor, temporary hearing loss."

"Thank God," Paul Rubenstein murmured.

"Yes—but also thank Herr Doctor Rourke for his tenacity while waiting for your God to point the way to his deliverance."

Paul Rubenstein started to laugh . . .

The wind of the desert blew cold and Akiro Kurinami stood staring into the night, shivering a little but not yet ready to return to his tent, shared with a Spanish biotech specialist named Juliano Alverez de Zaragoza, as fine a combat helicopter pilot as ever lived. Alverez de Zaragoza had died in combat with the now defeated, now vanquished Soviet attack force.

But they would be back. Four other Eden personnel had died, several others had sustained minor wounds, eighteen Germans dead and many others wounded.

How many of the attacking Soviet force had lost their lives was impossible to gauge.

The Russians were a threat from without.

But a threat from within somehow worried him vastly more.

The missing rifles, the other supplies. And there was Commander Dodd's cavalier attitude toward it all—or was it studied disregard, he wondered. The thought made him shiver all the more and he turned, startled, when he felt the touch at his shoulder, so lost in thought he had heard no approach in the night.

He turned toward the touch—the chocolate brown skin of Elaine Halversen was somehow well defined in the moonlight, accentuating her cheekbones, making her appear more beautiful than he normally perceived her. He realized on an objective level that she was merely pretty, but subjectively—

"A penny for your thoughts, Akiro."

He folded his arms around her and smelled her hair. He was familiar with the Americanism and whispered against her, "They have insufficient value, I think—not worth the penny."

"Ahh, but I have a yen to know," and she laughed at her bad pun and he held her more tightly against him.

"I'm worried. We shouldn't be sitting out here in these tents while construction is going on for a permanent base. We could have delayed construction for a week and completed temporary fortifications that could have been cannibalized later. But we didn't. And the missing weapons and supplies—Dodd didn't really seem to care at all when I spoke of them with him."

"He was probably concerned about the attack, that's all," Elaine told him. "You know—I mean I'm changing the subject," and she stepped back from him, holding both his hands out at arm's length. "When I was a little girl I traveled through this part of Georgia. It was never like this. There were people, road signs—there were even signs that said only white people could use a drinking fountain or a bathroom. Wasn't that silly?"

"What about Japanese—we are neither white nor black."

She seemed to ponder his remark, then laughed a little, a soft laugh that he had come to enjoy hearing very much. "I don't know if you would have been treated like a white man or a—well—they called us colored people, and sometimes worse."

"I like your color very much." And Kurinami drew her

83

close to him again, staring skyward as he held her. It was silly that she called herself black. She was brown and so much warmer than the night . . .

The shrieking riders were closer now. Michael Rourke realized that he and Hammerschmidt and Maria Leuden were all but ignored as the six men from the fire which had originally drawn them up onto the plateau frantically saddled their mixed-breed horses. Snapping a frenzied and largely symbolic shot toward the riders, two of the six swung up into their saddles. One of the men still on the ground who had been wrestling his rearing mount, abandoned the animal, vaulting up behind one of the already mounted men, bashing the man in the side of the face with a pistol butt, then goading the animal ahead as he threw himself over the cantle of the saddle, his feet never finding the stirrups as the animal leaped ahead.

Michael looked at Maria Leuden, then at Hammerschmidt. "We've gotta see where they're going and find out who those other guys are. Otto — keep down here with Maria and then as soon as everyone's past, get the hell back down into the valley. I'll use my radio to keep in touch. Good luck."

He started up from his crouched position behind the rocks where Hammerschmidt had taken shelter, Hammerschmidt giving him a nod. But Maria Leuden reached out to him, her hands touching his face, one of them gloved and itchy from wool, the other soft, cool more than cold. "Come back," and she kissed him hard on the mouth.

For some reason, he realized, he would always remember the look in her gray-green eyes at that instant. "I will," he whispered, not knowing if she heard him, not knowing why he said it. He broke into a dead run toward the last three of the men from the fire, the largest of them starting aboard the largest of the animals. Michael angled toward him, slinging the assault rifle behind him, jumping.

Michael's hands reached for the man's neck, peeling him away from the saddle, the animal the man had been about to mount rearing, Michael dodging left to avoid its flailing hooves. The big man came up in a roll, hurtling himself toward him. Michael spun left, his right foot snapping up and out, impacting the fur clad man at the throat and then at the forehead with the last beat of the double kick.

Michael turned, looking for the horse, seeing it, seeing the band of horsemen not far off now, knowing that in less than a minute they would close. Michael started for the horse, grabbing at the one piece rein, dragging the horse down by the bit in its mouth, the horse falling, Michael stepping back, throwing his right leg across the animal's saddled back as it rose, stumbled, regained its footing and reared. He tensed back the reins, digging his heels in, the animal bucking once, then starting to leap ahead and away from the band of horsemen, jumping the all but dead night fire.

And suddenly Michael felt a terrible weight pulling him from the saddle, twisting his head left, craning his neck, straining to see from the far edge of his peripheral vision. It was the man whose horse Michael had just stolen, clinging to the assault rifle, the sling from which Michael had suspended the German assault rifle cross-body now strangling him, pulling him from the saddle of the galloping horse beneath him. Michael's left fist snapped outward, hitting the man's face, but not dislodging him. Michael reached to his belt with his left hand, finding the butt of the knife old Jon the swordmaker had given him, unsheathing it, nearly losing it as the horse dodged some low rocks. Michael brought the knife up in his left hand — there was time for one thing only. In seconds, he realized, the pressure of the man's weight against the rifle and then the sling which was already gouging into Michael's neck would be so great as to pull him free. If he hacked outward with the knife and missed the man who clung to him, there might not be a chance to do anything else. He brought the knife up to where the sling was taut but away from his body and slashed, the sudden release of pressure almost causing Michael to pitch forward over the animal's neck, almost making him lose his grip on the knife. But neither happened, Michael half hanging over the right side of the saddle, the reins gripped in his right fist, the knife in his left, the rifle and the man who had clung to it gone. Michael looked back as he righted himself in the saddle, the band of horsemen less than fifty yards behind him, the last of the two men from the fire galloping past him. And for some reason, the little, dark amber skinned man in fur robes and astrakhan hat was howling with laughter. The man signalled the universal gesture for follow me and Michael, sheathing his knife, dug his heels in and lowered himself in the saddle, the horse surging ahead.

He looked back, the distance to the pursing band of horsemen not having narrowed. Reason told him their animals would be slowing from·the prolonged gallop. But gunfire was coming from the horsemen again, assault rifles, bullets churning the snowy ground beneath his animal's hooves.

About two hundred yards ahead across the barren plateau, dotted here and there with isolated stands of pine and low brush, were the other two men from the campfire, one of them hanging low in the saddle as though wounded, but his horse galloping ahead unimpaired.

The little man who had gestured for Michael to follow was veering his mount toward the other two ahead of them, Michael doing the same now, not eager for their company but eager to know their destination. The gunfire from behind him was intensifying, as were the shrieked battle cries of the riders, the sound of their animals' hoofbeats — there were at least two dozen of the pursuers — like thunder. And Michael Rourke smiled to himself — the "thunder of hoofbeats" was an expression he had always thought trite.

Apparently it wasn't, the ground seeming to rock with it, his ears vibrating with it. Clumps of snow and bits of rock and dirt streamed up around him from his animal's hooves. He had noticed as he had clambered aboard the horse that its hooves were shod.

He could hear the animal's breathing, feeling it as the animal moved. The largest of the horses at the camp, it was still smaller than he remembered horses being from the days before the Great Conflagration, and it should have been the other way around since he had been only a boy then and not fully grown. But what the animal lacked in size it seemed to compensate for with stamina. Like the Indian ponies he had read about. And he wondered if these men who looked for all the world like Mongols transplanted from some distant epoch would do like the Indians had done, ride their animals into the ground, slitting a vein for the moisture of blood while the animal was still on the move, and when it dropped and died, cutting off meat to eat raw as they ran on.

Michael twisted in the saddle to look back, his pursuers not hanging back. If these men rode their animals into the ground, he might soon find out.

He kept riding . . .

Maria Leuden let Hammerschmidt help her down from the breadloaf-shaped rock to the rocks beneath it, but looked back once through the cloud of snow and dust of the riders. But it was too distant now. She stood beside Hammerschmidt.

"Fraulein Doctor—we must move as rapidly as possible. More of these men may be in—"

He didn't finish his words as she screamed and drew back, Hammerschmidt wheeling around, swinging his assault rifle up, Maria Leuden going for the pistol at her belt. It was one of the antiques like the Rourke family carried, something called a Beretta or something and she tried getting the flap of the holster open to help Hammerschmidt as the five men dressed like the horsemen and the men from the campfire fell on him, his rifle discharging into the rocks, the butt of one of the five men's rifles swinging outward suddenly and catching him at the side of the head. She had her pistol free and she remembered to move the safety catch up as she tried to stab it toward the nearest of the five men.

He was her height, nothing more, but seeming huge under his layers of fur trimmed coats, his deep yellow face lighting with what seemed like a grin, a wicked looking long thin mustache starting at each side of his mouth and curling under his lips as his mouth opened and he shouted something at her. She recoiled from him, nearly losing the pistol. He was laughing at her as he reached out for her. She pulled the trigger of her pistol but he knocked it aside and blood spurted from his left cheek and he let go of her for an instant, then hammered his right fist forward and she felt an awful pain and knew that she had let go of the pistol, knew that she had lost. And she was falling . . .

He had read his chart, the technical medical German hard to get through but understandable enough. The chart confirmed his self-diagnosis. It essentially boiled down to exhaustion and muscle fatigue. John Rourke reflected it would not have taken a medical genius to deduce that. But Munchen was a more than competent physician. Rest, relaxation — it was what any doctor would have ordered. Rourke would allow himself a night of it. But there was still the question of the ultimate destination of Karamatsov's army in Eurasia, and Michael's quest for the destination which had taken him far into unexplored regions of Asia.

The resiliency of humanity to survive the unsurvivable had ceased to astound John Rourke, but rather in an odd way inspired him. His own resiliency this time had been pushed to the limit — or nearly, he told himself.

Sarah sat asleep in a chair by the foot of the bed, cocooned in a shawl. Annie had gone, with much protest, to seek out

Munchen to get his agreement to release him from the hospital. If Munchen did not agree, Rourke would simply release himself. His gear was stowed in the closet-like cabinet beside where Sarah slept, all except for the two knives he had used to extricate himself from the crevasse. These were on the small, utilitarian stand beside the bed. He reached for the larger of the two, the Crain System X, his neck, his left shoulder, his left forearm coming suddenly alive with pain as he moved. But his left fist closed over the knife.

Chapter Fourteen

The plateau had begun gradually dipping into a flat, natural ramp, leading downward. Michael Rourke urged his animal onward, a few of the pursuing horsemen having fallen away, their animals going down under them as Michael soon feared his would. The gunfire was more sporadic now, and the distance between Michael and his pursuers having widened by at least a hundred yards. The added freshness of his mount had been the telling factor, he realized, but now his own animal was nearly as dead on its feet as theirs seemed to be. But he kept the animal moving, its brown eyes bloodshot, red-rimmed, froth of sweat and spittle heavy on its muzzle, a spray on the slipstream of icy air around him, but his body hot with the exertion and from the heat of the animal.

The gap to the two men who had left the campfire first had closed as well, Michael riding almost neck and neck with the dark amber colored little man who had signalled that he follow. Michael's body did the work, his mind elsewhere, assessing his options—there seemed to be none at the moment, the countryside too open even to hope for breaking off, his ultimate goal still, if he survived, to follow these men to their base, their home.

But he also assessed the men with whom he rode and those

who pursued, trying to form some logical reason which would account for their presence here, their very existence. And were these men somehow linked to Karamatsov's march into Asia?

The man beside whom Michael Rourke rode was small in height, but seemed well-developed enough that malnutrition didn't appear to be a problem. The fur trimming of his clothes and the animal skin robe in which his body seemed all but engulfed, part of it trailing behind him on the wind, even the horse he rode, the saddle on which Michael rode, made of leather — all these factors bespoke animal life in such apparent abundance that its by-products could be used for simple, ordinary things. There was a water bag lashed to Michael's saddle, of animal skin, the fur rubbed away in spots, the contents no doubt frozen with the temperature, judging from the stiffness of the water bag. The bridle ornaments as some of the saddle trimmings were of silver, the silver worked into designs of Zodiac-like symbols and representations of animal heads. That all this had survived five centuries seemed unlikely, the silver work beautiful, but crude.

He smiled ruefully to himself — had his father been here in his stead and had Natalia accompanied his father, no doubt Natalia would have been conversing with these people by now in Chinese which he felt certain would be one of her many languages, gifted polyglot that she was. He spoke English and Natalia had begun teaching him some Russian and before — before Madison had, had died — before that he had begun learning some Icelandic. Kurinami had taught him a few expressions in Japanese. He doubted that his vastly less than meager knowledge of one principal Oriental language would be of any assistance with what was probably a dialect of still another.

He carefully took in each detail of his riding companion and tried using the details to construct a more complete overall picture. The clothing was almost too perfectly like that of the classic movie or history book Mongol warrior of ages past, almost as if copied or kept as some uniform for religious or cultural reasons. He had seen a flash of a saber-like blade, and the workmanship had seemed, at least from a distance, to bespeak quality. The rifles were either five centuries old or lovingly made duplicates of the originals; he could not be certain which without close range examination. The pistol he had seen one man brain another with was another story, clearly recognizable as something from close before the Night of The War, but perhaps also a copy. The pistol had appeared to be a Glock 17 9mm. Somewhere in his readings he seemed to recall that the Chinese army had begun issuing these as military standard before the unthinkable had become history.

Perhaps these strange men had a stockpile of pre-war weaponry from which to draw.

His attention was drawn back to the precarious reality of his own situation. The two riders in front of him were slowing, one man's horse dropping to its knees, rolling over into the snow, the other horse stumbling on ahead a few paces as its rider dropped easily from the saddle, then standing, swaying, falling over—dead, he presumed.

The men unslung their assault rifles, the first man pulling his kneeling horse fully down, the flash of a blade, the animal's head twitching upward, then sagging down, both men dropping behind their animals.

The man who rode abreast of Michael Rourke started slowing his own mount, the animal faltering slightly as it slowed. Michael had no intention of slashing his animal's throat. Animal life was still a rarity to him and the animal might be saved.

But abruptly, he realized he would have no choice to make, his animal starting to fall, its eyes wide open, a sound like that of regurgitation coming from deep in its throat, a mixture of blood and food leavings pouring from its mouth as Michael hurtled himself clear and into the snow. The animal's head raised once and then fell. Michael drew the .44 Magnum 629 from his belt and double actioned the revolver once, into the horse's brain. He started to run then, the riders in pursuit bearing down toward him, Michael discharging the revolver toward them, then emptying the cylinder of the remaining four shots as he threw himself into a dead run toward the two men who hunkered down behind their dead mounts. The third man, who had ridden beside him, sprang from his saddle as his faltering animal neared the other two, a blade appearing in his left hand, the blade catching a flicker of sunlight, then all but lost in a spray of red as he slit the horse's throat and dropped to cover behind its body even as it fell. Michael angled right toward the third man.

He holstered the emptied 629 as he ran, reaching first with his right hand and then with his left, snatching the Beretta 92 F 9mms from the double shoulder rig he wore, the shoulder rig like his father's but different, his own personal design. He thumbed up both safeties, jumping up, spinning around, bringing both pistols on line with the leading horsemen and firing, horses rearing, men going down, gunfire ripping into the snow at his feet. He turned, ran, snapping off two more shots over his shoulders, diving up, crashing down behind the dead horse beside the man who had ridden next to him. As Michael Rourke looked up, he saw the muzzle of the man's pistol staring at him, and above the muzzle of the pistol, above the hand which held it, the eyes.

Michael nodded his head toward the enemy riding down on them and the eyes of the little man filled with laughter and he turned the pistol away, firing it toward the riders. Michael Rourke edged up beside him doing the same, emptying both pistols, the leading edge of the band of horsemen turning back under the hail of pistol and automatic weapons fire, some of their horses stumbling, faltering, going down, men dropping behind the fresh carcasses and firing assault rifles and pistols.

As Michael Rourke rammed fresh magazines home in each of the Berettas, he noticed something. The man beside him had perfect, white teeth. Michael raised up slightly behind the body of the dead horse. The pursuers still mounted were urging their horses into what, if memory served, had been called a skirmish line in books he had read and films he had seen which dealt with horsemounted cavalry.

And suddenly, the Mongol beside him said in oddly pronounced but syntactically perfect English, "Save your pistols until they are closer."

Michael Rourke looked at the man, feeling his jaw drop. "Who the hell are you?"

"You had to be Russian or American—I hoped it was the latter. My name is Han Lu Chen. And I'm not one of these, but the other two over there think I am. If we survive this encounter, we can speak at greater length. And your name?" He added the question as if it were a polite afterthought.

"Michael Rourke. Nice to meet you." And Michael turned his attention toward the skirmish line, the horses were advancing slowly, blowing steam and sweat, Michael keeping one eye on the mounted men and the other on the box of loose 9mms taken from his musette bag, his hands almost mechanically reloading the spent magazines for his pistols. The skirmish line started to advance more rapidly, Michael noticing Han Lu Chen bringing his assault rifle up to the shoulder. Michael began reloading the cylinder, rammed the speedloader into the ejector star and pocketed the empty loader. Ammunition for his handguns was abundant because of the cooperation of the Germans, but not abundant here. He carried a box of fifty 9mms in addition to the already loaded spare magazines and three loaded speedloaders for the .44 Magnum revolver, all this in the musette bag slung under his left arm. The rest of his spare ammo was in his backpack, the backpack with Bjorn Rolvaag back at the

94

German vehicle in the valley — how far away? Maria Leuden would be there by now, with Otto Hammerschmidt.

Michael reached for the radio at his belt and started to speak as he depressed the push to talk button. "This is Michael — Otto — Maria — come in. Over."

There was static, then in a moment, the voice of Bjorn Rolvaag who spoke no English.

Michael spoke again. "Bjorn — Maria or Otto. Over."

Rolvaag's voice returned and as best Michael could decipher from his meager knowledge of Icelandic, Maria and Otto were not there.

He said abruptly into the radio, "Michael out." And he cut the transmission.

The horsemen were coming and already, Han Lu Chen and the two (legitimate?) Mongols were opening fire. Michael would have waited to open fire whether advised by Han Lu Chen or not. The range was still well over a hundred yards.

But where were Maria Leuden and Otto Hammerschmidt? Where was Maria? He exhaled, steadying his hands, thumb cocking each of the pistols, ready . . .

Otto Hammerschmidt's head hurt when he opened his eyes, and his left eye would not fully open — he assumed the cause was clotted blood. He realized his body was shaking with the cold and he realized the cause. Not only had he been stripped of his weapons but he had been stripped of his arctic gear, down to the lightweight thermal underwear he had worn beneath it. He looked beyond the fire a few meters from where he was — he was tied, he realized, with some sort of rope that felt too smooth to be natural fiber, but bound tightly nonetheless. Beyond the fire, Hammerschmidt could see one of the Mongol-looking men, and the man wearing Hammerschmidt's stolen arctic parka, but the pants that went with it were nowhere in sight.

Hammerschmidt closed his eyes against the pain — he remembered being struck by a rifle butt.

He opened his eyes suddenly, craning his neck, straining against the ropes which bound him — to the trunk of a pine tree, he realized. Where was Fraulein Doctor Maria Leuden?

The horsemen were in range now and Michael Rourke opened fire, double taps with each of the Berettas, one of the military 9mms in his right fist, the other spitting fire from his left, men and horses going down, but gunfire still pouring toward their position from behind the carcasses of the dead horses, the body behind which Michael and Han Lu Chen crouched rocking with hits from the .30 caliber assault rifles the attackers used. Michael ducked down, Han Lu Chen saying to him, "You are very good with those pistols, Michael Rourke. When I saw you with one in each hand, I thought that perhaps you over estimated your abilities, but in fact you apparently do not."

There was no need to reload — Michael had only expended eight rounds from each pistol, seven rounds remaining, having started with full magazines only and not loaded one into the chamber. "Who the hell are you and how come you speak English?"

"I told you my name. But I assume you wish to know more — pardon me!" And Han thrust up and fired a burst from his assault rifle, Michael looking over the flanks of the dead animal behind which he hid, the Mongol attackers retreating for the moment. He doubted it would be a lasting condition.

"They'll be back, right?"

"You are perceptive, American. Yes — they fight until they win or die. They are a simple people."

"Who are you?"

"I am a member of the intelligence service of the People's

Republic of China. I believe our peoples were de facto allies during the Great War of The Nations five centuries ago."

"They were—you fought a land war with Russia after my country got all but destroyed. But then when the Great Conflagration came—"

"The Dragon Wind—Ahh! It must have been an awesome spectacle."

"There was death everywhere—I remember watching my father's face as he watched it happening—"

"You joke, of course, although I see little taste in it."

"I was born in the twentieth century—it's a long story," Michael Rourke nodded grimly. "And I wouldn't joke about that. Why do you speak English?"

Han grinned, saying, "Because I presume you speak no Chinese," and he rattled off something totally incomprehensible to Michael, then laughed again. "And apparently I was right, American."

"But how did you learn it?"

"Before the Dragon Wind, so much of the scientific and engineering literature was written in English, that afterward what survived of it could not be trusted to translation, and ours, though more beautiful, is a more cumbersome language. We have kept your language alive. We knew life still existed in America. We thought, perhaps, that someday—well, and we have met, heh?"

"How many of you are there?"

"Several hundred thousand in our city alone. And in their city, nearly that many, perhaps more."

"Their city?" And Michael Rourke jerked his head in the general direction of their attackers.

"It is not their city, really, although they live there at times and lived there once long ago. Before the Great War of Nations, we of the People's Republic had determined that the Soviet Union was preparing for global thermonuclear war. We wished none of this, but desired to be prepared to survive it—"

"You'd like my father," Michael Rourke grinned.

"Perhaps I would. But we constructed three Underground Cities, as the story goes. But the records of the Third City were lost or stolen and perhaps it is only a myth. When the Great War of Nations began, radical elements—"

"Maoists?"

"You are indeed the student of history—these Red Guards seized the Second City, while the People's Republic maintained control of the First City. When the Dragon Wind came, it was impossible to venture forth, to contact the Second City. In the five centuries our cities went their separate ways. The First City evolved as had the original People's Republic before it. We are very democratic now. But the Second City, we learned, had devolved, returned to the domination of radical militants, seeking to return to the Communism of Mao while yet resorting to the tactics of the old warlords who dominated China before the Revolution. They developed in a rigid class society, and these who attack us are of their warrior class, as fierce as the Mongols whom their tradition emulates."

"What about these guys?" And Michael gestured with the gun in his left fist toward the other two men who had come from the encampment.

"Some soldiers learn that the only way to truly succeed at their craft is to sell their services to those who would pay most highly. Mercenary soldiers, they would be called in English. These men I travel with are mercenary soldiers in the employ of the First City. We were assigned to penetrate the Second City and I was to assassinate the leader of the Second City. His name is taken from his deity—he calls himself Mao, though it is really a much more ordinary name that he was given at birth, no doubt."

"What about your mercenary pals—just to get you into the city?"

"You have captured the spirit of the endeavor."

"How were you going to get out?"

The smile vanished from Han's face. He looked up over the back of the dead horse and then returned his gaze to Michael. "We are in a state of war with the Second City, and have been for some five decades. Two years ago, during one of the many invasive commando raids made by the warriors of the Second City, my wife and two daughters happened to be shopping in the central market. A bomb exploded and they were killed. The thought of leaving the Second City after succeeding in killing the one who calls himself Mao had not occurred to me," and Han smiled again.

"I understand you," Michael almost whispered. "We are at war with the Soviet Union. My wife and our unborn child — they were —" Michael Rourke closed his eyes for a moment, then felt Han's hand touch at his shoulder. Michael opened his eyes.

Han said, "You need say no more, American. But these Russians of whom you speak. We knew of their existence and tried to conceal our own. But how goes your war?"

"It goes, let's say," Michael smiled.

"Ahh —" And Han peered up again, over the back of the horse. "Our enemies return, I fear."

Michael rested spare magazines for each of the pistols on the small flat rock beside which he knelt, worked up the safeties of the twin Berettas, then raised himself up to look toward the attackers. Perhaps ten remained on horseback, a few more crouched behind their dead animals, but the animals the horsemen rode appeared nearly dead with exhaustion, whipped by their riders into a skirmish line.

"The horses. The animal skins — where do they come from?"

"We returned to the surface five decades ago, the Second City perhaps as much as a decade before that — but they are less cautious, less caring for the welfare of their people than ourselves. Animals of all types were maintained in small zoos within each of the cities, with their habitats such that they simulated wild conditions. The Second City began an ambitious program of return to the wild, as we did some years later. Wolves, rabbits, a wide range of species now roam in these mountains, and more are raised in the cities themselves to be added to the wild population. But the people of the Second City prefer to hunt these animals into possible extinction. We do not. It is all a matter of perspective, I suppose. And as to horses, they were raised, at least by ourselves, in the event of their being used should synthetic fuel research prove fruitless, as it has."

"I know some people who can help you there," Michael nodded. "Here they come!"

Han opened fire with his assault rifle, Michael biding his time until the attackers came into range . . .

Maria Leuden told herself she was behaving like a child — but she couldn't help herself, crying. She had been stripped of her winter gear and all of the clothing beneath it. But she had not been raped. Yet. But she knew it would come, from the way the men looked at her; the man who had knocked her unconscious stared at her and laughed.

She wondered if perhaps she were being saved for someone else.

She was freezing cold, the dirty blankets and animal skins she had been covered with dislodging each time she attempted to move, to restore circulation to her bound wrists and ankles. And it was hard to breathe, something around her neck constricting her. Also, her glasses kept sliding down her runny nose.

She had seen no sign of Otto Hammerschmidt since regaining consciousness. Perhaps he was dead. And Michael — she had fallen in love with him; she knew that. And he had no interest in returning her love, and with the recent death of his wife, she could not blame him. But it was all over now.

She would keep herself alive long enough to get at least

one of these men and kill him somehow. She had learned that from the Rourkes. Life was not taken cheaply.

She stared at the man who had hit her. And she turned her eyes away as he stood up and started to walk toward her. And she couldn't help herself. The tears came again.

Chapter Fifteen

Vladmir Karamatsov stripped away his parka. It was warm in the command tent with the chemical heater going as it was. Beneath it, he wore the shoulder holster with the five centuries old Model 59 Smith & Wesson 9mm which he had vowed to himself he would use to personally kill John Thomas Rourke. The moment was getting close when he would keep the vow.

His field grade officers were assembled and they sat when he bade them to sit and he began to speak.

"For some time I have concealed from you my ultimate purpose in leading our armies to the east. I shall reveal to you much of that purpose. Before the Night of The War, in my capacity with the Committee for State Security, I was privy to considerable information, much of which has helped our people to survive in these centuries since the fire swept our skies.

"All nations prepared for the war which some said was inevitable—" A younger officer cleared his throat and Karamatsov looked icily toward him. "Which some said was inevitable," Karamatsov continued, "and some said was unthinkable. I believed it inevitable. I devoted considerable energies to ferreting out the plans of other nations for the time when the war came. Our own great people had planned wisely with the Underground City, though its leadership has now become corrupted with its own power and would deny the very revolution which sustained it." None of this was really true, but he had never shared his reasons for attacking the Underground City and the seat of Soviet government with his inferiors and these words seemed as good as any to serve the purpose.

"Other nations, as you all know, had their special plans as well. The United States developed the Eden Project, at once the most daring and the most foolhardy of the scenarios. Five centuries of sleep in space. Our own nation conceived a project of equal daring and with considerably greater chance for success. But more of this when it is appropriate." He liked to give them a taste and nothing more. Men keen to know were willing to serve. "Our enemies, the so-called People's Republic of China, planned as well. They constructed their own versions of our Underground City, their spies stealing much of the needed technological information from our own heroic scientists and leaders. Two cities were completed." A third city was under construction at that time and he had no way of knowing if it had ever been completed and since his data was incomplete, he declined any mention of it to his subordinates.

"In the era immediately before the Night of The War," he told his officers, "the nuclear strength of the nations possessed of this power was assessed as follows. Both our nation and the United States had roughly over fifty thousand nuclear devices, distributed more or less evenly among the two largest of the nuclear powers. The allies of the Americans had little more than a thousand between them, exclusive of the Jew occupiers of Palestine, who had nuclear capability of their own which they chose to keep secret. But the so-called People's Republic of China had some three hundred nuclear devices. Aside from a few dozen which were used tactically during the land war our heroic ancestors fought against Chinese aggression when the so-called

People's Republic attacked us during our war for Communist liberation of the world, none of the remaining were used. But I know where they are. We go to claim these nuclear weapons and to utilize them against the enemies of the Soviet people if need be."

He heard someone from the back of the command tent breathe loudly.

Vladmir Karamatsov asked, "Are there any questions?"

The tent was deathly silent except for the night wind outside it. Finally, the younger officer who had cleared his throat raised himself to a standing position. It was what Karamatsov had hoped for. "Comrade Marshal Karamatsov?"

"Yes, Comrade?" Karamatsov felt himself smile.

"Comrade Marshal. What effect would the use of a thermonuclear device have on the current state of the atmosphere?" The young officer sat down again, his face pale.

"The use of ten moderate yield devices, I am told, could well bring about a destruction of earth's environment which would make all which has gone before, the Night of The War and the fires — all of it seem like a ripple in a stream. It would destroy all life forever, I am told." He made no pretense to scientific knowledge, but his scientific advisors had told him this and it seemed to make sense. The terrestrial environment, once hardy, had become fragile. They had spoken of things he had not heard of for five centuries — the total loss of the atmosphere, the inability for the surface to ever again sustain life.

The question lay unspoken on the very air that he breathed. And so, Vladmir Karamatsov answered it. "We will be the only ones capable of such destruction, hold the very power of life and death over all who live on the planet. Our enemies will have no choice but to acquiesce to my demands. If they do not, their world will end forever." And he knew his first demand. The surrender of John Rourke and his family. And Natalia, the woman he, Vladmir Karamatsov, had once called his wife.

What happened after that to the rest of humanity was of little consequence.

Chapter Sixteen

The attacks had come less frequently and less savagely throughout the day, but they had come. One of the two Mongol mercenaries had died in battle, the other, riddled with bullets when he had attempted to steal a wandering horse, its rider slain, rode off. The horse, dead too, had collapsed over his body.

Only Michael Rourke and the Chinese intelligence agent, Han, lived. At least ten of their attackers survived somewhere in the night.

"They aren't like Indians, are they?"

"Indian?"

"American Indians—the old legends said they wouldn't attack at night because they feared evil spirits."

"These men fear nothing," Han observed. And as he slapped at his upper arms for increased circulation, he added, "not even death by freezing, it appears."

Michael had tried contacting Maria Leuden and Otto Hammerschmidt again, but there had only been a response from Bjorn Rolvaag and Michael had gotten across to Rolvaag to wait where he was and remain on guard, Rolvaag getting across that he had seen nothing of Maria Leuden or of the German commando Captain Hammerschmidt, but that he would wait, at least until dawn.

By the time dawn would come, Michael Rourke was beginning to have serious doubts he would be in a position to worry over anything. The body of the dead horse was beginning to smell and for that reason he thanked the below freezing temperatures.

Han spoke. "I will confess that my brain is lacking in ideas for some means of extricating ourselves from this predicament."

The night was clear and cold, the clarity of the stars at night the one tangible benefit to the reduced density of the overall terrestrial atmosphere, Michael thought, staring up at them. He remembered the times during the five years his father had spent teaching them to stay alive while he again took the Sleep that sometimes he and his father and Annie had sat outside the Retreat at night, cold like it was now, his father smoking one of the eternal cigars, discussing the night sky.

John Rourke had liked to conjecture that somewhere up there — or out there, Michael corrected himself — there was more life than just that of the returning Eden Project. That millions of light years from this small planet there might be men such as themselves who knew the answers to questions we could not even begin to comprehend, men like themselves who had found ways to live without mutual destruction.

John Rourke had likened the Retreat to an island, saying that perhaps there were other islands on the earth, and likely there were other islands out there. Perhaps someday we would know more of them — the islands here, the islands out there.

Michael Rourke remembered that one evening as they had sat outside the Retreat, star watching as his father had called it, Annie huddled between them for their warmth, that he — Michael — had finally understood his father's obsession with survival. It wasn't just an indomitable will to live. It was an indomitable will to know. And all the fighting and the killing which had kept them alive was simply the means to an end, a time when all of that would be gone and there would be quiet moments to contemplate the stars, learn all that there was to learn from the vast cache of books and videotapes and computer files John Rourke had passionately preserved at the Retreat.

He had, many years later in his own reading, encountered a description which well fit his father — The Socratic Man.

And perhaps it was the ultimate irony, that a man of great wisdom was so embroiled in the violence needed to preserve life, that there remained no time at all to live life. Those five years before his father had resumed the Sleep were the only time in which he had ever known his father at all. He had liked John Rourke the man, the father, far better than he liked John Rourke the implacable hero of humanity.

"I said, I am suffering from a lack of ideas, American — ideas for surviving this ordeal."

Michael Rourke looked at Han. "Me too," and returned to field stripping the Chinese assault rifle. He had climbed over to the body of the dead Mongol mercenary who had gone down in battle and reclaimed the man's rifle, pistol and other gear that might be useful. The man's sword, on close examination, seemed satisfactory at best. The rifle was ill-kept but seemed serviceable. The ammunition was corroded. He had noticed an inordinate number of misfires and jams and he realized his enemies and his allies were shooting poorly preserved cartridges stored since before the Great Conflagration, and military ammunition at that.

Michael had been gently but persistently rubbing corrosion from the primers of the rifle ammunition. He began to speak. "My father taught me a great deal about staying alive."

"He taught you well, I have seen since our meeting."

"Thank you," Michael nodded. At one level of consciousness he was listening for the sounds of another attack, the Chinese beside him peering over the body of the dead horse behind which they had taken cover a short while after dawn.

"He told me that if all seems lost and it appears that you'll get killed anyway, that is the time for bold action. There's nothing to lose and possibly everything to gain. I would imagine that, translating that advice into terms relative to our current situation, we should attack. If all ten or so of them rush us, we'll be up shit's creek anyway."

"What is shit?"

"Feces."

"A creek of human waste—this would be a small river of human excrement?"

"Only figuratively speaking."

"Ahh—I find the dynamics of your language fascinating—Feces creek. I must remember this."

"Yes—hopefully you'll have the chance. Tell me how these Mongols fight—I mean, hand to hand fighting styles."

Han seemed to consider this, shifted his eyes toward Michael for an instant, then resumed watching in the likely direction of attack. "You have familiarity with the various fighting styles of—"

"The martial arts. To a considerable degree, yes. I had two fine instructors." First his father, and then a few lessons from Natalia.

"These men are experts at killing with the bare hands, and with exotic edged weapons. What is it exactly which you propose, American?"

Michael considered his words before uttering them. Then, "We crawl off directly opposite our friends out there—"

"Our enemies, yes?"

"And once we're far enough away, we start to circle around them and find the men farthest out from the main body. We kill them however we can. Silently is best. We keep whittling down—"

"The sculpting technique where special knives are utilized to form figurines and the like from wood. I have read of this."

"Right—well, we sculpture them down until we reach their main concentration, then just open up with all the firepower we have. We sneak up on them and murder them, basically. Hopefully. You got any problems with that?"

"When?"

Michael Rourke felt the corners of his mouth raising into a smile. "I like you — now!" He slipped the assault rifle's rusted magazine into position and handed Han the spare Glock 17 pistol. Loosening the knife old Jon the swordmaker had given him from its sheath, he started into the night, Han beside him . . .

Otto Hammerschmidt raised his head, the pain no better and the stiffness worse, but his body adjusted to the cold. He realized he was going to die.

It was imperative that he find a means of getting free long enough to kill Fraulein Doctor Maria Leuden. Better that than leaving her to be the sexual toy of these barbarians. He had been working to free his wrists throughout the day. He was nearly there . . .

Maria Leuden could see the great yellow tongues of the bonfire around which the men who had captured her now sat. They had dragged her nearer to the fire and for that she was grateful. She had ceased wondering when it would happen. The five drank something which smelled like rotted garbage from huge animal skin bags they passed around the fire. If they were saving her as some sort of prize for someone, their resolve might vanish with their other inhibitions — one of the men was dancing around the fire and waving his sword like some sort of madman. She was terrified. And no help would come. She had begun wishing that she had this religious faith that Michael and the Rourke family seemed to possess — she could have prayed that he lived. She decided to try it anyway . . .

* * *

If they had been detected, there had been no sign of this by the ten or so men who awaited in the night to kill them. They had belly crawled through the snow for a distance of what Michael estimated as an even two hundred yards before changing direction, the greatness of the distance an added margin of safety in the event they should be spotted. None of their attackers had impressed Michael with astoundingly accurate marksmanship.

The slightly sloping expanse was barren of any real cover or concealment except for the occasional stands of pine and low brush, some of their attackers hidden in similar stands, others hidden behind their fallen mounts.

It was in one of these stands, some three hundred yards from their original position that Michael rose wearily to his feet, the Chinese agent, Han, joining him.

"This is tiring work, American," Han observed.

"Are there more of these guys in close proximity to us?"

"I do not understand — but wait — yes — there are other units from the Second City which move in this area."

"I had some companions. I tried reaching them by radio."

"Unfortunately, your radio and the communications system of the First City are not even similar."

They had tried altering the frequency of Michael's radio in the late morning, after Michael's first unsuccessful attempt to contact Maria Leuden and Otto Hammerschmidt.

Han spoke again. "You fear they were waylaid or met with some misfortune."

"Waylaid more likely."

"A woman among them. That could indeed be very bad. Perhaps she was killed instantly. Some of us in the First City are Christian. I assume that you are as well. Pray to Jesus that she died quickly. Otherwise —" and the Chinese let the sentence hang.

Michael was not about to pray for Maria Leuden's death.

"When we get this business over with," Michael said, his

voice low, almost a whisper, "I'd like to see this First City of yours. But if it means going to the Second City itself, I've gotta find my friends."

"I will help you. But you walk a path which can only lead to tears, American."

"I'll walk it with you or without you."

The Chinese clapped his left hand to Michael's shoulder. "With me, then."

There was little danger of running out of the cover of darkness, the night just begun little more than an hour before. But Michael had no desire to prolong the task ahead of them. He decided they could risk a run when the few clouds which were moving in from the west would pass in front of the moon. He gauged the time as perhaps a minute before then. He turned to face Han. "We'll make a run for it to that stand of pines roughly parallel to their position. As soon as the clouds cover the moon."

"And what if the enemy lurks in the trees there?"

"Then we won't have to worry about looking for them, will we?"

Michael checked the luminous face of his Rolex, then glanced skyward, checking the watch again. He made it at roughly ninety seconds or so until the clouds which would soon be covering the moon would have moved off, roughly ninety seconds for the run. He didn't try estimating the yardage. They would either make it or get caught in the open. There were no other options. There were few other clouds.

"Ready?"

"Yes, American."

Michael had made it his play and it was not the time to let the Chinese make the first move. As the leading edge of the clouds obscured the three-quarter full moon, Michael ran from the cover of the trees and started into the open, the Chinese assault rifle banging against his right side, in his left hand the copy of the five centuries old Crain knife old Jon the swordmaker had given him. His father had one just like it, only larger. But Michael was content with his copy, as his father seemed to be with his longer-bladed original. His father had told him the story of the knife. A long-standing friend of the maker, Jack Crain, John Rourke and Crain had often spoken of designing the ultimate survival knife. It was the era for survival knives, every movie hero — Michael had seen some of the films — with this new one or that new one. And John Rourke, always the survival expert, had decided that indeed such a knife was a wise thing to possess, but that it should be the ultimate of its breed. He had always respected the basic design of Crain's Life Support series, but valued a longer blade for its psychological impact as well as its physical impact against an opponent. And John Rourke had always favored a style of knife fighting more similar to the art of Kendo, but Kendo was done with a sword. Hence he had required a longer haft which would allow the use of two hands when needed, but a haft not so long as to require two hands to use the blade effectively. They had called it the System X.

Michael Rourke's left fist balled more tightly to his knife, the bracken of trees and brush nearing, his feet hammering down the snow, sometimes slipping, Michael manipulating his body weight to keep his balance, sometimes a near thing. He didn't glance skyward, running at full speed as he was, the stiffness of the cold, the stiffness from crawling those hundreds of yards gone, replaced with a rush of energy, a pounding of the blood. But he would know if the clouds passed from in front of the moon — because he would be immediately visible for the enemy to see and fire upon.

A hundred yards, he judged it. He kept running, the smaller man, Han, beside him. A good runner, Michael Rourke decided. They were racing each other, he suddenly realized, Han trying to pull ahead of him, Michael Rourke almost starting to laugh which would have broken his stride. Instead, he used the last of his kick, the left fist with the knife in it extended at his left side, his right hand holding the muzzle of the rifle away from him, his head back and high, shoulders thrown back, mouth gulping more air than he should have, he knew.

The snow was washed with light. They reached the trees, Michael sagging against one of them, his lungs aching with the cold air he had sucked in. He was breathing so rapidly, he could feel his heart thudding in his chest and there was a moment of lightheadedness and then terrible chill. The lightheadness passed, but not the chill. Han was beside him, smiling.

Michael had won the race.

The next question dealt with staying alive, he thought ruefully, considerably less fun and vastly more difficult. He heard movement at the far side of the stand of trees, both he and Han so consumed with the run that neither he nor Han had swept the area for sign of the enemy they hunted. Michael Rourke edged to the side of the tree against which he had sagged, stripping away the assault rifle, passing it to the Chinese. Han took it, Michael making himself disappear into the snow laden trees, the snow falling from the pine boughs, dusting his face and chest and hair and shoulders. He shook some of the snow free and pulled up the hood of the parka against the cold. He kept moving.

He heard movement, from the same direction as before. He stopped moving, listening.

The sounds were of two men. He had learned how to use a knife — for killing and for many other purposes — from his father. And then Natalia had taught him refinements in the use of a blade for killing or disabling an opponent. Even his father conceded that Natalia was the vastly better of the two of them with a knife.

Michael shifted the knife to his master hand, flexing the fingers of his left hand against the cold, tightening his right fist on the knife, waiting.

Someone whispered something in a language sounding

114

unintelligible to him and he assumed it was one of the Mongols rather than Han speaking to himself. Michael waited. The sounds seemed to shift their pattern, as though one were moving to his right and one were moving to his left. He would have to rely on Han to take the one on the left, who would be nearer to the Chinese at any event. Michael Rourke began moving, dropping to his knees to stay below the level of the pine boughs and the noise they might make if he brushed against them and dislodged snow.

He kept moving, as swiftly as he could, more swiftly he judged on hands and knees than the Mongol would move on two feet. He heard betraying sound again, a twig breaking. The Mongol was almost even with him. Michael leaned against a tree trunk, beneath the level of the branches, closing his eyes for an instant, evening his breath. When he opened his eyes and looked to his left he saw the Mongol, coming, dodging pine boughs, his pistol in his left fist, a long, curved blade sword in the other. The curve of the blade was more pronounced than that of a saber, yet less so than that of a scimitar. There would be no wisdom in matching the man blade for blade, though Michael would have trusted the strength of his own knife over any blade except perhaps the one his father now carried. And the noise of a fight would betray their position.

He wished for Natalia and her Walther PPK/S and silencer, but he had neither. The Germans were good at that sort of thing. He made a mental note to see if they could build a sound muffling device that might work with one of the Berettas he regularly carried, but it would require a slide lock because of the open design of the slide. And he disliked contraptions which complicated the blissfully simple. He shelved the thought, returning to the tactical problem at hand. He would have to kill the man instantly. The question was how. He could think of no comparable situation related to him by his father. Michael Rourke looked at the knife in his hand. The first time he had ever taken the life of an enemy he had been but a little child, and he had used a boning knife that was simply a very sharp kitchen utensil and stabbed a man who had been about to sexually assault his mother. The kidney.

Michael closed his eyes for an instant, summoning all of his energy into his imagined center, to transmit it to his right hand and the knife. He opened his eyes, the Mongol dead even with him. If he could penetrate the neck at the spinal column and then quickly move to so immobilize the gun as to avoid a death spasm triggering a shot—

He lunged forward, the Mongol starting to turn, Michael's knife thrusting into the rear of the neck, a crack that sounded almost as loud as a pistol shot. But it was bone. Michael let go of the knife and reached for the pistol, dodging as the sword swiped toward him in the Mongol's spasm of death. But his left fist closed over the gun, the hammer falling against the web of his hand. Michael followed the dead man down, his right hand recocking the hammer—it was an old Government Model .45 with Chinese markings or a copy of one. He wondered if he were holding something which dated to World War II, ancient history to him. He raised the hammer, freeing his hand, then freed the gun, then lowered the hammer. He shoved the pistol into his belt, not desiring any spare magazines for it, simply getting the gun under his control rather than leaving it for someone else. He took the sword from the dead man's grip. The sword seemed unremarkable. But he took it anyway. He freed his knife from the dead man's neck, then made a quick search of his clothing. A picture of a naked girl that smelled vaguely like someone had ejaculated on it. "What a prince," he murmured. He unlimbered the assault rifle. It was like the one Han and the others carried, and if anything in worse condition. He wiped his knife clean of blood on the dead man's clothes, then wiped the knife clean of the dead man's clothes with snow. He held the knife in his left fist, the inferior but longer sword in his right, the assault rifle slung across his back, muzzle down. He had heard no sounds, which either meant Han and the second Mongol had not yet met or that one of them was very good. In the event it wasn't Han, he was doubly alert. He reasoned that had it been the Mongol who was very good, there would have been no need for silence and so he would have heard the fight. Unless the Mongol were really good.

He moved slowly, crossing a small path through the pines and stopping abruptly. Han stood bent over a dead Mongol, a long, thin bladed dagger in his right fist, literally dripping blood. It was apparently Han who was good. Or at least better . . .

His hands were free of the ropes, had been for, as Otto Hammerschmidt reckoned it, at least fifteen minutes. He had been massaging his wrists and flexing his fingers, at first painfully, ever since.

His feet were still bound and the feeling in his feet and legs was such that he doubted he could move very rapidly if at all. But his hands and arms would be all he needed now.

One of the five men — they all danced about a fire now some distance from him. He had seen Maria Leuden as they had taken her toward it. But one of the five, who had taunted him several times during the day, hooked the tip of a knife blade in Hammerschmidt's nose, laughed, punched him, slapped him. This would be the man Hammerschmidt would eradicate to get a weapon. He would be sure of that death at least before he took Maria Leuden's life. And Hammerschmidt, in that instant, questioned his own resolve. To kill Fraulein Doctor Leuden would be inexcusable, but to let her live for the fate these barbarians offered would be worse.

He wondered if he were a victim of the old thinking, that some beings, however human, were unremittingly inferior. He had tried to purge himself of these doctrines even as they had been taught to him under the old Nazi rule, ever since his earliest childhood memories in school, in pre-military training. He had somehow known this thinking was wrong, immoral. But these men who had taken him and Fraulein Doctor Leuden were human beings only because they walked about on two legs and could speak. But they were without any of the qualities which made humans human.

He was not a superman destroying a racial inferior, but a man destroying vermin for a cause that was good—to save Fraulein Doctor Leuden. And in killing her, he was giving her the gift of mercy.

Otto Hammerschmidt felt himself ready. He began to bend to work at the knots which bound together the ropes encircling his ankles, and the sudden change in posture made him lightheaded and he nearly fainted.

There was no hope of escape. Only to do what had to be done. With fingers that shook from cold and still felt thick from the constriction of blood, he began to work at the knots at his ankles, forcing himself to stay conscious. He must . . .

They had crossed from the pines to a large outcropping of rock, expecting that some of the Mongols might be hidden here, but there were none. Now, on knees and elbows, Michael Rourke, Han beside him, crawled the distance separating the rocks from the next pine bracken.

The enemy would be there. How many, how few. It was of no importance. He would fight and win or fight and die. And if he won, he would find—he realized that what he felt for Maria Leuden was more than friendship and he resisted this. He told himself he was tired, horny—love was something he had experienced once. He would not experience it again.

He kept moving, the liberated assault rifle strapped to his back, the one he had field stripped and reassembled and at least marginally cleaned in both fists now, at the level of his head as he crawled. He had seen the few movies his father had on tape which dealt at all with the theme of war, and in one he had seen men crawling beneath barbed wire during training, holding their rifles like he held his. His father had told him that live ammo was fired over the heads of the men. Michael had thought that sensible for realistic training, if somewhat reckless. It had seemed unpleasant to do. Experiencing it now, minus the machinegun fire, it seemed no more pleasant. They were nearly up to the pines, Michael starting to move into a standing position, taking cover at the farthest edge, Han beside him then.

Michael saw three of them here at the leading edge of the pines, huddled in blankets, their rifles leaned beside the trees against which their bodies leaned. Further out, huddled beside their dead horses, he saw at least three more.

A logical plan suggested itself, but with these ill-maintained long guns, its logic was more than questionable. Instead of long-distancing the three men who huddled behind their mounts from here, it would be necessary to get closer, at least as close as where the three men within the tree line lounged.

One of them sat down.

Another lit a cigarette.

Michael judged the distance to the three men by the dead horses as a hundred yards. If he could somehow fire from the position of the three other men, he would cut the range to fifty yards.

Michael Rourke drew the Chinese toward him, cupped his hand beside the man's ear and whispered, "When I say so, spray both your assault rifle and your pistol toward those three men there by the trees. Keep your fire concentrated to your right, their left. I'll be coming up on them fast from their right, your left. Once they're all down, stop shooting immediately. I'm going for the second three as soon as I can get close enough. All right?"

"Yes, American."

Michael nodded. "Give me about fifteen seconds, then go

for it."

Han looked puzzled for an instant, then nodded, a smile crossing his lips.

Michael Rourke left both Beretta pistols in the leather, the sound of unholstering possibly enough to betray their position.

He would draw them as he ran. He looked at Han, the Chinese raising the assault rifle in his right fist, the pistol in his left. Michael planned to use the assault rifles he carried not at all.

And Michael Rourke dodged left into the trees, beating his way through the pine boughs, drawing as much attention as he could, counting as he ran, "one thousand one, one thousand two, one thousand three." Gunfire came at him through the trees. Pine boughs laden with snow snapped and broke and slapped against him. "One thousand nine, one thousand ten." He ripped both Beretta pistols from the leather. He knew these worked. "One thousand fourteen, one thousand fifteen," and he dodged right, toward the gunfire, and now there was more gunfire, Han opening up with his assault rifle and his pistol, the gunfire that had been aimed toward Michael Rourke now aimed toward the Chinese intelligence agent.

Michael broke through the trees into the small clearing where the three Mongols huddled beside their trees, all three of their bodies clear shots. He fired both Berettas from the hip, double taps, the bodies of the three men lurching, twisting, one of the men making to fire toward him, Michael shooting him again.

Michael Rourke ran forward, safing both Berettas, kicking a pistol from the hand of one of the Mongols who might still have been alive, drawing the four-inch Model 629 from his crossdraw belt holster, bringing it up in both fists. The three Mongols beside the dead horses were at an angle to him, clear shots. He double actioned the first one, the Mongol's body twisting, lurching forward across the dead

120

animal behind which he had taken cover. The second man turned to fire at Michael and Michael shot him in the chest, the man's hands snapping out and away from his body, the assault rifle sailing into the night. The third Mongol started to run.

Michael Rourke thumbed back the .44 Magnum's hammer. It was the kind of shooting he had painstakingly taught himself over the years since he had first begun using handguns and practicing to be good with them. He adjusted for elevation by feel and squeezed the trigger gently, the 629 bucking in his hands for the third time, the third Mongol's body lurching forward into the snow.

He felt something—like someone staring at him and he dropped left and rolled, thrusting the 629 forward in his right fist, another Mongol emerging from the trees. Michael fired, then fired again, the Mongol's assault rifle discharging into the ground, then jamming, the man falling, the gun, silent, falling with him. Michael Rourke raised to his left knee, the 629 with one shot remaining in his right fist, one of the Berettas in his left. There was a burst of automatic weapons fire from the trees and then a single pistol shot. Michael was up, running.

Han shouted, "Do not fire!" then stepped from the trees. "When you said there were ten, I thought nine but chose out of politeness not to correct your oversight. But it appears that it was I who was in error." He nodded into the trees. "Ten."

Three of the dead men's horses were tethered at the far edge of the stand of trees, the stand like a small woods. Michael Rourke, reloading his revolver, said, "Let's take those horses. Let's find my friends. You're pretty good, you know," and he rammed the 629 into the leather and started toward the dead men's horses. There were no saddles in sight here and he assumed they were near the animals . . .

* * *

Maria Leuden had been watching the shortest of the five men, also the one who should have been the most drunk. But he was still standing, dancing around the fire, laughing, but his eyes were drifting toward her every few seconds and she knew the meaning of terror.

One of the five fell over, drunk. The others stopped dancing and stared at him for an instant, then began to resume their dancing. All but the short man who had been watching her.

He picked up the bag they had been drinking from — it looked to be almost eighteen inches in length and more than half empty by the way he handled it. He took a long drink from the bag, then wiped his mouth clean against his sleeve and handed off the bag to one of the three men who were still dancing.

He walked away from the other three and stood on the near edge of the fire to her, staring at her.

One of the three still dancing came toward him, grabbed him at the shoulder and shouted something to him she could not understand, but the short man shook him off. The other man shrugged, took a drink from the bag and went back to dancing.

Maria Leuden tried to avert her eyes but couldn't — when she looked back at the short man he was still watching her, and his eyes were lit strangely by the firelight and his mouth hung open and he was laughing.

Maria Leuden, tied, naked, helpless, screamed.

Chapter Seventeen

John Thomas Rourke had not been ready for sleep. He sat in a rocking chair on the porch of the dormitory near the presidential residence. The rocking chair was one of several.

One of the Detonics Scoremasters was stuffed in the waistband of his Levis.

His wife, Sarah, sat on the porch railing near him. Her dark brown hair was down, well past her shoulders and the way the shawl swathed her upper body, it would have been impossible to tell by looking at her, he thought, that she was pregnant.

"You're going back," she said, not a question.

"Tomorrow—after I see Munchen and he tells me I'll be stiff for a little while. Yeah."

"What happens after you get Karamatsov, John?"

Rourke smiled. "Maybe life will calm down a little. I think we could both use it. The three of us," and he looked into her eyes, then flickered his eyes down toward her abdomen. "Start over again, raise our children a little more normally this time. There'll be a lot to do. America begs rebuilding."

"And you're just the man to do it, aren't you?"

"In less than a century we could begin repopulation at a serious rate, especially if some of the Germans or the Icelandics or any other peoples we found decided to emigrate from Argentina or here. And then there are the Wild Tribes—Jea and his people will need a lot of help, but they'll bounce back. Civilization will start again in Europe eventually if we help them. I don't know if civilization is all that marvelous a goal, but at least it'll be better than what they've got now. And maybe we can avoid the mistakes we all made the last time."

"Does that mean us too," Sarah asked him. "Avoiding mistakes, I mean?"

"Come here. This rocking chair'll hold three," and she laughed, stood up, came to him, sat in his lap, Rourke putting his pistol down on the porch floor beside the rocker. She wriggled a little in his lap, and then her arms were around his neck, her hair, her clothing flooding over him, the smell of her. It was a good smell — woman. The shawl fell from her shoulders as he closed his arms around her and touched his mouth to hers . . .

Natalia Anastasia Tiemerovna thrust her hands into the pockets of her skirt. Tomorrow, it would be back to battle gear, but tonight she could feel more comfortable. She walked, the warmth of the air here at Hekla feeling good against her ankles. She wore no stockings.

She rounded the bend in the path through the garden which dominated the center of the Hekla community. And she saw John Rourke and Sarah Rourke sitting on the porch, wrapped in each others arms.

Natalia stopped walking. In one of her pockets she had a package of the German cigarettes and a lighter. She dug in both pockets, finding them, lighting a cigarette, inhaling the smoke deep into her lungs as she watched them. And very suddenly she felt dirty standing here, watching them, and she turned and started back into the garden . . .

Paul Rubenstein completed the entry in his journal. The entries were always longer here at Hekla or back at the Retreat. There was more time to write.

He could hear Annie in the shower. She was singing.

He put down his pen and stood, stretching. He wore the bathrobe Annie had made for him while he was gone. It had a hood like something a Christian monk might use and went to his ankles and folded over generously and was warm, but not unpleasantly so. He ran his hands through his thinning hair as he walked toward the window, staring down into the greenway which he could see when he stood at the far right side of the window.

It was Natalia. Walking alone.

He didn't know how long he watched her, but suddenly he was aware of the fact that Annie's little sounds from the shower had stopped and he started to turn around and she was there, her arms coming around his neck, her waist-length hair unbound, She wore only a nightgown, white, high necked and long sleeved, the neck and cuffs trimmed with lace, as he looked down at her thinking that she seemed to be suspended in air because he could not see her feet under its hem.

"Whatchya thinking about?"

He smiled. "That I've got the prettiest girl in the world."

"Well, you do—otherwise you've been lying to me."

"I haven't been lying to you," and his hands closed at her waist, the tips of his thumbs and the tips of his fingers almost but not quite able to touch. A man with larger hands could have touched, he thought absently. But Annie Rourke, now Annie Rubenstein, hadn't wanted any other man. And that made him very special, he realized, smiling as he leaned down and kissed her parted lips.

She kissed him back hard.

"You feeling better?"

"I'm feeling perfect—almost. And if you take me to bed, then I will feel perfect."

"You got to ahh—" Dr. Munchen had fitted her with a diaphragm.

"I already did that, Paul. Carry me?"

125

Paul Rubenstein took her up in his arms. She was a good sized girl, but he was stronger than he ever had been in his life and she felt like nothing in this arms. He wondered if that were merely psychological.

He carrier her toward the bed, her arms still around his neck.

She was the prettiest girl he had ever seen. He set her down on the bed, her hair flowing across the pillows like an amber wave.

She was the prettiest girl . . .

Natalia finished the cigarette, grinding it out under her heel, then carrying the dead butt in her fingertips until she passed a trash container. She deposited it there, then continued walking, hands once again thrust deep into the pockets of her skirt.

John Rourke would never be hers.

She had resigned herself to that sometime ago, but could not stop loving him. She knew she was beautiful, had always known that. At one time in her life, she had thought that loneliness for another human being could only afflict girls who were not pretty. But then she had married Vladmir Karamatsov, now the Hero Marshal of the Soviet Union, the most evil man she could have conceived of. And from the first time he had made love to her, she had understood loneliness.

It was a different loneliness now. John Rourke had taken away that first loneliness, though he had never really touched her with his body, having touched her more strongly than any man had ever touched her.

She felt stupid — Natalia realized that she was crying.

Chapter Eighteen

Otto Hammerschmidt's feet would not respond at all and so, along the snow covered, rocky ground, he crawled, moving inexorably toward the fire. Michael had used an expression once, like a moth to a flame. Otto Hammerschmidt had needed to have it explained to him what a moth had been, a type of insect. Otto Hammerschmidt had never seen one. He sometimes found himself wondering what the old world had been like before the Night of The War and the Great Conflagration.

Flowers were pollinated by artificial means, scientists having determined to release bees into an environment which was not balanced would have produced ecological disaster. But moths did not pollinate flowers. Otto Hammerschmidt had asked Michael Rourke if moths pollinated flowers. Michael had told him they did not—they flew into flames and lightbulbs and some kinds ate holes in woolen clothing. They seemed suicidal and without value. In his present condition, he was without value, and his act was premeditatedly suicidal, but necessary.

He kept crawling toward the flames . . .

Michael Rourke and Han had taken the two strongest

looking of the Mongol animals, all three of the horses looking still exhausted. But the horses had responded well, hardy beasts, Michael realized. In a way they were very much reminiscent of the little ponies of the plains Indians.

They had ridden back the way they had come during the chase, but such a frantic pace would have destroyed the horses before they had conquered half the intervening distance, and even with the light of the moon and stars, to traverse the sometimes uneven ground at such speed would have invited a fall.

But the animals made good time, Michael stopping to rest them after an hour's riding, wiping the animals down against the chill.

He took the opportunity to try the radio again. "Maria. Otto — this is Michael. Come in. Over."

But the only voice which came back to him was that of Bjorn Rolvaag. And Rolvaag was trying to tell him something. Michael realized his radio had been off during the time in which he and Han had counter-attacked — a logical if unconscious move to avoid a radio transmission signalling his presence. And he had forgotten to turn it back on.

Rolvaag spoke slowly, Michael trying to understand, having little success.

But at last he heard a word which he thought he understood. "A fire?"

Rolvaag saw a fire? Rolvaag seemed to be telling him yes.

Michael reiterated his earlier instructions. Stay by the vehicle and the supplies.

Michael closed the transmission, turning to the Chinese, both horses feeding from bags which were fitted to their heads like bridles. "My friend at our vehicle — he sees a fire. In the same place where we saw the fire last night. You don't suppose —" Michael left the question hanging.

Han nodded. "Is your friend in plain sight from the plateau?"

"Not from that edge of it. But further back, he would be.

128

But they'd have to look for him."

"He is very fortunate that apparently they did not. Wood for fires is scarce here and these men we fight are by nature lazy people, all their energy consumed with battle and in drunken revels. If there was wood at hand, from our campfire, they would merely have relit it if they wished to stay in the area. When my party and I came upon the plateau we searched for more than a half hour until finding the campsite we used, because it had been used before and there was some wood there. We hacked down a little more and set our fire. Our enemies have probably done the same."

"Stupid bastards—and I'm thankful they are." Michael Rourke worked the cinch of the saddle, having loosened it only slightly after dismounting to tend the horses. If Maria Leuden and Otto Hammerschmidt were alive, they would be there, he told himself. He swung up into the saddle. He had full loads remaining for each of the Berettas, fifteen rounds in the magazine plus an additional round in the chamber. A full cylinderful for the 629. If there weren't too many of them, it would be enough.

Han mounted. Michael said nothing, just dug in his heels and the little horse vaulted ahead . . .

Maria Leuden had fallen asleep—or fainted. She was not sure which. The little man with the hungry eyes had returned to his drinking after tugging the blankets and robes which covered her nakedness away, staring at her for a while and then covering her once again.

As she looked toward the dying fire, the little man stirred from sleep. He stood up and urinated, starting to close his pants. But then he turned back and looked at her.

She couldn't look away. He disgusted her, terrified her. He held his penis in his hand a moment and smiled.

Now she looked away.

He said something, and she tried to ignore him. He spoke

129

again. She turned and looked back at him. His penis hanging out of his pants, his hands rubbing it, he started toward her.

She screamed at him in German, "No—go away. Go away from me!" He only laughed. She tried English. He kept walking toward her.

From the shadows beside the fire, she saw a ghostly shape in white—Otto Hammerschmidt, she realized suddenly, stripped to his underwear, diving for the little man, throttling the little man to the ground. But it seemed that Hammerschmidt could not really walk. He pushed himself up, seemed to fall on the little man, the two of them rolling toward the fire. She was screaming, she knew.

Hammerschmidt's left fist thudded against the little man's face, then both of them, to their knees, hammered at each other, collapsing into the fire, Hammerschmidt's clothing aflame, the little man ripping away his robe, flames flickering from it. A pistol was in his hand as Hammerschmidt rolled himself in the snow to smother the flames. The evil little man thrust his pistol toward Hammerschmidt's head.

"Otto!"

Hammerschmidt looked up, the last of the flames extinguished, the little man laughing. Hammerschmidt shouted to her from the fire. "Fraulein—I am sorry!"

Then she heard another voice. It was Michael Rourke's voice from the darkness beyond the firelight. "Hello."

The little man turned toward the sound. The four others were stirring. Michael Rourke stepped from shadow into light. Maria Leuden felt a hand going over her mouth, covering it so she could make no sound, then a voice whispered in her right ear in English. "Make no sound. I am a friend." She couldn't see the face as she tried to turn toward the voice, but she nodded and the hand left her mouth and she felt herself being dragged back from the fire. Her eyes were riveted on Michael Rourke.

"Too bad you don't speak English. I could tell you what

real assholes you are. And as soon as I figure my friend Han here has dragged the girl out of the line of fire, you fellas are gonna be dead. Like that, huh?" And he smiled. The evil little man laughed. "Yeah, well, your mothers fucked you every night, right?" And there was more laughter. His hands were just at his sides, there was a smile on his face, the firelight making shadows there, making the smile look somehow like death. "And not one of you has the brains of a horse, huh? Well—looks like I kill you now." He reached for the pistols in the double shoulder holster he always wore.

The evil little man swung his pistol toward Michael and fired, but somehow the gunshot sounded too loud and she realized Michael's pistols had fired simultaneously and the little man's body fell backward into the campfire. The other four men made to fire their rifles and Michael just turned toward them, the pistols in his hands spitting tongues of flame against the darkness which framed him, gunfire from the four men, their rifles discharging into the ground, Michael's hands moving as he would fire at one man then another and then another.

His pistols were still.

The remaining four men were down, their guns still as well.

Maria Leuden breathed.

"Otto—you all right?"

"Michael—yes—where did you—"

"Tell ya later, huh—gonna check on Maria," and Michael Rourke stepped over the legs of the evil little man, the torso in the fire, smoldering, crossed the few yards to where she lay, her wrists already being untied. He stood over her for a long moment, his voice very soft when he asked her, "Are you okay?"

"I—I never saw anything like that in my life—Michael."

"My dad's done it a few times. Always wondered if I were that good. I guess I am," and he dropped to his knees, saying something to the man, untying her ankles, the man going off to tend to Otto Hammerschmidt. Michael closed the blankets around her and stood up, with her in his arms. "You'll be all right now, Maria. No one will hurt you," and he started walking away from the fire still holding her and she leaned her weary head against his chest and listened to the sound of his breathing.

Chapter Nineteen

Michael Rourke was reloading the spent magazines for the Berettas as Maria Leuden slept beside where he sat on the gound next to the German SM-4 vehicle, Bjorn Rolvaag tending Otto Hammerschmidt. It would be dawn in less than an hour and they would use the vehicle then to reach the First City. Some of Hammerschmidt's burns, to heal properly, would need better treatment than emergency first aid could offer. Michael had gone through more ammunition than he wished to count and he took the time while they waited for the dawn to clean the Beretta pistols.

His father had given the Germans a container of Break-Free CLP and asked them to duplicate it. It was one of these which Michael took from the vehicle, unloading both pistols — he still carried the 629 in the crossdraw holster — and beginning to field strip. Using the disassembly latch, he slid the slide forward and dismounted it. He separated the barrel from the slide and began cleaning. The Berettas disassembled like Natalia's Walther P-38, basically.

"You will like my city. And your friend — he will be well cared for in our hospitals. We have fine doctors and they practice their art with great skill."

"My father's a doctor. If all of this ever gets over with," Michael said slowly, running a patch down the bore of the disassembled pistol, "I'd like to try it myself. Seems a useful skill."

"My father too was a physician," Han said enthusiastically.

Michael scrubbed the feed ramp to get rid of powder residue, then took a dry patch to wipe out the bore. They had spoken throughout the day between attacks of the ongoing war with the forces of Vladmir Karamatsov and how Karamatsov's forces seemed to be coming this way. "I have watched you with your guns. You are by far the best man at arms that could exist," Han said suddenly.

Michael laughed so loudly that Rolvaag turned and looked up from ministering to Hammerschmidt.

"Why do you laugh, American?"

"My father is better with guns than I could ever be. Believe me."

Han said nothing for a moment, then, "And what if you were to discover that you were better than he? Would it disappoint you?"

"My father told me a story once. He and his dad used to arm wrestle, you know?" And he looked into Han's eyes for a sign of comprehension of the term. He saw it and went on. "My dad was always big for his age, strong, worked out a lot. A good natural athlete but he never went out for sports beyond the regular stuff every kid does. But he figured by the time he was sixteen he was strong enough to beat his father at arm wrestling. And so he never arm wrestled his dad again."

Han nodded. Perhaps it was something all sons could understand, Michael thought. He began reassembling the pistol . . .

Hartman had not requested that his sleep be interrrupted an hour before dawn, so when it was he came instantly awake. "Herr Captain—the Soviet forces are moving, more rapidly it appears than they have moved before."

He looked into the face of his orderly, the man apparently awakened as well.

Hartman sat up in his cot, rubbing his eyes. "Bring my clothes. Then alert the radio operator to contact Herr Doctor Rourke in Lydveldid Island immediately. I will require a meeting with my officers in ten minutes in my tent. See to it that the exact movements of the Soviet force are brought completely up to date. I will require the most exact information," and he swung his legs from the cot, his bare feet to the floor and stood up, the orderly moving about the enclosure and assembling Hartman's clothes. He blinked his eyes to focus better and looked at his watch.

He attempted from the outset of his assignment to command the forces of New Germany which monitored the movements of Marshal Karamatsov's army to analyze his opponent. War was much like chess, he had learned recently. And the Soviet leader's actions had become boringly routine.

He realized now that perhaps deceptively routine was more apt a description.

Chapter Twenty

It was not disobeying an order, but rather reinterpreting it. Doctor Munchen had left word with Major Volkmer that should any messages be sent to Doctor Rourke from the Eurasian front that he should be notified immediately because of Herr Doctor Rourke's exhausted state from the ordeal in the crevasse.

Major Volkmer had so ordered his subordinates and now Munchen had been awakened several hours before dawn with a message for Doctor Rourke. He did not presume to read it, but it was from Captain Hartman, the commander of the forces of New Germany on the Eurasian front, so it would be important.

Every moment of sleep he could buy for John Rourke would be that much more beneficial, and so he dressed at his usual pace after having showered first. He could be court martialed, he knew, but he was a doctor and doctors were assumed to act a bit rebelliously toward military orders at times for the continued well-being of their patients.

He did not call ahead for the helicopter, but instead went to the control center for the helicopter fleet and ordered one on the spot, which would take at least ten minutes.

When the helicopter arrived, he boarded it, not telling the pilot to make best speed to Hekla, but simply letting the pilot fly the short run as he normally would.

When the helicopter landed on the greenway, was met by forces of his own army and by Icelandic police, he told them he had a secret message for Herr Doctor Rourke and walked away from them, from the helicopter, toward the dormitory where Doctor Rourke and his wife, Rubenstein and Annie and the Russian woman Major Tiemerovna would be sleeping. He looked at his watch. He had consumed twenty-three minutes, so far, and could easily stretch that into a half-hour. He stopped, lighting a cigarette from his case with studied deliberateness, pocketing his lighter, then walking on toward the dormitory steps.

Munchen stopped at the base of the steps. There was no security for the building. He started up the steps slowly, mentally ticking off the seconds, then entered the dormitory hallway through the large double doors. He knew the door to their small apartment and walked toward it, the message in his inside pocket. He removed his uniform headgear and looked around the corridor, glanced again at his wristwatch. It had been nearly a half-hour.

Munchen rapped lightly on the door with the knuckles of his right fist. He didn't knock too loudly, wishing to prolong arousing the Rourkes as much as possible.

He waited a more than respectable time and knocked again, the door opening under his hand. John Rourke stood in the doorway, naked from the waist up, the muscles of his chest and arms rippling, his right hand behind him.

"Doctor—a house call?"

"So to speak, Herr Doctor."

"Come in—just a moment first though," and the door closed almost fully and he heard Rourke's voice just inside the doorway, then the door reopened. Munchen stepped inside as bidden. He noticed in the back of Rourke's pants a pistol, as though thrust there hurriedly. He imagined it was what had been in Rourke's right hand when the door had opened the first time. The bedside lamp was on and Frau

Rourke sat up on the edge of the bed, in her nightdress, a shawl about her shoulders as was the custom of the women of Hekla.

"Good evening, Doctor Munchen," she smiled. "Or good morning might be more appropriate."

Munchen looked away from Frau Rourke, into Doctor Rourke's eyes. The face was lined with what might have been a smile or might only have been amusement. Rourke was barefoot, but still well over six feet tall, lean, but not thin. His hair, above the naturally high forehead, was thick, tousled from interrupted sleep. Or from the look on Frau Rourke's face, perhaps something else interrupted which could be, he felt with his best medical opinion, nearly as salubrious as sleep and definitely more pleasant.

"I have a message for you, Herr Doctor. From Captain Hartman at the Eurasian front. I took the liberty of delivering it personally." He neglected to mention that he had done so in order to delay it and allow Rourke more time — for sleep or whatever.

"Thank you, Doctor," and Rourke took the message from Munchen's hand as Munchen offered it. Rourke didn't move toward the light and apparently in the semi-darkness it was not even necessary for his light sensitive eyes to squint. Munchen had once contrived to be allowed to test Rourke's vision. It was almost uncannily good. Munchen often found himself wondering if it were somehow to do with Rourke's light sensitivity.

Rourke passed the message to Frau Rourke, then turned to look at Munchen. "There was a time stamp on the message. Giving me more sleep, were you?"

"I am that transparent? Sleep or — "

"I am that transparent?" Rourke walked to the nightstand and took up one of the thin, dark tobacco cigars he habitually smoked. Munchen had tried one once but preferred his cigarettes. Frau Rourke took Rourke's rather battered looking cigarette lighter and lit the cigar for her husband. John Rourke seemed to study the tip of the cigar as he exhaled, then turned and said, "It appears I won't be around for that physical examination tomorrow. But, as one medical man to another, let me assure you that the patient is recovering nicely."

"May I say something, Herr Doctor Rourke—and please accept my comment in the spirit in which it is offered."

"Yes," Rourke nodded.

"You are not, in and of yourself, an entire army. Eventually, the laws of probability overtake us all."

Doctor Rourke said nothing, and Frau Rourke merely closed her eyes . . .

Paul Rubenstein heard the light knocking at the door and started to sit up, Annie still asleep, his right arm beneath her. He slipped his arm free, experiencing a tingling sensation, his arm partially asleep. She was naked beneath the blankets and he pressed the covers more tightly around her as he slipped, naked, from bed and took the Browning High Power in his fist.

He approached the door, the knocking coming again. He opened the door instantly, the pistol tight at his side as he stepped back. It was John Rourke.

"Hi—you'll catch cold that way."

Rubenstein remembered he was naked. He stepped a little left, partially behind the door.

"We have to go," John Rourke told him.

John Rourke himself was barefoot and naked from the waist up, one of the Scoremasters thrust casually into the waistband of his faded blue Levis. "I've got transport being arranged," his friend continued. "Meet me out front in twenty-five minutes," and he looked at his wristwatch. Paul Rubenstein did the same.

"To rejoin Hartman?"

"Yeah."

"You up to it?"

"I'll take it easy for a few days. Just some soreness, like that."

"All right. What's up?"

"Karamatsov's army broke off in what looks like a direct thrust for northern China. This could be it."

"All right. Tell Sarah good-bye for me."

"Give Annie a kiss for me," John Rourke smiled.

Paul Rubenstein nodded.

John Rourke started down the corridor and Paul closed the door, leaning heavily against it. He heard Annie's voice in the darkness. "Come and make love to me quickly."

"All right," he answered her, walked toward the bed and put down his pistol. He came into her arms and she drew the covers up over them both . . .

John Rourke knocked at the door. The door opened, Natalia beautiful in the pink floor length nightgown, a shawl pulled around her shoulders, her left hand going through her almost black hair, the surreal blueness of her eyes somehow tinged with something that reminded him of sadness. In her right hand was the stainless American Walther PPK/S with the custom silencer at the muzzle. Rourke smiled inwardly at the thought: If Natalia Anastasia Tiemerovna, Major, Committee for State Security, Retired, were forced to shoot someone at such an ungodly hour she would do so without awakening the neighbors.

"What is it, John?"

She didn't ask him inside. Even at Hekla, people talked, he realized. "We have to go. Do you want to stay here?"

"Do you want me to come with you?"

"Always."

"Then I will, of course."

"Twenty-five minutes, on the steps."

"Yes."

"You look beautiful."

"Twenty-five minutes," she repeated.

"Yes," and he smiled at her and turned back down the corridor toward the room he shared with his wife. He realized he loved them both, as equally as one man could love two women. And he realized what it was doing to all three of them.

He walked into the rooms he shared with his wife, closed the door behind him and closed his eyes, hearing Sarah in the shower.

Chapter Twenty-one

Michael Rourke had pictured it as something like the Soviet Underground City had appeared. But it was not.

The Soviet Underground City had been, when seen from a distance like this, merely a utilitarian tunnel, much like the railroad tunnels he remembered seeing as a boy and some of which still survived after a fashion today.

He saw the Chinese city first as they reached the summit of an almost unnaturally circular range of moderately high, jagged peaks. Beneath them in the valley was where it lay, rising out of the ground like some sort of magnificently geometric flower, segmented, each segment vastly large, a half-dozen segments already visible, others (he imagined perhaps a dozen in all) partially uncovered. The city had been buried, he realized, built, buried within the valley under what would have been millions of tons of dirt and rock, and was now, perhaps over the space of decades being uncovered.

"It's beautiful," Michael Rourke told the Chinese beside him as Michael rested his hands over the steering wheel and stared. The fully uncovered segments were a dark cream color, like the petals of a rose. Annie had grown some. Beside two of the fully uncovered segments were pagoda-shaped structures, some apparently completed, others seemingly under construction. The once buried segments of the city were forming the basis for a new city that was emerging before his eyes. Heavy equipment moved dirt and rock and what appeared, from the distance, to be thousands of men and women moved about the structure, working to complete them.

"I thought you had no fuel."

"Our heavy construction equipment is electrically powered, and must be recharged every several hours. We have electricity in abundance. Originally, our reactors were fission powered but in the third century of our confinement beneath the ground, fusion was at last conquered and we have clean, safe power to supply all our needs."

"How did your people get outside—if the city was buried, as it appears?"

"There are entrances throughout the mountains here, many of them since re-sealed, American. Many of them were large enough and designed to accommodate the transfer of construction vehicles like those which you see now. It was all planned by our leaders five centuries ago. And, thank God, it was successful."

Michael Rourke looked at Han and felt himself smile. "Yes—for all of us," and he started the vehicle down along what appeared to be a service road leading to a paved highway perhaps a quarter mile further down along the gently sloping side of the valley. The road was only one lane wide, but there was sufficient room on both sides of it to be broadened should it become necessary to do so. His father would like these people. They planned ahead.

Behind him, as he drove, Maria Leuden knelt in the vehicle's bed, Otto Hammerschmidt's head in her lap, Rolvaag and his dog with them there as well, Hammerschmidt sedated against the pain of his burns; some of the German spray which promoted healing had been used on his burns, but Hammerschmidt was feverish, the sedation necessary against what Michael judged must have been excruciating pain.

They had recovered Hammerschmidt's clothing and weapons, as well as those things of Marie Leuden, but neither wore their original clothes, Hammerschmidt's body unable to support the contact against his skin, and Maria Leuden declaring that the clothes would have to be sterilized before she would even touch them. Michael had loaned her a shirt and a pair of pants, miles too big except in the leg length, which was nearly right when rolled up six inches or so. She was quite tall for a woman. She had wrapped herself in the ultra thin survival blankets provided for them by the German quartermasters.

As yet, Michael had mentioned nothing to Maria Leuden of the fact that the radio transmission he had sent to her and to Otto Hammerschmidt, in addition to being picked up by Bjorn Rolvaag, should have been picked up by the pilot and door gunner of the German heliocopter which had brought them into this area and which should still be less than seventy-five miles away. That the messages had not been intercepted, indicated to Michael that the Mongol warriors of the Second City, which Han had described in more graphic detail than his own city, might indeed have been more active in the area than Han suspected.

But Michael had not been asked how they had gotten to the general area of the Greater Khingan Range in northern Manchuria and he had not volunteered the information. If the helicopter and its crew, or for that matter the helicopter alone, still existed, it might be useful to keep its presence a secret. He trusted Han but had never considered it deceitful to be prudent.

He could see railroad tracks now, and steam operated locomotives coupled to massive flat cars; and, leading from some of the flat cars, ramps. Michael assumed the Chinese had a source of coal to run the steam locomotives.

They reached the single lane highway and Michael turned down onto it toward the city, the road looping the valley several times before reaching the level of the city, but the drive easier and faster for Hammerschmidt than going cross-country. He slowly felt out the acceleration, driving the vehicle faster than he had ever driven it, but at what he considered a safe speed. It was gradually warmer as the vehicle descended, Michael throwing back the hood of his parka and freeing one hand from the steering wheel to open his coat. "Why did your people pick this area, Han—for the construction of their city?"

"The rail lines which once serviced Harbin were easily extended to service the construction site in those days and, it was felt, even if the more disastrous possibilities became reality following a nuclear war, the railroad beds would still exist and perhaps the rail lines themselves. As it happened, the beds indeed existed but were buried beneath generations of ice and snow and it required many years of work with explosives to make the new beds beyond our valley. We were able to construct rail lines leading to the sea and hope to construct ships. But this will not be in my lifetime. At least I presume not."

His voice sounded off slightly and Michael asked him, "Is something wrong?"

"Do your people have sea power?"

Michael saw no sense in a lie and evasion was a lie under some circumstances. It was not the same as just not mentioning the helicopter. "No—we don't. We could, I suppose. But there hasn't been time. Why do you ask?"

"There have been incursions, coming from the direction of the sea. Attacks on a distant outpost we have established by the Yellow Sea. It was thought wise for us to have a military presence on the seacoast. We have there a small town as well. For the most part the wives and families of military officers and the men who work on the new fusion generator systems live there. And this is where, someday, we will build our ships."

"Where do you mine your coal?" Michael asked. And Han began to laugh. "For the locomotives you run, I mean?"

"They are steam engines, but require no coal. The water is heated by fusion generators, American. We may have no synthetic fuel, but we are not entirely without resources."

Michael asked a question he had been dying to ask since he had field stripped the Chinese rifle. He slowed for a curve in the road and then began again to accelerate. "Why is it that you utilize arms from five centuries ago, and in such a poor condition?"

"Isolated as we were, there was no need for the mass production of arms, although we had the capability. When we re-emerged, it was practical to arm our military forces with the weapons from before the Dragon Wind, but as we realized we had a fierce and implacable enemy in the Second City, it became necessary to revise these plans. And the production of arms was begun. We have a well-equipped army, but to equip our Mongol mercenaries with the newer weapons would betray them as being in our employ. So the old weapons are still issued."

Michael started into the final straightaway which would feed into the city itself, Han saying to him, "The first petal, there—turn into the access route."

"The first petal?"

"Does it not remind you of a flower, our city?"

Michael only nodded, slowing, taking the turn, then accelerating only a little. He expected security at any moment to come crashing abruptly down on them, but none had yet and none seemed forthcoming. "How do you guard this place?"

"You will soon see."

Michael didn't like the tone of the remark, and slowed the vehicle still more. The access road was leading into a tunnel which seemed to feed into the "petal," as Han had called it.

"You should stop this conveyance here, American. Go no further."

Michael realized in the next second that Han did not comprehend how brakes worked, the front end of the vehicle slamming into something that seemed impossibly nonresilient, sparks flying, electrical current flashing from the hood of the German machine, the instruments on the dashboard going wild, beginning to smoke. Michael shuddered as the vehicle lurched backward, taking his hands involuntarily from the wheel, the "conveyance," as Han again had called it, dead.

"What the hell —"

"You did not stop rapidly enough, American," Han groused.

Michael Rourke looked at him. "Do you know the expression 'Shove it up your ass'? What the —"

Maria Leuden shouted forward, "What is happening?" Bjorn Rolvaag's dog growled menacingly.

Alarms were sounding now, armed men appearing from inside the tunnel which seemed to lead inside the petal, the assault rifles they carried decidedly different in profile from the five centuries old weapons he had seen earlier.

Han stepped out of the vehicle and began speaking in a loud voice, one of the armed men, but carrying a pistol and apparently an officer, signaling the others to stop their advance. Michael's hands were on the butts of his Berettas beneath his coat. He didn't draw them.

Han stopped speaking to the soldiers and turned to face Michael as Michael climbed out, the two staring at each other across the dented and wrinkled hood. "The current will be shut off momentarily," Han smiled. "I told the officer in charge you are the ambassador from the United States of America and that the woman, the injured man and the green clad giant are your staff. We can clarify the details later."

Michael shrugged, then started toward the rear of the vehicle to start moving Otto Hammerschmidt.

He wondered if Rolvaag's dog, Hrothgar, had been elevated to ambassadorial rank as well?

Chapter Twenty-two

Everyone pulled guard duty from time to time and Akiro Kurinami, not liking it, didn't resent it. He imagined it was simply his turn to be unlucky.

The guard posts were divided equally among the Germans who supported their otherwise untenable position at Eden Base and the Eden personnel, every other post German, every other post Eden. Because of the international composition of the Eden astronaut corps, few called themselves Americans.

Kurinami, huddled in his parka, gripped the M-16 that was slung to his body merely by the pistol grip, his gloved trigger finger alongside the trigger guard. He expected no trouble. The German surveillance devices would have detected it. But guard tours were necessary — as John Rourke would have put it, "It pays to plan ahead."

Soon, he would see John Rourke again, and Paul and Annie, and Sarah, and of course Natalia Tiemerovna. What an exquisite creature, he thought.

They would come for the wedding.

He had drawn perhaps the most remote of the guardposts and with the heavy snow that had begun a few hours before, visibility was less than a hundred yards. But it was, in one respect, a good time for security. Every guard would be awake and moving, patrolling his post, since it was the only way to keep from freezing. The abrupt change from cold to below freezing with snow had been unexpected. But he supposed that with the radical change in the earth's environment, the unexpected was to be expected. Had it been less nearer to dawn, he doubted he would have been able to see his hand in front of his face.

His thoughts focused on Elaine Halversen, soon to be Elaine Kurinami. Thinking of her somehow kept him warmer. Someday, he knew, they would both look back on this as they told their children of the early days of the return to earth, of having to stand guard in the middle of what could soon turn from a heavy snowfall into hard blizzard conditions, and the children would stare at them, agape at such an existence—

He thought he saw something moving as a gust of wind cut through him like a knife and temporarily cleared the air of snow.

"Halt! Who is it?"

There was no answer.

Kurinami licked his lips beneath the toque which covered his face except for the eyes. His right first finger slipped into the trigger guard, his right thumb finding the safety tumbler and moving it into the full auto position. "Who is it?"

It was too early for his relief to come, wasn't it? He refigured the time, not daring to shift his eyes to his wrist to look at his chronometer. "Who is it?"

Kurinami saw a shape—not definable enough to be certain what it was, and he wheeled toward it, bringing the muzzle of his rifle up, then feeling it as something hammered against his right shoulder and his right arm went numb and the rifle fell from his grasp and he started to fall forward into the snow. But he caught himself, realizing that something had struck him, rolling to the ground, blinking his eyes against the cold wetness of the snow, the sling of the rifle being twisted away from him, a foot suddenly visible inches in front of his face. He dodged it, losing the rifle, grabbing the foot with his left hand and twisting it hard, seeing someone in a hooded parka and ski toque and white snow smock tumble into the snow near him. Kurinami was up, moving, his right arm still all but paralyzed, another figure lurching at him from the snow, Kurinami wheeling, his left foot snapping out, a double Tae Kwon Do kick to the face and chest, the attacker falling back.

Kurinami reached to his hip for the Government Model .45 there, but his right hand still wouldn't respond. He now saw the wisdom of the Rourkes, all but Paul Rubenstein carrying two handguns at all times.

The first man—was it the first man, the one he had tumbled into the snow?—was coming for him and Kurinami tried another kick, but felt something—a rifle butt?—sweeping him off balance and down into the snow and then they were on him.

He didn't know how many there were. His good hand flailed toward faces, punching, his feet kicking. He felt a sudden dullness and then a warmth that he knew somehow was unnatural and the whiteness of the snow which swirled around him was turning to blackness and he thought of Elaine.

"Elaine . . ."

Chapter Twenty-three

When his eyes opened — but they didn't open and he knew he was blindfolded — Akiro Kurinami thought of Commander Dodd and the stolen guns.

He didn't move, lest he betray that he was awake. It was warm, so he knew that he was inside, somewhere. But where?

They — whoever they were — could not have risked taking him to the Eden Base. What if they were discovered.

And he realized where he had to be. Where the missing weapons and supplies and computer files had been taken. And he knew why he was here — for the duplicate files which showed the locations of the supply caches. He knew why . . .

Maria Leuden resisted it, but then, as she dressed before the mirror, she tried to search out for Michael Rourke's thoughts. She was obsessed with knowing if he loved her, she realized. Ever since he had taken her up into his arms and carried her as if she were just some tiny child —

The clothes given her were beautiful to wear. But she

didn't care about them.

She closed her eyes, thinking of Michael Rourke.

She had not seen him since they had passed through the tunnel, some of the soldiers carrying the stretcher they had placed Otto Hammerschmidt upon, then an electrically powered vehicle of some sort which was like an ambulance coming for him and Otto Hammerschmidt disappearing inside it. She had been given over to a woman named Toy, and facilities for bathing, for washing her hair, fresh clothes, all had been made available to her. She assumed Toy was some sort of intelligence agent, much like Han.

She could not use her mind like Annie Rourke could. And she had forced herself to stop reading Michael's thoughts. She put on her glasses. Wearing nothing but panties and a bra, she sat on the edge of the rather ornately styled bed. Her glasses had been placed on the small table next to the bed, Maria still utterly surprised that they had survived through her ordeal. She looked at herself in the mirror. A tall, skinny girl in love with a man whose mind she could read. But only when she was with him, really. She feared that she would, as time went by, be able to read his thoughts even when they were separated by some distance, as she had been able to with her father, her friend Elsie who had died. And what she feared most was that, if Michael refused to care for her, that she would be able to feel his thoughts forever, even when he was with another woman.

And that would drive her mad.

She decided to get dressed. The Chinese girl, Toy, very pretty, had promised to wait for her in the corridor outside the room she had been given. Maria Leuden had wondered if that translated to standing guard over her?

But she would dress and then Toy would give her a tour of this petal, because that would be all there would be time for before the dinner that would be tonight and she would need the time to change.

She exhaled. She should have been tired. She wasn't tired.

She was exhausted in a way she had never been.

She stood up and started to dress . . .

The SM-4 had been completely disabled and they had left it at the energy field barrier leading into the tunnel, Michael having taken up his pack and the spare assault rifle, an M-16, then proceeding through the tunnel and into the city in the company of Han and some eighteen soldiers and an officer. The tunnel had been far less than remarkable except for the smoothness of the joints where it was sectioned.

But once through the tunnel, he had been even more impressed than he had been at his first somewhat distant view of the First City. The tunnel had been steeply down sloping and Michael Rourke had assumed that he would enter the city at its lowest level, but instead they had emerged before a roadway, and beyond the roadway were towering buildings rising to a height he had judged as several hundred feet, the tunnel mouth at the level of their pinnacles. There was something like a train station near the tunnel mouth. He had remembered, when a boy, his mother taking them to Atlanta and parking the car in a large parking lot and then boarding a train at a station like this. She had called it a subway.

But the train, which came to the station and stopped and Michael, Maria Leuden and Han had boarded, after Hammerschmidt had been placed aboard what looked to be an electrically powered ambulance, was a monorail. And as it crossed from the tunnel mouth over much of the petal, as Han had called this wing of the First City, Michael had been amazed.

He had considered it a symbol of friendship that he had not been asked to turn over his weapons, and perhaps also a symbol of Han's eminence in the city. For that reason, he had elected, after showering, changing to fresh clothes from his pack, to leave the assault rifle and the 629 in his room, wearing only the double shoulder rig with the Berettas, but beneath his leather jacket so they would not be seen.

Han had been waiting for him when he emerged from the suite of rooms he had been given, the rooms in a large building that seemed at once to house offices yet be some sort of official residence. Han had changed as well, his skin several shades lighter than it had appeared, his stubble shaven away and only the thin mustache remaining, his clothes consisting of a gray suit with a collarless jacket and conventional shoes rather than boots. He looked anything but the Mongol warrior that he had appeared to be when they had first met a day before.

"You appear renewed, American."

Michael rubbed his face with his left hand. He had shaved and was clean and wore clean clothes. "I suppose I'm renewed. If you can be renewed when you are too tired to sleep."

Han laughed. "Tired or curious, American?"

"Both."

"Then come and meet our chairman. You are awaited. The pistols under your coat will be acceptable as long as they are not drawn."

"Five points," Michael Rourke told him . . .

None of the new German J-7Vs had been available to speed their flight to Iceland, but one had been available on the coast of Norway and Rourke, Natalia and Rubenstein had transferred from the German helicopter to the versatile aircraft with its dynamically rearswept wings and rear mounted jet driven propellers which allowed it to change from horizontal to vertical flight mode almost at will, as fast as a conventional jet but with the manueverability of a helicopter gunship.

John Rourke had resisted the temptation to ask to be allowed in the cockpit and, when the invitation to do so had come, he had refused it as well, forcing himself to sleep, knowing that he would need it.

As the J-7V changed flight modes for landing, he awakened, Paul asleep in the seat opposite him, Natalia beside him — Rourke — with her long legs stretched out and feet crossed on the seat next to Paul. She was not asleep.

"We are just going into landing mode," she told him. "While you were asleep, I went forward. They let me try the controls for a few minutes. These machines fly beautifully. I have to check out on one. It might be a useful skill."

Rourke looked at her. "Yes. I feel the same way."

"If Vladmir has finally changed directions, perhaps we can somehow more effectively anticipate him."

"I hope so. Gotta find out how Michael's doing, too."

"Yes. I think our Fraulein doctor likes him quite a bit."

"Maria Leuden?"

"Yes. It would be good for him. Michael is too young to be alone."

"Chronologically, he's older than you are."

"I think he'll always be little Michael to me, but he wasn't little, really. Was he even big as a baby?"

"Nine pounds and four ounces — and not an ounce of flab. Yeah — he was a big baby. Then he hit a growth spurt and it seemed never to stop."

"What are you and Sarah hoping to have — or don't you care whether it's a boy or a girl?"

John Rourke looked away from her and out the window. "So long as it's healthy, we'll be happy," and he looked back at Natalia. "I'm sorry I messed you up. I didn't mean to do that to you."

"You don't mean you and Sarah having the baby — that —"

"No — I didn't mean that. I meant, well — falling in love with you. You loving me. I left you holding the shit end of the stick and I'm sorry. If I could — but I really don't know what."

"I always love you and I realized — realized a long time ago

155

I could never have you. I won't lie and say I'm all perfectly adjusted, John—but I'll survive. Maybe you did that for me."

John Rourke touched his right hand to her left cheek and kissed her lightly on the lips.

The aircraft touched down . . .

Captain Hartman seemed weary, Rourke thought. "There have been many developments, Herr Doctor. The gunship which carried your son and Fraulein Doctor Leuden, under the command of Captain Hammerschmidt, has been out of radio contact for some twenty-four hours. We have no idea why. At the last report, your son had determined that the search might best progress on foot and they left with one of the SM-4s, the Icelandic policeman Bjorn Rolvaag accompanying them. The last communication from the SM-4 vehicle was prior to young Herr Rourke, Fraulein Doctor Leuden and Captain Hammerschmidt climbing a high escarpment toward what appeared to be a fire of other than natural origins."

"Damn," John Rourke almost whispered. "Not a word since?"

"Not a word since, Herr Doctor."

Rourke felt suddenly warm there inside the command tent, but realized it was not the temperature. "What about the direction Karamatsov's forces are moving in?"

"That is rather disconcerting—it roughly approximates the direction from which your son's last radio transmission originated."

"At his present rate of movement," Paul Rubenstein asked, "how rapidly would Karamatsov be able to reach that general area?"

Rourke felt Natalia's right hand finding his left, squeezing it tightly.

Hartman answered. "Approximately seventy-two hours,

were they to stop for two rest periods of six hours each in that time."

"With no rest periods," Natalia began, "they would reach that general area in two and one-half days. That is very little time."

John Rourke chewed down on the tip of the unlit cigar between his teeth. "Time enough. We'll take that J-7V if you don't have any objections."

"I will dispatch Lieutenant Schmidt to assist you."

"No—we'll need a pilot, co-pilot and a small security team to secure the immediate area where we touch down. Those special items I asked for—have they arrived?"

"Yes—but they have not been field tested, Herr Doctor."

"We'll field test them in the field. Get them loaded aboard," and Rourke turned away from Hartman. "Paul—see to it that we've got all the ammo and spare magazines we can carry. Replenish anything that's running low. Natalia," and he turned and looked into her face. She stood beside him still—always, he wondered? "Marshal together extra clothing, rations, medical supplies. Let's be airborne in a half hour—they were already fueling the J 7V when we left the field." And Rourke turned to Captain Hartman. "That enough time for you?"

"Yes, Herr Doctor."

"What are the chances of getting reinforcements from the Complex in Argentina to assist us against Karamatsov?"

"Not very good, I am afraid. But I shall endeavor to get what reinforcements I can. It appears we will be fighting soon."

"We'll see—I want to let him get where he's going, and then stop him. That's the riskiest way of doing it, but the only way. If he has another supply of that gas, or something worse—"

"I will make certain, Herr Doctor, that an adequate supply of masks are available to you. It is my intent to keep moving our main body up behind Marshal Karamatsov's forces while still maintaining a defensive posture in the event he turns his army and attacks. I have units monitoring the Soviet forces constantly so we should have adequate warning."

"Let's make a pre-arranged transmission schedule," Natalia said, taking out a cigarette, Rourke lighting it for her in the blue-yellow flame of his battered Zippo, then lighting his cigar. "Every six hours once we're on the ground. Then if you do not hear from us—" She didn't finish.

Paul Rubenstein smiled, then, his voice cheerful, said, "We're up shit's creek?"

John Rourke smiled.

Chapter Twenty-four

Akiro Kurinami writhed, trying to escape the electrical shocks as they came again, his body slamming hard against what could have been a wall or only a wall of rock. Then the electrical charges stopped coming and he heard the voice again. It was through a synthesizer, sounding like the voices of persons who had no voice, an artificial larynx, metallic, grating, and, blindfolded and bound and helpless as he was, terrifying.

"Lieutenant Kurinami. Where are the duplicate files?" It was the same question they had begun asking him hours ago—or was it longer than that? He could no longer be certain. He could smell his body, during one of the sessions with the electrical prods that were used against his body, his muscles had involuntarily relaxed. His bladder had emptied and that wasn't all.

The files contained the locations of the supply caches where weapons, food, building equipment, and medical supplies had been buried five centuries before for use after their return. The original files had been wiped from the Eden Fleet onboard computers and Kurinami's copies were the only one which existed, except for the copy whoever had cleared the files had taken. If he surrendered them, whoever possessed the files would control Eden Base unless the

Germans stopped them. And if the Germans were unable to do so—

"Kill me—but you won't get the files," Kurinami said, noticing that the resolve in his voice sounded less firm than it had when they had begun the torture. "If I die you will never get them."

The synthesized voice came again in his darkness and pain. "We will take Elaine Halversen—perhaps she will answer us."

"No!"

"Then tell!"

"No!"

The voice stopped. There was no renewal of the pain and he thought he heard a sound, after a moment, like feet moving across a floor. Then there was nothing but silence. He shouted into it. "I'll kill you if you harm her. I will kill you! I will kill you if you—"

No one answered and Akiro Kurinami realized he was alone.

And they were going after Elaine . . .

Michael sat in a straight backed chair in the middle of a high ceilinged room at what he estimated to be the exact center of the building. Another straight backed upholstered chair, empty, was a few feet from his, facing him. Han stood beside him.

"You straighten out this ambassador stuff?" Michael asked him.

"I said that it was meant figuratively, rather than literally. Do not worry, American."

The room was utilitarian in its furnishing, the walls a subdued shade of red with black trim, looking to be made of something like marble. Michael reflected that perhaps it was marble. Han had said nothing which intimated anything about the person whose room this was, whose empty chair now faced Michael Rourke. In books, the person would have automatically been some wizened old man who spoke in riddles but exuded wisdom. Or perhaps a woman, albeit more mysterious seeming and more seductive looking than Lydveldid Island's Madame Jokli.

He had seen Bjorn Rolvaag and the dog, making a point of stopping to see them on the way here, Rolvaag sitting calmly reading one of his inevitable books, the Icelandics historically among the most literate people in all the world. He had nodded, said little, stroked the head of his dog Hrothgar between the ears, then leaned back against the wall and continued to read as Michael had left. Rolvaag had apparently preferred the hardness of the floor to the softness of a bed or even a chair.

And he had stopped to see Hammerschmidt. Hammerschmidt, the doctors had said in their quaintly accented but perfectly understandable English, was making good progress. The healing agent in the German spray had been the perfect thing to administer. Michael was flattered at his own diagnostic abilities. But Hammerschmidt had still been sedated.

The walk to this room where Michael now sat had been long, but pleasant, Han explaining that indeed this building was the seat of government of the First City, as well as the residence of the chairman. The additional apartments, like those occupied now by Michael and Maria Leuden and Rolvaag and his dog, were just three of more than two dozen kept on hand for government officials to use in times of emergency when their special abilities might be required by the chairman at any hour of the day or night.

When they had left the building, briefly, to journey by monorail again to the hospital where Otto Hammerschmidt was being treated, Michael had again marveled at this city within the earth. At first glance, past the beauty of its architecture, it might well have seemed forbiddingly uniform, as if all its inhabitants were like ants in a tunnel.

Michael remembered ants.

But there was individualism, subtle, yet definite, every-where he looked, no two gardens alike, no two buildings identical and, in the hospital, in the monorail station, on the monorail car itself, this a public unit and not the private unit which had originally brought them into the city, the faces of the people bespeaking happiness without anything vacuous, a dignity of personal identity.

The Chinese, he felt based on his readings, had indeed come far.

The doors at the far end of the room opened. They were black, looking to be of lacquered wood but logic dictating rather some sort of synthetic. He had seen few trees and he doubted such a precious commodity would be wasted for ornamentation.

Through the doors walked a man. He was tall, as tall as Michael or his father easily, and thin without, at the distance, appearing painfully so. His hair was steel gray rather than white, and full but cut short, seeming to crown a craggy face which looked at once Oriental yet western as he approached. His body was covered in a black, ankle length tunic that rustled slightly as he drew near. Michael wondered if it were made of silk, something for which the Chinese had always been famous in his day and before.

The man, his eyes rock steady, hands folded in front of him, stopped some six feet behind the vacant chair. Michael stood.

"I am Lin Tsao Tang, Mr. Rourke. How do you do?"

"An honor to meet you, Mr. Chairman."

"The honor is mine. Please be seated. I have recently left a rather pressing meeting and find it more comfortable to stand after so much time seated. You and your friends were the subject of the meeting. But rest assured, the meeting was a pleasant one. You are indeed an American?"

"Yes, sir," Michael nodded, still standing.

"An informal ambassador, I am told—meaning I take it

162

that you and your friends were exploring this portion of Asia and since you have 'discovered' us, shall we say, you would represent your people to us. But let me assure you, we were not lost," and the chairman smiled.

"I hadn't thought that you were, sir. But you presume correctly. We were exploring and it was then when we encountered Mr. Han and learned for the first time that your people had survived what we call the Great Conflagration and you call the Dragon Wind."

"Both rather picturesque terms, Mr. Rourke. You were just exploring?" And he emphasized the word 'just'.

"As you no doubt know, sir, we—meaning the few surviving Americans, the people of New Germany in what before the Dragon Wind was called Argentina and the people of Lydveldid Island, have formed an alliance against the Soviet Union forces under the command of Marshal Vladmir Karamatsov, a man of unspeakable evil, like myself, my father and mother, my sister, my sister's husband and a family friend, a survivor from the period before the Night of The War."

Lin Tsao Tang reached out both his hands as he stepped forward, appearing to steady himself against the back of his chair. "I have misunderstood," he said in his deep, rich baritone.

"I fear you have not misunderstood, sir. Through a process known as cryogenic sleep, myself, my family and some others, both from among our enemies in the Soviet Union and from among the persons living now in the United States, survived. I was born in the last quarter of the twentieth century, and it is now the twenty-fifth in our reckoning."

"If you do not wish to sit down, I at least do," and the chairman eased himself into the chair.

Michael sat down opposite him, feeling it rude to remain standing.

"And you fight a war with the Russians?"

163

"There was an attempt at a coup in the Russian camp, an attack by the army of Marshal Karamatsov against his government leadership at their Underground City in the Ural Mountains, a less elaborate structure to be sure, I understand. The position of the actual Soviet leadership within the city is unknown, but a state of war exists between ourselves and the forces of Marshal Karamatsov. He took his vast army to the east and I and my companions travelled ahead of his advance to determine his possible destination. I believe we have found it, sir."

"Indeed," the chairman said wearily.

Chapter Twenty-five

The J-7V landed, John Rourke and two men from the four man security unit being the first to disembark the aircraft; the helicopter was some fifty yards away and no sign of anyone around it. Nor was there any sign of the SM-4, the jeep-like vehicle with which Michael, Maria Leuden, Hammerschmidt and Bjorn Rolvaag had set out.

Rourke looked behind him once, Natalia and Paul Rubenstein disembarking, clad in their arctic gear, two more of the German security team with them.

"Paul, have those two men stay with the plane!"

"Right!"

Rourke took the senior of the two Germans with him by the arm. "Fan out to both sides of the helicopter and keep fifty yards back from it and find some cover in case it's wired to detonate or something. Move out!"

"Yes, Herr Doctor Rourke!" And the first man nodded to his fellow soldier and they split to right and left as they broke into a run, their weapons at high port.

Rourke slung the M-16 forward on its sling and worked the bolt, charging the chamber. He moved the selector to auto, his right first finger, gloved, just outside the guard. "Natalia—take my left. Paul, on the right!"

An icy wind swept across the plain as he walked, the plain longer by far than it was wide, the helicopter pilot having chosen his landing area well. It was moored against the high winds, but already its runners were partially drifted over with snow, the windshield partially covered as well, snow drifted beneath the craft and all but obscuring the chin bubble. It seemed clear the helicopter hadn't been moved in at least twenty-four hours.

"I should go in first—I'm better with explosives," Natalia called to him.

"We'll both go in—Paul—keep an eye out on the outside."

"Be careful, guys," the younger man urged. Rourke had every intention of doing so. As he glanced toward Natalia, she was slinging her rifle across her back, diagonally, muzzle down, and unlimbering the German explosives detector. Rourke had little faith in such contraptions, although he had seen it work and was impressed by the results. But the mind was a better machine by far, and he trusted Natalia's knowledge of explosives and demolitions far better than any machine.

They were within fifteen yards of the helicopter now, Rourke pushing down the hood of his parka, the cold stinging him even through the toque he wore beneath it. He pulled the toque off over his head and stuffed it into a side pocket. He wanted his hearing unimpaired, as well as his peripheral vision. The wind seemed to increase, howling loud near the derelict helicopter, the rotor blades locked down, but still being pressured by the incessant wind.

Rourke opened the front of his snow smock and his parka, so he could have more rapid access to his handguns. He started ahead again, seeing Paul Rubenstein out of the far right edge of his peripheral vision running toward the chopper at an oblique angle, covering the hatchway with an M-16.

Rourke stopped beneath the main rotor blades and peered inside. He saw no sign of life, but the glass itself was steamed and frozen over and to see in any clarity was impossible without opening the sliding door. Natalia was beside him. "Are you ready, John?"

"Yes—don't touch anything yet. Let's get up closer." He started to close the distance between himself and the machine, Natalia sweeping the German explosives sniffer ahead of them over the snow and ice, the tone it emitted even, unchanging. If the tone's pitch increased, explosives would be near. As she swept toward one of the weapons pods, the tone increased, Rourke saying, "That's normal, isn't it?"

"Yes. If the tone gets any higher, we've got something out of the ordinary." As she continued the sweep and moved the device away from the weapons pod, the tone dropped in pitch. She elevated the device and swept it over the skin of the craft, near the hatchway. There was nothing. She reached out to work the door.

Rourke pushed her back, safing the M-16 then taking the butt of it and rapping it hard against the door. Nothing happened.

He let Natalia work the door handle as he worked the safety back to the auto position.

She threw open the door, stepping back, Rourke thrusting the muzzle of the M-16 through the opening and inside.

The frozen body of a dead man lay in the widest beam section of the fuselage. But the dead man wasn't Michael. It was one of the German aircrew, and from the rank, he assumed it had been the gunner.

"Throat slit, it looks like."

"Yeah."

"Nothing's been touched and it doesn't—" she peered inside. "There's no sign of the pilot—or anyone else."

"No. Run the sniffer."

She swept the interior of the fuselage from the outside, then nodded to him and he helped her step up and inside, Rourke following after her, his eyes narrowing as he scanned the interior more closely. There appeared to be no damage to the instruments, almost as if whoever had killed the gunner had wished to keep the helicopter in good condition—for use?, Rourke wondered.

"Did you sweep the corporal's body?"

"Yes—and he doesn't look rigged. But don't turn him over. I want to check first."

"All right," Rourke nodded, but dropped to his knees

167

beside the dead man. With the conditions of extreme cold, even a detailed autopsy might not accurately fix time of death. There was a bruise on the man's lower left cheek which appeared to have been incurred just prior to death. With his gloved right hand he felt at the back of the dead man's neck, just above the hairline. The German military wore their hair short and he could see most of the bruise easily enough. "I think he was hit with a rifle butt or something like it. On the face, then on the neck."

"His throat was slit after he died," Natalia said over her shoulder, Rourke looking up at her.

"That's the way the wound to the throat looks. And the lack of bleeding seems to go along with that. He was stone dead and someone either slit his throat because they were too dumb to know for sure or just out of the desire to do it."

"Who, John? An advance party from Vladmir's force?"

Rourke considered her words for a moment. Then, "I don't think so. For one thing, they would have stolen the helicopter or destroyed it."

"Whoever it is, I don't think we'll find the pilot's body outside."

"Neither do I—he's probably a prisoner." And John Rourke wondered at the fate of his son. When Natalia had asked about Michael as a baby, Rourke had started remembering things he hadn't remembered in years—the real years, the ones he had lived, not the centuries he had slept. It was too easy to forget that because a son was a grown man, how it had been once. He closed his eyes for a moment. "We'll find him," Rourke told Natalia. And though he cared for the welfare of the pilot, that wasn't whom he meant . . .

Akiro Kurinami struggled against the ropes which bound his wrists and he could do nothing, the knots positioned so that he could not reach them with his fingers.

He had heard no sounds other than his own breathing and

the periodic actuating of a heater. Apparently his captors didn't wish him to freeze to death. The blindfold puzzled him. It seemed obvious that they intended to kill him if he revealed the information they sought. Perhaps the blindfold was only for the purpose of further inducing terror.

He had had several American friends when he was a boy in Japan and he had played blindman's bluff, as they called it, and never really liked it because there was always someone who—Akiro Kurinami thought of something he had not thought of for years. It was a trick he had learned as a boy. His uncle was a police inspector and he had asked his uncle, begged him, to let him see his handcuffs. His uncle had laughed and put the handcuffs on his wrists and Kurinami, always the agile athlete, had promptly worked his wrists beneath his rear end and up along the underside of his thighs and slipped his legs through the handcuffs to the delight of everyone watching. He had asked to be allowed to do it again, but his father had sternly said it was very undignified and he had not been allowed to do it.

He considered the memory of his father and felt that under these circumstances his father would not object. Kurinami began flexing his stiff shoulder and arm muscles, trying to loosen them, working his legs as well . . .

Vladmir Karamatsov had ordered the meeting for the short interval while the central element of his force stopped for refueling, the lead element moving ahead, the rear element paused as well. He remembered the Americanism, "leapfrogging", as the most apt description for what he was doing. This central element would become the lead element for the next leg of the journey.

Before him, in the open, a cold wind cutting across his exposed skin with the sharpness of a razor, stood Colonel Ivan Krakovski, a man he did not trust except for ruthlessness which nearly rivaled his own. With Krakovski stood fifty members of the new Elite Corps, Krakovski at their head.

"You may stand at ease," Karamatsov shouted over the keening of the wind. "I have something to tell you. Doubtlessly, you have heard by now rumors that we go to obtain the nuclear stockpile of the People's Republic of China. I will tell you things which you need to know before setting out on your mission.

"Before the Night of The War," he began, "the Chinese emulated the preparedness of the Soviet people, and constructed two cities, a third under construction but never completed, lost to time. The Chinese had a formidable nuclear arsenal, not nearly so formidable as that of the people of the Soviet, or our enemies in the United States, but substantial. The Chinese realized that sheer force of numbers of their people could not win a war against the superior technology and the superior will of the Soviet war machine. And so, it was decided that these cities would be built. And, ten per cent of their nuclear arsenal was taken off line and placed deep in an impenetrable storage vault, in the event that the two cities which they had designed to survive should find their very existence threatened . . ."

The Chinese premier had barely touched his food. Maria Leuden watched Michael, trying to resist reading his thoughts. But the thoughts were sometimes of her, and when he looked at her he would sometimes think the word 'privacy' and she would close her eyes and force herself to think of anything, from the color of the silk or silk-like slippers she wore on her feet to the way the frogs which closed her green Chinese dress had been so awkward to close, to the flower arrangements which seemed everywhere in the long, narrow, rich wood-grained walled banquet room in which they now sat, before a black lacquered table on chairs that at once seemed delicate yet very comfortable.

The Chinese premier began again to speak. "Our leaders planned with great wisdom. They realized that in a post-holocaust environment, loyalties could well be sacrificed in the lust for power, for domination of the ruins, as it were. And so, the secret to the location of the vault in which thirty-three state of the art nuclear weapons were cached was broken into three parts, the leadership of each of the three cities entrusted two of the parts, thus in the event that one of the cities was destroyed and the location of the nuclear warheads was needed, two of the cities would have the ability to jointly find the cache."

The chairman paused and Michael, seated across from Maria Leuden and beside Bjorn Rolvaag, asked, "Was it considered that in such a manner it would be possible for two of the cities to join in league against the third?"

"But if each city had possessed only one portion of the secret, then the destruction of one city would have resulted in the secret being forever lost. There is an expression in English, I believe — 'The lesser of two evils'?"

Michael nodded, Rolvaag struggled with his chopsticks, though Michael had taught him their use as he had, indirectly taught Maria Leuden.

The chairman continued to speak. "The Maoist reactionary government of the Second City clearly wishes to possess our two portions of the secret, and with these and their two portions, have all three."

"Two plus two equals three," Michael smiled.

"Quite, young man. Indeed, two and two do equal three in this context. And with this sum, the leader of the Second City would spread his barbarism over the face of the earth. If the world beyond our city is as you tell us, Michael Rourke, the three segments of the secret could well be the goal sought after by your vile sounding Marshal Karamatsov. The great majority of the thermonuclear devices held by the People's Republic of China were never used and are hidden in their silos and storage bunkers beneath the ground and might well be usable to someone ingenious enough to find them. With the thirty-three warheads dangling over the collective heads of the peoples of earth, at his leisure, an unscrupulous man might be able to locate the remaining more than two hundred and fifty warheads. Indeed, it is said by some that in the cache of the thirty-three weapons, there is a map by which could be found the remaining weapons."

"A sword of Damocles," Maria Leuden said, speaking for the first time since they had seated themselves around the black lacquered table and begun their meal, the chairman seated at its head like a father.

"World War IV," Michael Rourke almost whispered. "World War Last."

She put down her chopsticks, having lost her appetite for the appealing looking vegetables and thin strips of fowl . . .

Ivan Krakovski watched the Hero Marshal, hatless, his black hair moving in the wind, his figure straight and tall and imposing, his dark eyes burning with the fire that inspired those about him. The Hero Marshal Vladmir Karamatsov spoke again. "And so, under the leadership of our trusted Comrade Colonel Krakovski, utilizing the information I alone possess from before the Night of The War, you fifty will go forth to the secret hardened site where ten percent of the Chinese warheads can be found. You will inspect the warheads, ascertaining that they can safely be moved, and then rendezvous with our force at the predetermined coordinates Comrade Colonel Krakovski will possess. Go forth in the name of the Soviet people to the greater glory of scientific socialism, to fulfill our historic destiny. I will speak with Comrade Colonel Krakovski alone."

Krakovski called the Elite Corps to attention, and as the Hero Marshal retired, he turned to the captain beside and slightly behind him. "You will prepare for the mission." He did another about face and angled off after Marshal Kara-matsov. Already, in his mind, he was composing how he would record this moment for posterity. For surely, this was the greatest of all moments in the history of the Soviet people and it had been entrusted to him. And he wondered why, because clearly the Hero Marshal seemed jealous of his abilities.

The Hero Marshal had stopped beside his command helicopter and Krakovski approached, saluted, and then followed the Hero Marshal beneath the slowly turning rotor blades and inside.

No pilot sat at the controls. The Hero Marshal seated himself in the co-pilot's chair, but it seemed odd because Krakovski had never seen the Hero Marshal fly.

"Krakovski. I am entrusting you with something of vast importance, as I am sure you understand. Sit down."

Krakovski took the pilot's seat, studying the Hero Marshal's face.

Karamatsov looked away, snow starting to fall almost lazily, but then caught up in a gust of wind, swirling cyclonically, then lazily falling once again. "You will be tempted, Krakovski, to keep the power of these weapons for yourself, as well any man might be. But you do not know the secrets which I know which will enable their use if need be, make them the palpable threat to humanity which I intend they be. If you do my bidding and remain loyal to me, you will eventually know these secrets and share with me power greater than even you can imagine there could be.

"I had," the Hero Marshal continued, now turning, look-ing at him, "foreseen much of what might transpire. My great enemy, John Rourke, it is said has an expression he uses often. 'Plan ahead'," the Hero Marshal said, slipping into English. He cleared his throat as if to cleanse the words from his mouth. "I foresaw and planned that one day I would triumph. That day is nearly at hand. The setback at the gates to the Underground City was a costly one, one for which I can again give credit to John Rourke. The gas which we still possess will enable us to easily overwhelm small forces or fortified positions, but the power contained in the vault of the Chinese traitors is an irresistible power which can sweep continents to our will. If you keep faith with me, you shall triumph with me. If you betray me, you will never know a night's sleep again, for someday I will vindicate myself even though it might cost my own life. Do you understand me, Comrade?"

Krakovski understood and said that he did.

The Hero Marshal entrusted him with the map coordinates which would lead him to the thirty-three nuclear warheads. The cyclones of snow intensified and the black of the Hero Marshal's eyes deepened . . .

Akiro Kurinami lurched forward and his face impacted heavily against the hard surface and his breath left him in a rush, but his hands were in front of him. He lay there for an instant, regaining his breath, then moved his hands to his face and pulled away the blindfold. He squinted against a light which was not there, in total darkness except for the glow of the electrically powered heating unit at the far corner of the enclosure. But he was certain it was a room.

His teeth found the knots of the ropes which bound his wrists and he began to gnaw at them.

Elaine—he had to save her, to free himself before the men who had taken him prisoner and even now would be bringing her here returned . . .

Paul Rubenstein had found them. He hadn't believed his eyes. Now, John Rourke and Natalia Tiemerovna stood flanking him, staring at the ground.

"These animals are small—Asian horses. They're shod. One of them," and he outlined one set of hoofprints in the snow with the tip of his right index finger," was carrying double, or an extraordinarily heavy rider. But I prefer the latter."

"The pilot," Natalia whispered through the scarf which masked the lower portion of her face.

They had found the remains of a fire nearly a quarter mile from the abandoned helicopter, John Rourke having deduced that the captors of the pilot had spent the night there after seizing him. Paul had agreed with John's logic. Had the men who had taken the pilot stayed there before attacking the helicopter, their fire would have been clearly visible and given the pilot and co-pilot either time to lift off or in some other way ward off the attack, the gunship heavily armed. At the least, time for a distress signal.

John Rourke rose to his full height, taking the German radio from beneath his parka. The cold was intense and earlier John had expressed concern that the batteries for their radios might be ill-affected by it.

John Rourke spoke into the self-contained microphone. "This is Rourke. Rourke to Courier, come in. Over."

The J-7V was designated with the code name "Courier."

There was the crackle of static and the voice of the co-pilot came back. "This is Courier. Receiving you. Over."

"Courier—I want those three crates opened and have the security team start preparing the contents. Rourke out."

In a strange way, Paul Rubenstein had found himself looking forward to this.

Chapter Twenty-six

Michael had eaten the dinner, not enjoying it although the quality of the food was impeccable. The conversation had turned his appetite.

The chairman had been required at another meeting, had left the dinner table with profuse apologies and requested their presence for a late night drink in his private apartment.

He had looked even more tired when he had rejoined them.

The room in which they sat, a library, was modestly furnished, almost spartan, except for the books it contained. The languages were in most cases recognizable to Maria Leuden or to Michael himself, and Rolvaag had smiled when he had spied several books in the Icelandic tongue.

There was a smallish, low table around which they clustered, the table black lacquered like the dinner table, but covered with glass and pressed between the glass and the table surface dried flowers of some sort, or perhaps they were silk. Michael was uncertain.

The chairman had spoken of many things, most trivial, but at last, making a tent of his fingers and placing the tips of his index fingers to his eyelids, he addressed a question which Michael had been searching to introduce throughout the evening but had not.

"It was called Lushun before the Dragon Wind obliterated it from the face of the earth," and he made a sweeping gesture with his hands and his great, somehow sad eyes opened. "Of all nations, China's loss was perhaps the greatest, our population all but totally destroyed. When we determined some years ago that it would be to our interests to have available ships with which to cross the seas, Lushun was determined as the place to undertake this endeavor. We have small ships there even now, but no true ocean-going vessels as once crossed the waters. To facilitate this program, we constructed a rail line to reach Lushun, completed several years ago. But a short time after we established a presence at Lushun, the attacks began. Men came out of the sea, heavily armed but in small numbers, placing explosives, killing. It was debated whom these men might be, perhaps Americans, perhaps others. None has ever been captured and those few killed in battle with us have never been identified, except as Westerners. It was debated as well that we might best serve our goals by abandoning our port. I personally spoke against this, although I have no love for warfare. The reactor was nearly completed by the time the next series of attacks came and it soon became the target for these mysterious interlopers. Perhaps they will some day attack in force, or perhaps they cannot."

"You say they came from the sea," Michael pressed. "In ships, I presume?"

"No. They literally come from the waves."

"In scuba gear," Michael volunteered.

"Self-contained underwater breathing apparatus—the acronym, yes."

"When was the latest attack?" Maria Leuden spoke.

Michael looked at her, smiled.

The chairman spoke again. "Five days ago. Some among

177

us thought that you might be part of these attackers. I argued against that."

"If Karamatsov had sea power," Michael mused aloud, "I'd think we would know about it. Are there markings on the scuba gear taken from the dead?"

"There are none. Nor on the weapons, which are very sophisticated, I am told. So, you see, we fight a small but bloody war with an unknown enemy, and a continuing battle of harassment with the Second City. We need no more war, but I fear it has been thrust upon us. Tell your people — these men of Iceland, these new Germans of Argentina and the people of your Eden Project." Michael had explained the Eden Project and the use of cryogenics, including his survival and that of his family. The chairman had seemed amazed, but accepting. "Tell them that they have an ally in the People's Republic of China, here in the First City. This, indeed, was the topic of the meeting for which I left so hurriedly. I shall dispatch Han to accompany you."

Han had not joined them in the chairman's apartment. Michael decided now was the time. "We came by helicopter. You are familiar with these devices, I am sure."

"The term is not unknown to me, though I have never seen an aircraft of any type. I suppose our engineers have the abilities to construct such machines, but we have consumed their talents with other, more pressing concerns."

"Our helicopter dropped out of radio contact about the time Doctor Leuden and Captain Hammerschmidt were taken prisoner. It is possible your enemies from the Second City are responsible. I would like to request that you dispatch a modest number of troops with us when we attempt to return to the helicopter. And I would further like to request that Captain Hammerschmidt be allowed to remain here until he is fully well."

"But of course. Then you will carry our embassy of good will to your allies?"

Michael, his voice low, nodded as he said, "I will be

honored, sir."

And he noticed Maria Leuden was looking at him . . .

Akiro Kurinami had found the second knot to be more difficult than the first and he felt certain that he had loosened at least two of his teeth. But he told himself that they would tighten. He had to wait until the heater, thermostatically controlled, flared again in order to have light, needed for the third knot. But then the third and last knot had come out easily and, still by the light of the flaring heater, he unbound his ankles.

He had strained muscles he had not been aware of having, and he had not stood on his own two feet for—how long? he wondered.

But he stood, having crawled to the nearest wall and used the wall to support him. As he touched the surface of the wall, Kurinami realized he had been taken to the construction area. And he knew the construction area well.

The heater's level dropped and there was little but gray haze through which to work his way along the wall, partially because of the darkness and partially because of his unsteadiness. But he found the airlock hatchway. He summoned his strength and found the wheel-like handle and began to turn it. The door had not been sabotaged, the wheel turning freely and, as he wrenched against it, the door opened and he half fell over the flange.

It was only these outer compartments which would be entry ways which sealed in such a manner and precious few of them were finished, but Kurinami had still contended that to shelter here against Russian attack would have been a wiser choice by far than their tent village.

And he suddenly wondered if somehow there was a motive behind Commander Dodd disallowing the use of the facility.

There was stronger gray light here and he started along the access tunnel which would upon completion, have its own massive airlock, the airlocks and all of the construction site modular sections having been buried five centuries before and the pieces transported from the central storage site in what had been South Dakota to here by the German forces. But because of their war effort, the supply of cargo helicopters available to the task was erratic. Logic might have dictated moving Eden Base to South Dakota, but it was above the permanent snow line.

He moved along the corridor, the light intensifying as he neared the exit to the outdoors.

The airlocks, the very design of the pre-fabricated city they were building, had been conceived as insurance against a hostile atmosphere and severe weather. The planning had been well-conceived.

Kurinami was very near the mouth of the tunnel now, the tunnel itself like a massive, sectioned storm drain, the temperature colder here; Kurinami, freezing already in his sweat and waste stained coveralls, had no idea what had become of his arctic gear. He had known better than to even consider the fate of his M-16 and Colt Government Model .45.

It had seemed odd to him during the brief firearms familiarization course he and the other members of the Eden Project corps with prior military service had been given, that there were two Government model pistols in the inventory of the United States, the Colt 1911A1 .45 ACP and the Beretta 92F 9mm Parabellum. But then one of the Americans had told him that indeed there were .38 Special Smith & Wesson revolvers and various other handguns, all to lesser degrees, that were, in a manner of speaking "Government Models." He wished he had any of them now. Soon, the men who had attacked him — he thought two of them, but perhaps three — would be returning. And what he did would determine if Elaine and he lived or died. And more importantly, he realized, even than the life of the woman he loved and his own life, the fate of Eden Base.

Near the entranceway, snow falling heavily outside, swirling in what seemed like a strong wind, the howl of it filling the tunnel mouth, he found what he had sought.

And now if the battery for the bulldozer was not too cold . . .

The motorcycles had been designed for uneven terrain, drifted snow, for traction on ice. John Rourke had taken the best features of twentieth century motorcycles with which he had been familiar and conferred with German engineers, the same team which had designed their mini-tank, and they had produced something beyond which he had thought possible.

Four of them to be precise, he thought, three of them here now, the fourth in Argentina being tested for improvement before actual production.

The German engineering team had asked him what he wished to have the motorcycle called. He had deferred to them to decide as the persons who had taken ideas and hastily sketched drawings and hastily listed specifications and turned all these into reality.

They had simply called the motorcycles "Specials."

They were that.

John Rourke was the last to mount, Natalia and Paul already having climbed aboard. "Remember," he cautioned, "on level terrain when it's dry, these things will do 160 or better which is a lot more speed than you'll ever really need."

"If I find any dry level terrain, I'll remember that," Paul Rubenstein observed.

Rourke started to laugh.

Word from Captain Hartman was that heavy snow was falling, slowing the advance of Karamatsov's army, which was good. And that six gunships, obviously heavy laden, had lifted off into the worsening blizzard conditions and headed toward Manchuria.

As yet, the storm, which was moving eastward, had not reached here, but the temperatures were dropping, the wind velocity increasing. There would be little time to follow the hoofprints left in the snow before the wind obliterated them all or new snow filled them in.

Rourke mounted his machine. It was the same general size as his Harley, but in his heart it would never take its place. It was built to run on synth fuel and was more fuel efficient than conventional machines which had been built to run on gasoline. The faring was contoured to body shape, protecting the lower body, armored as was the high rising windshield, the windshield fitted with defogger coils, the fairing on each side fitted with twelve-inch barreled hybrid "machineguns", like submachineguns in their size, but firing the major caliber caseless round utilized in the German assault rifles, the firing mechanism concealed within the handlebars. Storage capacity for gear was located both behind the saddle on both sides and, to a lesser degree, in compartments incorporated into the fairing. Behind the rear storage compartments were two compartments which were capable of launching, from the left, high explosive mini-grenades and, from the right, smoke or gas grenades.

When he had first explained the concept of the new machine to Paul and Natalia, the younger man had said, "It sounds like something James Bond would have used in a movie." Natalia had remarked, "It sounds like something our Research and Development people were working on at the Chicago espionage school in the Soviet Union before the Night of The War." In either case, Rourke had not been certain the comments were complimentary. He had ordered the prototypes, as these three of the total of four were, to be color coded. Natalia's was a dark green, Paul's a medium blue and Rourke's own, of course, a gleaming jet black.

He had tried the machines, each of them, in Iceland before returning to the Eurasian Front, then ordered them transhipped. They had sat in storage crates ever since.

The tires, the entire bodywork of the machines was armored against conventional small arms ammunition. The suspension was self-adjusting for highway or flatlands use or for steep or rugged terrain.

It was as close to the perfect means of overland transportation as possible, able to go places where no vehicle could go, in theory, and outrun most conventional vehicles as well.

His parka hood was down, the black helmet, which had been built specifically to accompany the motorcycle, in his hands. He pulled it on, electro-chemical energy of the body powering the short range radio headset built into the helmet, enabling him to speak at will to anyone similarly equipped or hear them within maximum distances of four miles.

He had designed the machine despite his natural dislike for things less than straightforward. Such a machine had been necessary. And, using it now to overtake the horsemen who had captured the pilot of the helicopter, he would find out if the machines were practical.

He almost whispered into the microphone built into the helmet's rigid chin guard, the visor having started to steam but the same electro-chemical energy of the body which powered the radio powering the visor's defogging system. It was already working. "All right—everybody hear me?"

The system was multi-band, enabling two speakers to be heard at once. Natalia and Paul spoke almost simultaneously. "Gotchya," Paul said, Natalia whispering, "Affirmative."

Rourke spoke again. "All right—remember, these things are fast and it's slippery. Be cool."

"Be cool—with the windchill, the temperature must be forty below."

He told Paul, "Instruments aboard the J-7V indicate a windchill closer to minus fifty. Let's go." Rourke revved the machine and gradually let it out, starting away from the German aircraft, the security team and the pilot and co-pilot staring after them as Rourke looked back once. At his right,

Natalia, at his left Paul Rubenstein. The machines were vastly different than the Harleys stored at the Retreat, but the feeling was the same. With the two best friends he had every had, riding . . .

Akiro Kurinami huddled beneath the dashboard of the bulldozer and he saw them. And his heart sank. Three men, carrying M-16 rifles. And between two of the men, their rifles slung across their backs, he saw a body being carried by wrists and ankles, as though dead. The body was Elaine's body.

She was clad in her arctic gear, which was green unlike that of the three men, theirs covered with white snow smocks. He fought thinking that she was dead, because to keep his head, if she were alive, was the only way to keep her alive.

The third man walked at the head of the file, his rifle carried in his right hand by the carrying handle, like someone might carry an attache case and just as casually.

They would have to pass within ten feet of the bulldozer.

He had started the machine, let it run, elevated the shovel, moved the machine slightly closer to where they would walk. Prayed they would not notice the changed position of the machine.

Less than a dozen yards to go now, one hand on the starter, the other on the control which would drop the shovel.

And he realized his hands trembled. If he miscalculated or the shovel did not drop instantly, he might crush Elaine.

Less than a half dozen yards, his grip tightening on the release lever for the shovel. He inhaled, waiting, released part of the air, the lead man just beneath the shovel, almost past it.

Akiro Kurinami hit the starter and it turned over and his other hand worked the shovel release as he flung himself off the right side of the open-cabbed machine, the scream that had started from the leader dying as the steel of the shovel slapped against the concrete floor. Kurinami dove over the shovel and toward the forward-most of the two men who carried Elaine slung between them, his muscles not responding as they should, he knew, the jump short, his hands barely reaching to the shoulders of the man who was his target, his feet slipping in something like glue which he realized inside himself was bodily fluids from the man he had crushed beneath the massive shovel.

His right fist curled into the fabric of the man's snow smock and suddenly both of them were slipping into the ooze which seeped from beneath the shovel, Kurinami realizing only split seconds were left before the last man opened fire.

Kurinami's left hand moved for the throat, his fist closing over it as he wrenched his body sideways, throwing his entire weight behind his hand as they slammed into the puddle of oozed human remains. There was a scream from the man's throat, Kurinami's right hand grabbing for the head, the man's hands pummeling him, Kurinami twisting his body away from the man, still grasping throat and head. There was an earsplittingly loud snap and the body went limp under his hands. He was on his knees.

Elaine had been thrown down like a discarded rag doll, the last man struggling his rifle forward on its sling. Kurinami summoned all the strength inside him, as he had been taught to do when he had been taught the martial arts by his grandfather. He hurtled himself to his feet and then forward, his head impacting the last man at the abdomen, his hands going for the knees, behind the knees, ripping, the man's body toppling rearward, Kurinami rolling over him.

As the third man came to his knees, his assault rifle coming up, Kurinami, on his right side, snapped his left foot up and out, into the throat, then into the face. The body toppled back, Kurinami throwing himself over the man, hauling his right fist up, snapping it downward into the exposed throat as the rifle discharged beside him,

185

Kurinami's ears ringing with it.

He fell over the third man, collapsed, unable to move, barely able to breathe.

He closed his eyes.

He forced himself to roll free of the man, disentangling the man's neck and right arm from the sling. He held the M-16 in his right first, on his knees, crawling now, to reach Elaine.

He pulled her hood back. He ripped the toque from her face, his ear going to her lips. She was breathing, shallowly but evenly. He curled back her left eyelid, the eyes glassy looking, the pupils dilated.

"Drugged," he gasped.

He fell back on his haunches.

Beside him was the second dead man. He pushed back the hood of the snowsmock and the parka, tore the white toque from over the face.

The face belonged to a man he had never seen before. Not Eden Project. Not one of the Germans.

Who, he almost whispered . . .

The wind had erased the hoofprints in all but those areas which were sheltered from its force by natural windbreaks—rock overhangs, narrow gaps. The helmet radios proved invaluable as they would split up, making ever widening interlocking circles, searching in the likely areas for the next scattered sets of hoofprints, then at last finding what they sought, then moving ahead, only to repeat the laborious process time and time again.

The last set of prints—Natalia had found them—seemed deep and fresh. The darkness and the swirling snow had made finding them consume nearly two hours.

Rourke, Natalia and Paul Rubenstein flanking him, sat aboard his Special and spoke into the headset microphone. "They must be stopping for the night soon. If they build fires typically like the remains of the one we saw near the helicopter, we'll spot them. Unless we stumble right on them, let's stick to the plan."

Both Paul and Natalia uttered their agreement.

Rourke started them ahead, into the night . . .

He had been told there was a snowstorm outside. But inside the petal of the First City, all was serene and the artificial light was unchanged.

He had felt Maria Leuden's eyes on him all night.

After the drink with the chairman and his ambassadorial charge, he had taken Maria into the corridor where her apartment could be found and then left quickly, going to see to Hammerschmidt's condition.

Michael Rourke had found his way to the monorail and to the right stop for the hospital without incident, searched out the equivalent of the charge nurse—he had encountered the term in a book or videotape—and asked concerning the welfare of the German commando captain. He had been told that Hammerschmidt was progressing extraordinarily well and, though no miraculous overnight healing could be expected, Hammerschmidt rested comfortably and the burns seemed less severe than originally thought.

Contented, Michael had returned to his apartment, showered, attempted to leaf through a book. Rolvaag, despite being nearly as long without sleep as Michael, had been sitting in the spacious waiting room at the end of the hall reading as Michael had entered and called out to him. The dog had stirred, Rolvaag had waved, then returned to his book, one of the Icelandic volumes Michael had arranged that Rolvaag could borrow from the chairman's private library. If the chairman spoke Icelandic, he had not evinced it at the dinner party.

The book was a nineteenth century English novel, and though Michael had read other works by the same author, it did not capture his interest.

Sleep was what he needed, but it wasn't in him.

He thought of Maria Leuden. She would probably be asleep by now.

In less than twelve hours, they would be leaving to link up with the helicopter and find out why it had gone out of radio contact.

He began to pace the bedroom.

He looked at the two Beretta 92Fs in the double shoulder rig hanging on the headboard post. He could always clean them again, but the interval since the last cleaning had been so short that powder residue could not have sweated out of the bore and the cleaning would be essentially useless. The 629 hadn't been cleaned since he had used it against the Mongols.

He started for the elaborately painted cabinet in which he had stowed his pack and his other gear.

He opened the double doors.

He closed his eyes.

He closed the doors and leaned heavily against the cabinet.

He was naked except for a pair of underpants and he walked back toward the bed, skinned into his blue jeans and the shirt he had just worn and ripped both Berettas from their leather, stuffing them beneath his shirt butts, outward against his kidneys.

Michael Rourke started from the bedroom, across the sitting room, snatching up the key from beside the door, opening the door, slamming it overly hard behind him. He didn't worry over the lock. If it locked, he had the key. But the door and the lock were so flimsy no one with any determination would have been kept out.

Down the corridor.

Michael Rourke stopped at the door, so much like his own.

He knocked at the door.

He waited.

He started to turn away.

The door opened.

Maria Leuden wore a blue silk-looking robe, tied about her waist, her glasses on, her eyes huge seeming behind them, her left hand pushing her hair back from her face.

"Michael — I —"

He stepped inside the doorway, his hands touching at her waist, then his arms encircling her. "I love you," she whispered.

Michael Rourke brought his mouth down on hers, molding her body against his . . .

When they reached the top of the rise, it was at first hard to tell how far away the fire really was because of its size. But after some observation, Rourke decided the captors of the pilot were a little over a mile distant.

He pulled the helmet from his head, taking the radio from beneath his parka. "Rourke to Courier. Come in. Over."

There was static, then the voice of the pilot. "This is Courier, Herr Doctor. Come in. Over."

"I'm leaving this frequency open. Are you ready to fly, over?"

"Ready, Herr Doctor. My co-pilot stands by. Over."

"I estimate your ETA —" Rourke rolled back the storm sleeve and looked at the luminous black of the Rolex Submariner on his wrist. "ETA in sixteen minutes from lift-off. Rourke out."

He pocketed the radio, leaving the frequency open to serve as a homing beacon.

He replaced his helmet, his ears numb with the cold from the brief exposure, the shield before his face steaming, then the steam starting to dissipate as he spoke to Natalia and to Paul. "With them out in the open like that, we won't be able to accurately judge their strength until we're right up on them. There shouldn't be more than eight or nine at any event. We need the pilot alive. That's why we're here. And we need one of whoever they are alive to find out who they are. Like we planned it, up the middle, Natalia gets the pilot. Right?"

"Like we planned it," Paul answered.

"Yes," Natalia murmured.

"Nice and slow until we're close. Once the superchargers on these bikes kick in, they'll hear it. Now we sit here for twelve minutes." He slung his M-16 forward, removing the magazine, working the action several times to be certain the cold hadn't adversely affected it.

He replaced the magazine, wishing he could have lit a cigar, but the cold was a more powerful motivator than habit.

Chapter Twenty-seven

John Rourke had judged the time needed to cross slowly to within two hundred yards of the camp and then accelerate into the camp as about three minutes. If these people had not stolen the helicopter or damaged it, there was substantial reason to believe they were not familiar with aircraft to any substantial degree, if at all. The fact that they rode horses, the inefficient but deadly means with which they had dispatched the gunner, all pointed to a certain primitiveness.

He wondered.

Rourke checked the face of his Rolex. It was nearly time.

He spoke into the helmet microphone. "Let's start out nice and slowly," and he throttled up and let the machine rumble forward, Natalia moving into the center position, Rourke to her left, Paul to her right, Rourke checking the gauges on the Special's instrument panel. He ruled out using the explosive charges which could be expelled from the bike, and with the rising force of the wind and the snow it drove, smoke would have been of little effect.

These were hardy men he would soon face, living here, camping out of doors in weather so horrible severe. But he realized he could never be so naive as to regret killing them any more than he regretted killing anyone. He had known a man once who had told him something invaluable about

191

killing. "Once you get to liking it, there's only one more kill you should rack up — yourself." He had known men to whom the advice should have been meaningful.

They had crossed half the expanse separating them from the campfire, Rourke increasing speed slightly, Natalia and Paul following his lead.

He armed the twin machineguns in the fairing.

He consulted his wristwatch — the helicopter would be due, barring the unforeseen, in one minute, the J-7V timing itself to sweep in from the opposite end of the plateau sixty seconds after the helicopter. He swung the M-16 slightly forward, charging the chamber, leaving the safety set to safe.

"Now," he whispered, revving the machine, giving it what he still mentally called "gas," the speedometer bouncing upward, the supercharger kicking in with a loud whine.

Men were rising from around the fire, great mounds of snow falling from the lean-to shelters in which they had protected themselves, Rourke seeing the outline of rifles coming up.

He fired a burst with both faring machineguns, intentionally firing wide to the left of the camp to avoid inadvertently killing the captured German pilot, Paul's machineguns doing the same. Natalia accelerating past them dead for the center of the camp, Rourke giving the machine full acceleration, the Special skipping over the hummocks of snow and the rocks beneath them, Rourke twisting the fork, cutting into the camp to the left of the fire, not using the machineguns, stabbing the M-16 forward, working off the safety tumbler and firing into the moving shapes of men.

A bullet whined as it ricocheted off the faring, Rourke firing another burst. A man shape bundled in blankets — and furs? — brought a rifle that looked modern yet looked oddly familiar to his hip, tongues of flame flickering from it as Rourke fired again.

The man went down. As Rourke wheeled the Special, he saw Natalia in the center of the camp, a man swinging a burning club toward her, snatched from the fire. She dodged, the Special she had been dismounting collapsing against her. Rourke throttled out, riding from the camp, Rourke arcing it in a tight loop, wrestling the fork as he accelerated the machine out of the curve of the loop, aiming himself and the machine toward the center of the camp, the motorcycle lurching beneath him, Rourke letting go, diving from it and tackling the man with the burning club as he swung it down toward Natalia.

Rourke hammered the man into the snow, the fire extinguishing with a loud hiss, the man wriggling away from him, Rourke rocking back, the M-16 too far back to get fast enough as the man drew his pistol. Rourke drew the Python from the flap holster at his hip and doubled actioned it twice, then twice again, the man's body snapping back into the fire.

Rourke was up, to his feet, wrestling the Special free of Natalia. "Are you all right?"

"Yes—winded—yes—" He left her, stabbing the revolver into its holster, the helicopter roaring in overhead, machine-gun fire strafing the snow on either side of the camp, the defenders of the camp screaming in panic, some dropping to their knees, others running.

A man dove from the shadows beyond the fire, a long bladed, curving sword in his right hand, Rourke dodging back.

But Rourke realized he wasn't the man's target. The sword was raised, ready to hack down into a long, formless looking shape at the opposite edge of the fire.

Rourke sprayed the M-16 into swordsman, the .223 bucking in his right fist, the swordsman's body spinning, falling away.

Natalia was beside him then, both her revolvers in her fists as she approached the formless thing on the ground.

Rourke let the M-16 fall to his side, opening his parka, ripping the twin stainless Detonics pistols from the leather.

"John," Natalia screamed over the roar of the helicopter

overhead. The downdraft making a blizzard which swirled around them. "He's alive. It's the pilot."

The J-7V streaked overhead, dipping its wings, the slip-stream around it tearing at Rourke's face and hair as he pulled the helmet from his head.

And he dropped to his knees beside one of the dead men. For all the world, the man looked like a Mongolian warrior.

"Right place, wrong time," he said under his breath.

And then he heard Paul Rubenstein. "I got one! I got one!" And Rourke looked around, Paul Rubenstein dragging a man through the snow by his heels.

Chapter Twenty-eight

Natalia spoke to the Mongol, having tried several different dialects of Chinese, none of which she considered herself speaking well, until at last there had been some flicker of recognition in the man's eyes.

He seemed terrified, she thought, terrified not at anything a rational man would have feared, but at being taken inside the German helicopter gunship.

"Now that he knows this thing flies, he is afraid of it, more so than of any of the guns he has seen, or any of us."

John Rourke said to her, "Ask him if he knows what happened to Michael."

She tried the dialect that had seemed to stimulate recognition. And he answered her, in such a rapid fashion that she could barely understand every third or fourth word he spoke.

"He says, I think, that he knows nothing about anything."

She watched John's face as he lit his cigar, the cigar having been in the left corner of his mouth unlit for some time now. "I'm going to ask him why, if he knows nothing, he tried killing the pilot," she said, then proceeded to translate her own question as best she could.

The Mongol didn't answer.

She looked at John Rourke. He winked and looked at Paul

for an instant. She sat back.

Paul stepped forward, taking the black catspaw handled Gerber MkII from his belt, almost shoving her aside, grabbing the Mongol by the front of the man's tunic-like shirt, the knife in Paul's right hand going to the Mongol's throat. "Then Peter Piper picked a peck of pickled peppers," he snarled. "And Mary had a little lamb! And what about Mother Goose!" He shook the man and brandished the knife, Natalia looking for the look of fear there.

She found it, then stood, grabbing at Paul, making herself sound frightened, saying to him, "You almost started me laughing, Paul! That could have been terrible! You could have at least said something threatening to him!"

Paul, with overly dramatic reluctance, she thought, stepped back, feeling the blade of his knife and smiling wickedly, John making a show of holding him back.

She looked meaningfully into the eyes of the Mongol and told him, as best she could, that she would let the man with the knife carve him to pieces as he had wanted to do, would not be able to stop his vile temper, if the Mongol remained silent.

He told her that he was a soldier of the Second City. He told her he knew nothing about the tall man's son or a woman with green eyes or a man with blond hair or a huge red-haired man with a dog that looked like a wolf or a cart on wheels that needed no horses to pull it. He told her he would tell her nothing more.

She asked where the Second City was.

He said the evil man with the knife could kill him, but he would never tell.

She recounted this to John Rourke.

Paul started into his evil man with the knife act again, but John pulled him back.

John turned instead to the pilot of the helicopter, the co-pilot of the J-7V. "Take her up—just straight up into the air and hover."

"Yes, Herr Doctor!"

The rotor blades, which had turned lazily before, began to beat in earnest.

She could feel it in her stomach as the aircraft began to rise, the look of terror in the man's eyes rising with the regularity of an altimeter.

John Rourke, his voice low, told her, "Translate for me. And tell him I mean it, because I do."

Natalia began to translate.

"He'll tell me the location of this Second City, he'll tell me everything he knows he thinks I might want to know . . ." And he paused as she caught up with the translation. "He'll tell me everything right now, or . . ." She translated, huddling into her parka as John Rourke tugged open the fuselage door, the wind and snow swirling inside like needles of ice. "Or I'll throw him out into the air and he will fall to earth and die in such an evil way his spirit will know no peace. Tell him."

She told the Mongol. And the Mongol dropped to his knees, one of the German security team starting to grab for him, but Natalia waving him back. The Mongol touched his forehead to her feet.

She closed her eyes, hearing John Rourke closing the fuselage door.

Chapter Twenty-nine

Ivan Krakovski had taken personal charge of navigation for the fleet of six helicopter gunships, trusting no one with the coordinates given him by the Hero Marshal.

For a short while, the fleet of gunships had passed out of the teeth of the blizzard, but now the snow swirled around them maddeningly, crusting over the bubble, Krakovski taking the controls of the gunship for a time to relieve the pilot of the strain. The windshield wipers raced crazily, but could not compete with the rate of snowfall and wind driven snow as it lashed against the machine, the five other machines barely visible even by their running lights.

The Hero Marshal had told him that the cache of some thirty Chinese weapons was near the city once called Lushun, in what had once been a mine, the interior of the main shaft reinforced with concrete and steel and capped like something the Hero Marshal had called a well. Krakovski had not asked what this "well" thing was, assuming he would recognize it when he saw it.

It was cold, and colder still from the feeling of fear which he unashamedly admitted consumed him. The machine which he flew was buffeted by winds of what he estimated to be gale force, and the controls had to be manipulated with the greatest precision, not just to keep on course, but to keep from being thrown into an uncontrolled spin and the machine destroyed.

He used the radio and ordered all pilots to transfer controls to their co-pilots for periods of at least thirty minutes while they rested from their ordeal.

He would find the coordinates, but if the storm intensified, he doubted he would be able to take off. And the Hero Marshal and the destiny of the Soviet people depended on him . . .

Michael Rourke studied Maria Leuden's face in the gray light of the room in which they lay. And his thoughts were consumed with his dead wife. It was not rationalization. She had cherished life and would wish him to do the same. Had he celebrated life by invading Maria Leuden's loins, or had he merely satisfied lust, he asked himself. He was drawn to her, and for the first time since Madison's death, there had been a moment when he had felt real happiness. Maria Leuden had cried as she held him, Michael for the first time appreciating the sadness which had consumed her as well. The rape she had endured years before, the scorn of her lover because somehow he had blamed her for it or not having the grace to die during the process. She had whispered to him, it was the first time she had ever been loved willingly by a man and he had wondered at how close she had been to her fiance. It was then she had cried, her body trembling beneath his, and her very trembling drawing him deeper into her — spiritually as well, he wondered?

It was more than unnerving to consider loving a woman who could read your thoughts. If Annie could actually read what Paul thought, she never alluded to the fact. But with Maria, he had known from that first moment aboard the aircraft taking them to Egypt that she could see inside him. He wondered if it had brought him closer to her, or kept him away.

Madison's body had been more beautiful and he doubted he would ever see a woman who could compare to her in her beauty or her compassion. But he realized, he loved this woman now as well.

He pushed away the sheet and as he started to rise, Maria Leuden came softly against him and he held her in his arms for a time, kissing her lightly on the forehead.

There was something he had to do. And he needed to escape the sensation of being beside her.

Michael Rourke left the bed and skinned into his pants and shirt, taking his two pistols as well. He left her apartment and walked as quietly as he could down the corridor. Rolvaag and his dog were nowhere in evidence and Michael assumed that at last the giant man in green had retired. Michael let himself into his rooms and stripped away his clothes, showering quickly, his body still remembering Maria Leuden's touch. He towelled his hair as dry as he could make it, then dressed in fresh Levis and fresh shirt and his arctic gear, except for the parka which would be too warm to wear until he left the petal. He had a pass from Han which would allow him to come and go at the main entrance.

He took only the Beretta pistols and slung the shoulder rig in place. The parka over his arm, he left.

He found the monorail station again. It was fully automated and summoning a car at any hour of the day or night, he had been told, would cause a car to arrive within ninety seconds or less. It was forty-five seconds. He boarded the car and signalled his destination by pressing the spot on the map located beside the sliding doors. The car sped along its single overhead track, the petal of the First City over which he rode all but asleep, some workers moving in a long, narrow street, an electric car crossing an intersection, the lights in most of the residential structures extinguished.

The monorail stopped by the main entrance tunnel and he exited the car, slipping his parka on, but not closing it. He started up the tunnel.

The guard patrol at the tunnel. Two men with rifles stepped from the shadows beyond the yellow light through which he walked, evidently recognized him, one of them nodded, both moving away.

When he reached the end of the tunnel, he found that there was a storm like none he had ever seen. There were several guards clustered about the energy field which formed the main entrance, snow sparking in the field, the invisible barrier crackling, flashing. He could not converse with the officer in charge of the detail. Unlike the Germans, English was not a requirement for the officer corps. It was merely a language of the learned. But with gestures, Michael at last made clear his intent. And it was clear to him that the Chinese guards thought he was a madman to venture into the storm.

The cold that was somehow blocked by the energy field was suddenly there, and a wind which howled maddeningly and hammered at the barrier crackling into place behind him, through him.

Movement along the road surface was difficult because it was so slippery, and slow because of the pressure of the wind, but his meager transmitter would have no effect without his getting far enough into the open. He had told the chairman his intention and the chairman had told him somberly that most likely his companions from the flying machine would be dead, the prey of the soldiers of the Second City who roamed the wildly frigid terrain and would kill without provocation.

Michael Rourke kept walking, the radio handset safely beneath his parka and close to his body to prevent damage to the batteries.

He estimated another hundred yards through the already thigh deep snow would be adequate distance from interfering structures.

He kept moving, fatigue setting in more quickly than he had imagined. Four hours of sleep had all but restored him, the first relaxed sleep he had experienced since the death of his wife and unborn child. Madison would have wanted this, he suddenly realized. His happiness, such happiness as there could be while an evil of unspeakable proportion prowled the earth and casually claimed the lives of innocent women and babies.

He had made his hundred yards or close to it and Michael Rourke, at peace with himself oddly, took the radio set from beneath his parka and turned it on.

The voice he heard belonged to Paul Rubenstein, caught in mid-transmission. ". . . can hear, respond. If your receiver is incapable of clear sending, open and close the frequency in series. Over."

Michael Rourke raised the machine to his lips, pulling away the flap from the hood which protected his lower face. "This is Michael. Paul? Come in. Over."

It wasn't Paul's voice which came back, but his father's. "Michael—this is Dad. Are you all right? Over."

"Dad—I'm fine. Where are you? Over."

"Flying the chopper you and and the others left behind. Heading for someplace called the Second City with a prisoner aboard who looks like some kind of movie lot Mongolian. Over."

"The crew. Over."

"Gunner dead, pilot in serious condition from beating and exposure and some burns, apparently torture. Over."

"Do you know your position? Over." It was a ridiculous question to ask his father.

"Prepare to copy," and John Rourke gave coordinates, Michael Rourke committing them to memory, telling his father to hold that approximate position while he got precise coordinates—for the First City . . .

John Rourke rarely looked tired, Paul Rubenstein reflected. But he looked tired now. "He's all right—"

He watched John Rourke's eyes as his friend shifted them briefly from the swirling blizzard through which they flew and to his face, then away again. "You don't realize how much you love someone," John began. "Well—you know what I mean."

"He's all right," Paul Rubenstein said again. "That's what matters."

The radio crackled but it wasn't Michael's voice, but Natalia from aboard the J-7V. "Thank God, John."

"Amen," Rourke said into the microphone near his lips.

"I've got something on radar. It probably has me. No—wait a minute. It was one blip just a second ago. Now I have five—no—make that six."

Paul Rubenstein began working the radar console and picked up the six blips as well. "Look like helicopters," he said. "Agree?"

"Agree," Rourke said.

"Agree," Natalia's voice came back. "They aren't German or we'd know. Logic indicates they're the six Soviet gunships Captain Hartman spoke of."

"Shit," Rourke snarled. The gunships were nearly off screen. "How's your fuel, Natalia?"

"We won't have to set down for six hours and we have plenty of reserves."

Paul Rubenstein watched John Rourke's face. Then John Rourke spoke. "All right. Let's do this. If Michael is with friendlies, we can get the pilot of the helicopter to medical facilities. Can you fly above the Soviet gunships and keep them in your radar without being detected."

"We've lost them on our scope," Paul interjected.

"We've lost them just now, Paul says—you have a better reach. Still got them?"

"Affirmative, John," Natalia answered. "Checking with the pilot now." There was static, then her voice came back. "The pilot tells me we can do it, but we'll have to fly tight circles like we have or we will outdistance them just like we would have outdistanced you."

"Do it," John Rourke told her. "Do not engage. Just follow. Stay on this frequency and we'll monitor it. Be careful. I almost lost someone I love tonight. I don't want to repeat the experience. Rourke out."

There was a pause, then, "Natalia out."

Rourke, his face lit by the reddish glow of the overhead, looked at Paul Rubenstein. "Maybe we've got them."

The radio crackled again, Michael's voice, a little less clear than the last transmission, but Paul Rubenstein could read the transmission clearly enough and started logging the coordinates.

Second City. First City. It reminded him of the rivalry between Chicago and New York. He felt the change in rotor pitch, the change in wind as John Rourke called to the J-7V and simply said, "Breaking off—good luck. Rourke out."

Six Soviet gunships, a blizzard, Chinese cities—Michael had said that in the second series of transmissions—killer Mongols and Karamatsov's army still coming. Paul Rubenstein suspected that more than luck would be required.

Chapter Thirty

At high altitude, the modest irregularities in the terrain features would never have been detected, she felt. She remembered discussing the subject with Annie and with several scientists from the Icelandic community at Hekla. The Eden Project personnel had detected what had appeared as a power source and, really by accident (she was not about to call it serendipity since Eden personnel had nearly taken her life), had sent Elaine Halversen and Akiro Kurinami to the surface to investigate. She had seen charts on computer screens showing their orbital paths, and she had realized at once that had a similar power source been detectable from space anywhere within all of Eurasia, it would likely have been missed.

The J-7V had no instruments specifically designed for probing for power sources, and simply because of its terrain following features was it radar sensitive enough to have picked up the quite definite signs of human habitation the screen now revealed.

Coastlines had changed over the five centuries since the near total destruction of life, the advancing poles lowering sea levels dramatically, but the concussive effect of the bombings on the Night of The War itself having caused earthquakes more severe than she had previously realized. With the coordinates as reference, a superimposed map of the area from the pre-Holocaust period revealed a vastly altered shape to the land. There had, in the past, been a bay and peninsula here at the tip of Manchuria near what had been North Korea. But no longer. The peninsula was now a land bridge to a radically altered coast of China.

And the six helicopters were traveling into this area with what seemed from the pattern of their flight a quite definite destination.

Their radar would not as yet have acquired the evidence of human habitation just acquired by the J-7V, but would soon acquire it. She was curious if they were aware of it, her faceless adversaries.

She spoke into her headset to the pilot. "Lieutenant?"

"Fraulein Major?"

"Can you circle widely enough around our quarry that we can still keep them in definite radar contact but get well ahead of them? That series of terrain features. It seems to clearly suggest human habitation near what was once the city of Lushun. If that is the Soviet destination, perhaps we can guess their purpose if we get a closer look."

"Yes, Fraulein Major." And immediately, the young pilot's fingers began punching a new program into the navigational console. She glanced back along the length of the fuselage. The six men of the security detail, a bit white faced from the bumpiness of the flight, seemed alert enough, the Mongol-looking prisoner, bound with disposable, synthetic plastic restraints, squatted on the floor between them, his face a mask of terror. She called out to the Mongol, telling him that if he behaved himself, the machine which flew through the sky would bring him safely to earth again. He said something to her, essentially thanking her for her kindness.

It was not politeness which motivated his response, but

fear instead. The J-7V banked sharply to port, implementing the course change . . .

It was barely possible to land the German gunship, the storm seeming to have intensified if that could have been possible, John Rourke thought.

"You're going to have to help me, Paul," Rourke shouted, bypassing the radio. "As soon as we touch down there, get Michael and whoever else you can and get those guy wires attached to the fuselage to anchor this thing. She'll flip on us otherwise. The wind is too strong. Be ready!"

The younger man was already freeing himself of the restraint harness, Rourke glancing back once, seeing Paul checking that the injured German pilot was secured, then going to the fuselage door. "Don't open it yet, Paul!"

"Right — tell me when, John!"

He was playing with the pitch control, trying for something similar to level flight, the wind slamming at him from all sides, no matter which way he oriented the helicopter. Beneath them, near the shelter of a massive looking ramp, one of several partially drifted over with snow leading to flower petal shaped structures which began above the surface and disappeared below, he could see people, at least two dozen of them. Details were impossible to see.

He spoke into the headset on the frequency established with Michael's radio. "Son — you hear me? Over."

"I hear you, Dad — looks like you're having problems with the winds. Over."

"Affirmative on that. As soon as I touch down, Paul's jumping out with the guy wires to anchor this down. Otherwise, the helicopter will flip over. Can you get him some assistance? Over."

"Gotchya. We'll be ready to move as soon as Paul is out the door. How's the pilot doing?"

"All right last time I checked, which wasn't too recently.

But Paul just looked at him. You said Hammerschmidt was injured. How's he doing?"

"Better all the time. Hang in there. Over."

"Out," Rourke snapped back, working the stick, playing the instrument switches like a rock singer on an electronic keyboard, as soon as he had the machine stabilized, another gust assaulting the aircraft. He was dropping, the descent less than perfectly controlled. Rourke powered up, taking the chopper out over the valley in which he was trying to land. "Hang on tight, Paul!"

He banked, letting the wind play with the machine for an instant, then levelling off and increasing rotation, sweeping downward toward the flare lighted landing circle, the wind gusting more heavily, Rourke sliding the helicopter down, ready to reduce power. "Hang on! Going in!" He cut power, letting the machine's weight take over, upping power just slightly, touching down, the machine vibrating around him, killing tail rotor power, the machine lurching sickeningly, a howling scream from the storm as the fuselage door opened, Rourke feeling the cold and the wind assaulting the exposed skin of his neck. He increased rotor speed just slightly, the machine lurching again as another gust assaulted it, the clipboard with the maps blowing from Paul's seat, Paul visible now by the chin bubble, gusts of wind and snow blowing him back as he made to secure the line to the grommet, Michael to starboard, securing a line, Chinese soldiers surrounding the helicopter, Rourke fighting the uncomfortable feeling they gave him.

His eyes found Michael again, Maria Leuden beside him. Rourke found himself smiling.

The buffeting of the wind did not decrease, but the erratic swaying of the German gunship stabilized, then stopped, only the strongest of gusts rocking it now, and only slightly.

He killed power, unstrapping. The rotor blades had to be attended to quickly . . .

Father and son stood by the monorail station. Except for the few strands of gray in the elder Rourke's hair and that John Rourke needed a shave and Michael Rourke did not, the two men, in height, in bearing, in the subtle mannerisms and looks which accompanied their speech, even in the timbre of their voices, seemed to her identical.

Between them stood the chairman, his own considerable height all but diminished. Maria Leuden hugged her arms to her breasts, shivering from the remembered cold they had just quit.

As she made to join them, the Chinese agent, Han, ran from the tunnel, slowing as he approached the leader of his government. She could hear him as he spoke. "I have monitored the radio frequency Doctor Rourke asked be monitored. There is a message coming in from a woman."

"Natalia," John Rourke murmured, then broke into a long strided sprint back up the tunnel, the parka he wore still dark stained with wetness, Michael behind him, then running even with him, Maria Leuden following after them. As she glanced back, the chairman, not running, but walking briskly, was also coming.

A radio had been set up just beyond the electronic barrier, a portable antenna wired to it, the location selected because the signal could not be picked up on Chinese radio, the frequency range different. It was a field radio from her own country, she recognized.

She could hear Natalia's voice. "This is Courier. Come in Watchman. Over." She assumed Watchman was a code designation.

John Rourke took the microphone, saying into it, "This is Watchman, Courier. Reading you with heavy static. Over."

Snow and wind lashed them, Maria Leuden closing her parka quickly, pulling the hood up. Suddenly Michael's arm was around her and she leaned her head against him. Paul Rubenstein stood beside John Rourke. She noticed the chairman crossing past the barrier, one of the officers giving the chairman his parka, the chairman hugging it around him, his long robe blowing in the gale force wind like a woman's skirts.

Natalia's voice came again. "Have located what appears to be an aggregation of pre-fabricated structures near location of pre-Conflagration Lushun, on what is now a very narrow isthmus between a large lake and the Yellow Sea. There is a rail line here. The six gunships have landed at approximately seventy-five miles northeast of the city along the rail line. We are landing out of their radar range and will proceed toward their location to observe using the Specials. Over."

"This is our outpost," the chairman said, his body visibly shaking with the cold. "Are these gunships — aircraft?"

"Yes," John Rourke told him. "Russian gunships. Looking for something."

The chairman seemed stricken, sagging against the officer near him, Han going to his aid. John Rourke spoke into the microphone, "Stand by, courier. Do nothing. Stand by. Over."

The elder Rourke attended the chairman, the man shaking his head as if to clear it. "What is it, sir," John Rourke asked, his voice barely audible over the wind. Michael walked forward, to stand beside his father, Maria's right hand locked in his left in tow to him. She followed. "Why did you react like that?" John Rourke asked.

The chairman drew himself up to his full height. "The cache of nuclear warheads we spoke of earlier," he said, addressing the remarks toward Michael, toward her, then looking at the elder Rourke. "Thirty-three nuclear warheads. A secret broken in three parts, two possessed by ourselves and two by our enemies of the Second City. The two parts of the secret which we possess indicate that the cache of warheads may be hidden near the sea."

"Shit," John Rourke hissed. She watched as he licked his

lips, looked at his son, then at Paul Rubenstein, then at the chairman. "That helicopter won't get off the ground again. What do you have that can get us to this area Major Tiemerovna spoke of? Somebody answer me." There was a look of desperation in his eyes she had not seen before. She had seen it in Michael's eyes when he had come to her door hours ago and taken her into his arms and taken her to her bed and made love to her in a way she hadn't thought would be possible.

"We have no aircraft," the chairman began.

Michael spoke. "You spoke of trains that traveled to Lushun, sir. Your agent, Mr. Han—he told me they were steam powered. How, without wood or coal?"

"When we mastered fusion power, the miniaturization of fusion reactors was quite simple, the requirements for shielding comparatively non-existent. The engines are powered in this manner."

"What?" John Rourke bit down on a cigar. "Fusion powered trains? That's crazy—no offense, sir."

"But it is reality, doctor."

John Rourke looked at the radio set. "How far is Lushun and how fast do these locomotives of yours go?"

"Nearly a thousand kilometers—"

"About five hundred and fifty miles," Rubenstein said. "We'll never make it in time."

"The trains, sir," the chairman said, "will travel at speeds in excess of 250 kilometers per hour."

"The Tokaido Bullet Train—Holy God," Paul Rubenstein whispered.

"What is this?" Maria Leuden asked, her curiosity forcing her to interrupt.

John Rourke looked at her. "Before the Night of The War, the Japanese had conventionally powered rapid rail service consisting of hundreds of trains—two hundred and two, I believe—which ran in regular service at surface speeds in excess of 155 miles per hour. Everything changes and nothing changes," he smiled.

Michael's eyes were elsewhere for an instant as she looked up at him. "About four hours or a little better. We can work it out to the minute," he volunteered.

John Rourke lit his cigar.

His voice was, again, like a whisper. "We'll need troops, if you can spare them. I don't know how many of Karamatsov's people are in those six gunships. We'll just have to pray that in four hours he can't locate the warheads and get them moved and get airborne or we've lost it forever. Once the Russians have nuclear weapons again, the game is up. Karamatsov will use them. And now I've gotta do something I don't want to do."

John Rourke looked at the chairman. "How long, considering the weather, before we can be aboard one of those trains? There literally isn't a minute to lose. And will they travel at high speed under these conditions?"

The chairman spoke in Chinese with Han, Han running to a telephone located just inside the tunnel mouth. It seemed an eternity to her as she looked from Michael to his father, to the chairman, to Paul Rubenstein, then back to Michael. But when Han returned she realized it was perhaps no more than three minutes.

The chairman nodded and Han addressed them all.

"I have been informed that indeed the train can run unimpaired and, on order, can be readied for boarding in less than ten minutes. The train can be reached within five minutes utilizing the monorail system. One hundred crack troops under the command of the Intelligence Service will be in full battle gear and at the train within twelve minutes. I will personally command them."

John Rourke only nodded. He took the microphone from the enlisted soldier standing beside the radio. If he— Rourke—was cold, he didn't show it, his parka open, his hood down, his cigar clamped in his teeth. "Courier, this is Watchman. Come in. Over."

Natalia's voice came back, the static worse this time. "This is Courier, Watchman. Reading you with heavy static. Over."

"I have to ask you to do something that I could regret for the rest of my life. There is strong reason to believe our friends are about to unearth thirty-three thermonuclear warheads, Natalia. Paul and Michael and I are coming with a large force to stop them, but won't arrive for four hours or a little over that. They can't be allowed—" He stopped for a moment.

Natalia's voice came back over the radio. She knew enough about radios to realize they were broadcasting on one band, receiving on another. "John. I'll love you with the last breath of my body and after that. I understand."

John Rourke handed the microphone to Paul Rubenstein and shook his head. Maria Leuden watched the father of the man she loved, a father who a moment ago had seemed young enough to be his brother and was, in fact, that young. But as he closed his eyes, John Rourke now suddenly looked very old and alone.

She never wanted that for Michael, his son.

Chapter Thirty-one

She had picked the two most competent of the security team, the commander who was a lieutenant and a corporal. They were preparing the Specials. Since there were only three of the motorcycles, only three could go.

Natalia Anastasia Tiemerovna girded herself for battle. The shoulder holster with the stainless steel Walther PPK/S American was in place, the Walther's silencer affixed. She snapped it out, giving the silencer a good luck twist to make sure it was secure, then reholstering it in the Ken Null holster.

She had removed her gunbelt when she had taken the co-pilot's seat for added comfort. She now put it on, securing the double billeted belt with the matching black leather Safariland full flap holsters. She checked each of the twin stainless Smith & Wesson L-Frame revolvers in turn, the guns custom action-tuned and polished, the four-inch barrels slab sided and American Eagles emblazoned on the right barrel flats by Metalife Industries as a gift to Samuel Chambers who eventually became the first and last president of United States II. He had given them to her for her efforts in aiding with the evacuation of combatants and civilians from doomed peninsula Florida five centuries ago. She holstered the guns.

In her backpack was the Walther P-38 9mm she had 'liberated' from the Place, the place of Madison's birth. Pretty Madison, who had carried Michael's baby, who had died so senselessly. Soon all who lived on the battered earth might die.

She put the pistol under her belt against her abdomen.

She hugged her arms to herself, shivering with cold. But it was not cold in the cabin of the J-7V. It was the cold within herself.

She checked both M-16s carefully.

She pulled on her parka, then tied the silk scarf over her hair, the second scarf over the lower portion of her face.

Natalia Anastasia Tiemerovna, daughter of a Russian ballerina and a Jewish Soviet dissident, raised as the niece of the commanding general of the Army of Occupation of North America, Ishmael Verikov, wife by act of insanity to the Hero Marshal of the Soviet Union Vladmir Karamatsov — Natalia Anastasia Tiemerovna, Major, Committee for State Security, opened the fuselage door and stepped into the howling winds of the blizzard. But she knew where she was going — to meet her fate.

Chapter Thirty-two

It was comfortably warm inside the train, Rourke stripped off his parka and sweater, the seat opposite him occupied by his guns and gear.

Natalia—if she too died—

He exhaled so loudly that Paul, seated opposite him, in the aisle of the passenger car, looked across at him. Rourke simply looked away.

He was tired of it all. Very tired of it. War, for as long as he could remember. When he had been in the CIA as a case officer, he had fought terrorists and those who would steal his nation's secrets. When he had left CIA and freelanced to teach and write, it had always devolved to him teaching in the field and that had always meant—

Then the Night of The War had come. And since then—

John Rourke began the mechanical things which were needed, which logic decreed he do. He began with the twin stainless Detonics mini-guns he had carried—for how long? Their principal designer had been an old friend and designed a .45 ACP pistol which was as ultimately reliable as such a machine could be because he knew the same things Rourke knew. The Python, its action more watchlike than other revolvers of its type and demanding more careful maintenance, but unmatched for what he carried it for, accuracy. The Scoremasters he had taken from the Place, from where Michael had taken his bride who was now dead.

One by one, all of the guns he checked and, satisfied, put them down.

The two knives which had saved his life the last time — in the crevasse. The custom Crain Life Support System X. The little A.G. Russell Sting IA black chrome which he had carried almost as long as the little Detonics pistols.

Faces. Friends. Memories.

John Rourke sat alone. He had learned throughout his life one thing. For him, it was a natural state. He closed his eyes and leaned his head back. He would not sleep.

Chapter Thirty-three

Vladmir Karamatsov had cursed the night because the snow had become so heavy that his helicopter gunships were grounded and his vehicles could barely move along the roads and his army had ground to a halt.

He stood in the radio truck, the static making it hard to hear. He strained his ears, wanting not to miss a word.

Ivan Krakovski's voice came to him, like a longed-for spirit in the night. "We have located the cache and are proceeding at this hour with removal of contents. Conditions too severe for flight. Have located train tracks and a high speed train. This is part of a Chinese civilization found near the site of the cache.

"Train personnel," Krakovski's voice continued, "indicate larger city to northeast of current position, some one thousand kilometers. Storm seems to be breaking from the north. Can you pick us up? Over."

"Tell him to go on. I wish to know more," Karamatsov snapped to the communications officer, the officer repeating his words into the table top microphone.

Krakovski's voice resumed. "Intend load contents of cache aboard high speed train and proceed northeasterly at best speed. Will keep this frequency open. Requesting airlift approximately five hundred kilometers from current position when weather breaks. Leaving small complement with helicopters in the event weather information incorrect and storm breaks from south. Awaiting further orders. Krakovski over."

Karamatsov thought for a moment. The weather had been breaking from the north. He had been told that in a matter of perhaps an hour he could risk getting gunships off the ground and taking them northward.

He took the microphone from the table and held it in his hand. "This is Karamatsov. Proceed with train to position five hundred kilometers northeast of your current position. Maintain constant radio contact. Am sending gunships within one hour to circle north of the storm and retrieve your personnel and your cargo. Was it all there?" He forgot to use the right words. "Over," he added lamely.

"This is Krakovski, Comrade Marshal. Affirmative. Contents of cache as expected. No map. I say again, there was no map. Over."

Karamatsov threw the microphone to the table and stormed toward the doors of the truck, throwing them open, snow and cold and wind almost consuming him as he shrieked his rage into the night.

Chapter Thirty-four

The Specials had been built for rugged terrain and high snow, but not for this, the going slow, so very slow, sometimes the drifting snow forcing them to dismount and struggle ahead, on foot, virtually carrying the machines only so they could ride again when the drifting was less great.

Time was fleeting and it was her obsession. If Vladmir were to possess thirty-three nuclear warheads, he would rule the entire world or destroy it.

An hour into the crossing to the point where the Soviet gunships had landed, she ordered a halt.

There was the perfunctory encoded radio contact with the J-7V, no fresh news of John Rourke and the fabulous sounding high speed train, no fresh news of any change in the radar profile the J7-V was barely able to hold of the six gunships.

The German corporal came to her and offered her hot coffee from the thermos-like canteen he carried and she took a sip of it, telling him, "Thank you," leaving the scarf down, struggling to light a cigarette if she could only fight the wind long enough. The German corporal cupped his hands over hers and the lighter and, by sucking in her breath as hard as she could the instant there was flame, she had the cigarette lit. "Thank you again."

"You are most welcome, Fraulein Major."

He was practising his English on her, she knew, English a requirement for the officer corps of New Germany and, with the war, the chances for attaining rank faster, better. He had a nice face, what she could see of it. She offered the cigarette to him.

"No thank you, Fraulein Major—I do not cigarette smoke."

"You do not smoke cigarettes, not 'do not cigarette smoke'. Okay?"

"Yes—okay, Fraulein Major."

"How old are you, corporal?" They were sitting in the shelter of some rocks, precious little shelter, his lieutenant scouting ahead at the man's own request.

"I have nineteen years, Fraulein Major."

"You are nineteen years old—not what you said."

"Thank you once more, Fraulein Major," and he laughed, then told her, "Forgive my talking, but I think that the Fraulein Major is very beautiful."

She leaned toward him quickly and touched her lips to his cheek and then pulled away. "Thank you, Corporal," she told him.

It was time to go and she stood up, dragging heavily on the cigarette. If her calculations were correct, in twenty minutes the gunships and the rail line near which they had landed should be in sight . . .

It was a rail terminus, she realized. Several train cars and what appeared to be an engine, long, sleek, drifted with snow, stood off on a siding beyond a small, low prefabricated building and beside that a tower, which she assumed oversaw the switching. A second engine was hissing steam on what appeared to be the main track, several transport cars and what might have been passenger cars already coupled to it, Soviet personnel boarding the train. She realized she was too late. With the night vision turned on, through the German binoculars she could clearly see a vast crater some two hundred yards beyond the rail line itself, apparently freshly blasted since much of the dirt was still uncovered by snow. It was here then that her husband's personnel had found their thermonuclear warheads.

Beyond the crater, the sea rose in a mighty fury, whitecaps gleaming with what seemed their own luminescence, on the near side of the isthmus, less than a hundred yards from her, a lake, whitecaps here too, the lake's farther shore further than she could reach even with the aid of the powerful German optics.

The corporal whom she had helped with his English was at her left, the officer at her right, the three of them crouched beneath the crown of a small ice-slicked ridge, her body shaking with cold but the shaking still managable, survivable.

What transpired below seemed clear to her. The storm precluded the possibility of safely taking off with the cargo of nuclear warheads aboard. Logic dictated that the alternative to evacuation of the site would have been fortifying it against attack until the weather cleared. Logic. But perhaps the Soviet commander was privy to meteorological data to which she was not. The rail line could go only northeast from here, and if he knew the weather were breaking from the north, and if the front were as distended as it appeared, then it would be logical to assume that even now some of her husband's gunships from the main body of his force significantly to the north and west, would be able to get airborne. Circumstances suggested a rendezvous to collect the thermonuclear devices. She could not imagine her husband wasting the time and manpower and fuel merely to rescue men under his command.

Lights burned in the gunships, and she knew from observation and from analysis that the Soviet field commander would have left the flight crews and perhaps some few additional personnel to guard the gunships until weather conditions moderated to the point where they could lift off. Insurance in case the front stalled and the weather cleared from the south.

She had lived with her husband, worked with her husband, been taught by her husband and knew his thinking, knew the way he expected his subordinates to think, because once she had been chief among them.

Natalia Tiemerovna made a decision. "Lieutenant. I will need you to accompany me. Corporal, you must wait here, guard the Specials as they are called and monitor the position of the six gunships. Should that position change, notify the commander of the J-7V immediately that he may relay the information to Doctor Rourke. Your role is vital." She looked away from his young eyes and told the lieutenant, "Work your way to the right, I'll work my way to the left. We'll rendezvous by the switching tower."

"Yes, Fraulein Major," and he said a word in German to the corporal, then started working his way along the ridge and down.

"Fraulein — why —"

She looked at the corporal. "Live, instead, hmm?" And she smiled at him. He was a very pretty boy, she thought, and some girl would surely be waiting for him and though the girl would never know, Natalia had just saved his life.

She touched his arm with her left hand, then started past him into the storm . . .

The lieutenant's last name was Keefler and she huddled with him from sight of the men who guarded the train tracks

223

behind one of the drifts that had molded itself to the conformation of the tower supports.

"There is a ditch there, Lieutenant—you see?"

"Yes, Fraulein Major. What do you suggest?"

She had gestured toward the very rear of the train and what appeared to be an open drainage ditch some fifty yards further back at the very end of the track section before it bridged into the switching yard proper. "I suggest the only alternative. We must get aboard the train. It is guarded from all sides, but not from the rear. If we can get aboard, we can perhaps sabotage it."

"I have explosives, Fraulein Major."

"Explosives might cause one or more of the nuclear warheads to detonate. We cannot risk that." She spoke with him comfortably in German, easier for him and not really considerably more difficult for her than English, English and German her primary languages during her course of studies at the Chicago espionage school, Spanish learned more rapidly and less grammatically perfect when necessity had demanded it. The other languages with which she was familiar were the result of happenstance and spare time and opportunity.

"When I give the word, we move out separately toward the ditch. You will cover me, then I will cover you. Once we have reached the ditch we will move along its length until we reach its furthest extent, then make for the train."

"Yes, Fraulein Major."

She slung both M-16s forward, trying to wait for the split second that seemed better than the last and perhaps better than the next. But the guards, despite the cold, seemed immutable in their positions. She pushed herself up from behind the drift and ran now, her tiny fists balled on the pistol grips of the M-16s.

The snow made movement feel sluggish, slow, awkward, but she reached the ditch, throwing herself down into it after a glance, the snow so deep here that she almost smothered in it, the snow crusting over her eyelashes as she blinked it away.

She set one of the M-16s on safe, thrusting the second one over the lip of the ditch as she waited for Lieutenant Keefler. Most of the Soviet personnel were boarded on the train, and she saw among them an officer, in high collared greatcoat rather than a parka, his black uniform denoting to her, even after five centuries, her husband's KGB Elite Corps. He rose to the steps of the lead car. She could barely see him now. He seemed to look along the length of the train front and back. Though she could hear nothing over the keening of the wind, she realized he had issued a command, his form disappearing inside the car, the guards which flanked the train on both sides peeling off and clambering aboard.

Keefler was coming, in a dead run, his German assault rifle in both hands, his body vaulting into the ditch beside her.

"They prepare to move, Fraulein Major."

"Yes," she nodded. "And so do we. Catch your breath."

Her heart sank, a guard armed with an assault rifle appeared in the rear door of the rear car, yellow light backlighting him for a moment, then the light gone, but the guard remaining. There was nothing for it but to do as planned. Natalia moved the second M-16's selector to safe, telling Keefler, "I will go ahead of you. I have a weapon for the job at hand." From under her parka, not bothering to reclose it, she extracted the silenced Walther PPK/S .380. She pushed herself up, running through the snow toward the rear of the train car, the Walther tight in her right hand, the thumb safety off.

Forty yards. Then thirty. Then twenty. The guard turned. He tried to move his rifle. She threw herself to the snow and fired, the Walther's sound barely audible as the sounds of the train increased, the squeak of wheels, the groan of metal against metal. The man's body lurched back, then flopped forward as she shot him again, the body falling over the side and into the snow.

To her feet, running, the train starting to move. There was no time to look for Keefler. If he made it aboard, he did. If not, she was alone. It was a natural state for her.

Chapter Thirty-five

Natalia Tiemerovna would have no choice but to enter the rail car. And the German, Keefler, had not made it aboard, the train picking up speed so rapidly that it reminded her of one of the Japanese bullet trains from before the Night of The War. As she entered the car, slowly, her silenced pistol in her left hand, her M-16 in her right, she had no plan. Only to live long enough to accomplish her mission of stopping or slowing the train so that John Rourke and the Chinese military force that was accompanying him could reach it and prevent the nuclear warheads from falling into her husband's hands.

Realistically, she doubted the warheads would be serviceable as they were, no matter how carefully they had been stored. But the plutonium used in them would still be usable in freshly constructed weapons and this was obviously what Vladmir Karamatsov sought.

She had seen only two of the Elite Corps enter this last car, the car's purpose uncertain to her. As she entered the car, she realized its purpose. Two men on each side of the car crewed one light machinegun respectively, each mounted on a tripod and aimed to the flanks of the railcar, the windows in front of the muzzles closed but easily enough smashed or shot through, a female officer, pretty, walking up and down the center aisle. Was she Vladmir's woman?

The female officer wheeled toward the sound of the opening door and Natalia fired as the woman drew her pistol, Natalia firing before the woman's handgun cleared the holster, a double tap to the forehead and nose, the woman's body falling back. One of the LMG crewmen at Natalia's left tried to swing the weapon in the direction of the doorway through which Natalia had come. Natalia snapped the silenced muzzle of the Walther toward his head and fired again, a single shot through the left cheek and into the eye.

She thrust the M-16 toward the remaining three, in her most vulgar Russian snapping, "Move and your fucking brains will be all over the walls!"

The three men froze, Natalia's mind racing, the Walther in her right hand down to three shots remaining. It was murder, but if she tried to have the men bind each other or tried to force them to exit the train by the doorway through which she had come, she might be forced to use the M-16, and the sound of gunfire would bring more of the at least forty men she had counted outside the train. She eyed the three men. In one man's eyes, she could see that he knew. He made for the assault rifle on the car floor beside him. Natalia fired, the hollow point into the left nostril, Natalia wheeling left, a single hollow point into the second man's right temple. The third man had an assault rifle swinging up toward her and she fired the last round from the Walther, impacting his throat just below the chin, his head snapping back against the wall, his body sagging to the floor.

Natalia lowered the muzzle of her pistol and breathed . . .

Michael Rourke had asked to be allowed to ride in the engine with the train's engineer and although the noise of the train speeding over the rails was intense, he didn't regret it. The machine was a marvel of simplicity. The entire forward four-fifths of the engine comprised the fusion reaction chamber, water passed through the chamber and converted to steam, steam driving the pistons which made the train move. The instrument panel looked like the instrument panel of one of the J-7V fighters or one of the German helicopters. The engineer, rather than looking like the crusty fellows he had seen in videotapes of western movies, was a slightly built Chinese who wore wire rimmed glasses similar to the type Paul Rubenstein had worn before the Sleep. His appearance seemed more appropriate for a professor rather than a man who drove a train such as this through the night.

Han had accompanied Michael in the cab, to serve as translator to the many questions, Han had remarked, he knew Michael would have. And questions Michael did have.

How could they speed along the tracks when heavy snow was drifted on all sides—the tracks were clear? The engineer had explained, Michael realizing that in fact this man was an engineer in the truest sense of the word. The Chinese had electrical power to waste with their conquest of fusion power. The tracks, whenever there was snow anywhere along the line and the snows here were heavy, were utilized as convection coils and melted the snow from the bed over which they travelled. He had perhaps noticed that the cross ties were of steel as were the rails. Wouldn't such a system be dangerous to animals, as he understood there were, or to the inadvertent rail worker who might contact the rails? But the system used such a low charge, electrical hazard was out of the question and the heat produced would feel pleasantly hot to the touch, not burningly hot. Where were the water towers which would be necessary to replenish the supply needed to produce more steam? The system was totally enclosed and once charged, never needed replacement of the water unless the entire system was to be dismantled for periodic maintenance.

As they entered the second hour of the ride, the engineer asked Michael if he would care to take the controls. Michael had begun to laugh at himself. He had stopped being a kid

229

so long ago he had almost forgotten what it was like. Almost. He took the controls . . .

The Schmeisser, the M-16, all were cleaned and checked. With time on his hands, Paul Rubenstein drew the battered Browning High Power from the black ballistic tanker holster he wore for it and popped the magazine, then worked the slide to clear the chambered round. Mechanically, he started to disassemble the pistol, moving the slide rearward so he could lock the safety into the proper notch to hold the slide back while he began to tug out the slide stop.

If Karamatsov had nuclear weapons, it would all be over. Paul would fight beside John Rourke until the last and then, if all were lost, he would take Annie and find the last place on earth that would be destroyed and stay with her there and die with her there. He wanted children. She wanted them. He worked down the safety and eased the slide forward off the frame, then jiggled the barrel free of the slide and began wiping the bore.

John Rourke had been silent since boarding this bizarre train. And Paul Rubenstein knew why. Normally, John would have been in the engine cab with his son, just as eagerly asking questions and learning the workings of the new magnificent machine. But the silence. John Rourke thought that he had sent Natalia to her death, perhaps, and already, before the fact, blamed himself.

Paul wondered if he could have told Annie that for the good of all mankind she should put her life in almost certain terrible jeopardy. It required a strength Paul Rubenstein prayed he would never have to find out if he possessed or not. He began reassembly of the High Power.

Chapter Thirty-six

John Rourke opened his eyes.

He realized that he had subconsciously accepted the fact that there was nothing which could be done to avert Natalia's possible death, that there was no way to more quickly intercept the oncoming Soviet train.

John Rourke stood up abruptly, snatching up his guns. "Paul! We've got a chance!"

He thrust both Scoremasters into his trouser band and began buckling on the pistol belt with the Python and the Sparks Six-Pak of spare magazines for the little Detonics pistols.

"What—"

Rourke shrugged into the double Alessi rig, the weight of the twin stainless Detonics .45s somehow more comforting to him than it had ever been.

"The J-7V. We can use it. Save Natalia. Stop the Russian train and keep Karamatsov from getting the warheads." He picked up the little Sting IA Black Chrome and positioned it in its sheath inside the waistband of his Levis, then took the massive Crain Life Support System X from the seat. He wore the sheath on his trouser belt and had simply unsheathed the knife rather than removing steel and leather. He stared at the twelve-inch blade for a moment, then looked at Paul Rubenstein, standing almost beside him. "The J-7V. If it can get off the ground and that pilot is as good as he seemed, we've got a chance. A damned good one." He sheathed the knife.

He caught up his parka and started for the rear of the car shrugging into his parka, finding the radio transmitter in the interior pocket, working up the antenna as he stepped into the arctic blast, Paul Rubenstein beside him.

"Courier. This is Rourke. Come in, Courier. This is Rourke. Do you read me? Over."

He closed his eyes and prayed. There was static and when the voice finally came it was almost impossible to hear over the roar of the slipstream around them, but it was the pilot's voice. "This is Courier, Herr Doctor. Reading you with some static. Over."

"Listen, Courier. Can you get airborne? Over."

"This is Courier—affirmative. Can be airborne in under sixty seconds. Over."

"Get airborne—" John Rourke looked at the younger man beside him, then embraced him . . .

Because of the high speeds at which the Chinese train traveled, the track ahead was constantly scanned by radar and by other more sophisticated means for obstructions and the like. Trains on a parallel track could scan the second set of tracks in order to warn oncoming trains of perils. This system John Rourke ordered implemented to watch out for the oncoming Russian controlled train. But he had hoped it would not have to be used.

If the J-7V's pilot was good enough . . .

Natalia Anastasia Tiemerovna worked the Soviet light machine gun free of its mounts. The ammunition was belt fed from a box, but the box made the weapon so muzzle heavy that despite the fact that she considered herself considerably stronger than the average woman, she realized that manipulation of the weapon would be impaired. She dismounted the box and started pulling out the link belt. She discarded the box, then took the box from beside the tripod and began to open it to do the same. With the ammunition link belts draped around her shoulders, she could carry more.

She picked up the reloaded Walther PPK/S from the floor beside her and holstered it in the Ken Null rig, then went to the second LMG and began to systematically disable it, to have left such a weapon operational behind her the sort of unpardonable sin that only heroes of twentieth century American adventure films survived.

Natalia draped the belts criss-cross fashion over her, her parka discarded, stripped down now to the black battle gear she normally wore, a loose-fitting black woolen turtleneck sweater over it, the shoulder holster concealed beneath the sweater, the P-38 in the center of her abdomen under her gunbelt, her revolvers at her hips, the M-16s slung across her back. The weight was still enormous as she added the musette bag with the spare magazines for the M-16s.

But the weight would diminish rapidly, as soon as the battle was joined. She started for the next car in the train.

Chapter Thirty-seven

The Soviet controlled train had passed through Lushun, Chinese troops forming a *cordone sanitaire* around it, leaving the train and its occupants unmolested, Han had told them. The German J-7V dual mode fighter radioed that Lieutenant Keefler and the corporal with him had radioed that Major Tiemerovna had boarded the Soviet-controlled train, and that Keefler had been unable to get aboard in time, the train accelerating so rapidly under the control of a captured Chinese engineer, apparently.

The second train, carrying them, Rourke had ordered to proceed at maximum speed until it was sighted by the J-7V, then begin braking.

Michael, Paul and John Rourke himself took turns enduring the terrific cold and 150 mile per hour slipstream, fortunately partially shielded from the full force of the wind by the body of the train, alternating on the radio until the J-7V reported having them in sight.

As the train began its braking action, John Rourke bundled into his parka, leaving the snow pants behind, intending to ditch the parka as soon as he was aboard the train, Michael and Paul opting for the same, Han and his troops readying themselves in the next two forward cars.

As the train slowed, John Rourke reviewed the plan, such as it was. "When we get aboard the other train, Paul—you and this man Wing who speaks English like Han—take the six men we spoke about and cut through the train to find Natalia. Don't be diverted by anything else no matter what happens. When you get her, signal on Michael's radio. I'll be ready to receive you. Get a defensible position near an exit and be ready. Michael and I, since Michael has been learning how these trains run, will go after the engine. Once the engine is secured we stop the train. Han has ordered his men to kill every Russian trooper aboard the train. As soon as the train is stopped, Michael and I will look for the warheads and if they aren't already secured, take out whoever is guarding them and hold the area until the resistance is crushed. Things may change rapidly. We have to be alert for that." And John Rourke unfolded the map of the rail line given him by Han, the three of them crouching beside the seat on which Rourke had previously laid his weapons. "Now—again to review. The train carrying the Russians will be crossing this forty mile stretch where the Yellow Sea has formed a natural reentrant just north of forty degrees latitude—here," and Rourke gestured with his right trigger finger. "A plate shift or some other geologic activity has altered the coastline here drastically from the pre-war geography we're all used to. Originally, we were going to block the tracks to slow down the train and board it, but that could have given a desperate man all the impetus needed to try to get one of those warheads going and that would have been all he needed to get them all to blow. But this way, whoever their field commander is shouldn't have that much advance warning. Michael—you checked with the engineer."

"This train can go just as rapidly in reverse, but it's dangerous because the radar and sensing equipment aren't operational that way."

Rourke nodded.

"All right—right here then, with the sea on one side and the mountains on the other side. Any Russians who get off can be killed or captured. They'll have nowhere to go. And there won't be any place to haul one of the warheads off to, either. If the scale on this map is correct, and Han assures me it is, for this forty mile stretch, the distance from the wall of granite where they blasted into the mountains to form the road bed and the water is a maximum of thirty yards, the two tracks less than five yards apart. This is the only place. Karamatsov probably had gunships enroute to rendezvous with the train just beyond here, about where we're at now. If any of those warheads gets airborne then the entire thing— well, we all know that," and John Rourke folded the map and stood to his full height. "Ready?"

The train was nearly at full stop. Paul nodded. So did Michael.

John Rourke started for the rear door of the car, the train all but stopped as he clambered over the railing and dropped to the snowy ground, the wind howling across the icy wilderness, the J-7V starting its vertical descent, Han and his men, armed with caseless ammo bullpup style assault rifles and submachineguns, piling out.

Rourke broke into a run for the J-7V. It could only hold him, Paul, Michael and fifteen others, Han among them. If eighteen men weren't enough . . .

Natalia's left hand was bleeding where a flying splinter from one of the seatbacks had grazed her, but she had killed sixteen men in this second from the last car.

But now she was pinned down, men from the forward cars having poured back, smoke grenades used, acrid smoke which burned her eyes and stung her throat and her nostrils, filling the car even though she had shot out three windows. And it was bone-chillingly cold, the wind of the train's slipstream lashing at her as she huddled behind three dead bodies and two crates of rations, the bodies riddled with more bullets than she could have counted, the gunfire from the front of the rail car incessant.

She pushed up, firing the LMG, the cyclic rate amazingly fast because with caseless ammo as was used in all of the Soviet weapons, there was no true ejection cycle. She had fired through the first of the belts, the discarded links clustered around her everywhere as profusely as pine needles in a forest.

She could have withdrawn to the last car, but it would have accomplished nothing. There was no place to go, and even if she were able to escape the train, doubtful at the enormous speed at which it traveled without sustaining fatal injury, her mission lay ahead. She fed the new link belt into the action of the LMG.

Another smoke grenade, then another and still another, were hurtled toward her. As she coughed, closing her eyes against it, but firing a burst with the LMG to keep her attackers away, she knew they could not try high explosives. Not with the cargo in the boxcar two cars ahead. Natalia kept firing . . .

The J-7V lifted off vertically, then changed into its horizontal flight mode, seemed to hesitate for a brief instant, then shot ahead, Rourke feeling himself pushed slightly back against the co-pilot's seat he had expropriated for the flight to the Russian-held train.

"I saw it, Herr Doctor. It appeared to be moving at best speed."

"A hundred and fifty miles per hour or so. Can you match it?"

"To match their speed exactly considering the power of the slipstream around them will be most difficult, Herr Doctor."

"If you don't we will have lost the war — and Major

237

Tiemerovna."

The German pilot's face split with a grin. "I said difficult, Herr Doctor. I did not say impossible, nor did I imply that."

Rourke nodded to him. "Good man."

"There!" Paul was crouched between the pilot's and co-pilot's seat and gestured toward the southwest in the distance. And Rourke saw it too. The Soviet-controlled train, nearer than expected.

The train was about to enter a steep walled mountain pass that the map had indicated ran for some thirty miles.

And beneath them, in the grayness now that despite the still swirling snow had replaced the darkness of night, Rourke could see the forty mile expanse that was their target zone.

Sheer walls of granite rose hundreds of feet into the air, the newness of their peaks sharp, threatening, and at the very base of the granite walls, the rail bed, two tracks looking from this elevation to be side by side, and a short distance beyond them to the southeast, waves lashing furiously high, was the Yellow Sea.

The pilot circled the J-7V and then banked to the east, Rourke squinting against the pencil thin line of sunrise beneath the gray blanket of the storm, the aircraft banking steeply again. "These winds will not help us, Herr Doctor."

"I know that. You've got to do it."

"And I know that, Herr Doctor," the pilot nodded somberly.

The aircraft banked again, behind the Soviet-controlled train now, following it along the tracks still at least a quarter mile below them.

Rourke's eyes moved to the altimeter. It was dropping rapidly.

The map Han had given him showed the mountain pass through which the tracks now crossed, but even from the map, Rourke had never envisioned it as this narrow, the J-7V dropping into it, flying on an angle because level flight would have brought the wingtips within mere feet of the rock wall on either side of them.

The pilot was slowly dropping speed as the J-7V overtook the train, almost matching it now, matching it, the rear car beneath them, the mountain pass extending for several miles yet. "Can you get us over the car just rear of the engine?"

"Yes, Herr Doctor," and almost imperceptibly, the J-7V moved ahead, a pale shadow of it visible on the snowless roofs of the cars over which the aircraft passed, the granite walls suddenly closer together, the pilot increasing air speed, rocketing ahead and up and out, passing over the engine. From the front car, immediately behind the engine and ahead of the solitary boxcar, there was gunfire coming now.

"It was too narrow, Herr Doctor."

"You've gotta try it, man!"

The pilot looked at Rourke, then at Rubenstein between them, then at Rourke again, his eyes wide, his tongue darting out to lick his lips. He nodded, the plane banking sharply, diving, back into the pass, flying, it seemed, mere feet over the tracks now, smoke billowing from the second to the last car of the train from windows that appeared shot out. Natalia? — Rourke wondered.

The aircraft was over the last car, over the second to the last car, the rock faces to either side of them seeming to squeeze together again, the angle of flight changing sharply, the pilot not flinching. Paul Rubenstein clung to the two seats between which he crouched, Rourke looking to the younger man's face, Rubenstein's eyes seeming to say, "It'll be all right, John." Rourke prayed that it would.

The J-7V was over the boxcar now, gunfire coming at them from the lead car just behind the engine, Rourke hearing the sounds of ricochets off the J-7V's armored skin.

The German aircraft was over the lead car now, the end of the mountain pass just ahead.

"As soon as we're through," Rourke shouted. "Then go to it."

"Yes, Herr Doctor."

They were through, the J-7V's angle of flight changing abruptly and sharply, level now, the speed seeming dead even with the train. And suddenly the J-7V shot ahead. "What are you doing?" Rourke shouted.

"I fly my aircraft to perform your mission, Herr Doctor. Trust me, Herr Doctor."

The pilot manipulated a bank of switches and suddenly the J-7V seemed to stall, switching into the vertical mode, the train nearly beneath them as the J-7V dropped, the aircraft buffeted and veering to port, the pilot playing the controls, the vertical descent continuing, and suddenly stopping.

"We have landed. Hurry and good luck, Herr Doctor!"

Rourke was already out of his seat, Rubenstein ahead of him near the egress hatch, Rourke clapping the pilot on the shoulder. "Thank you."

Rourke and Rubenstein together jumped through the egress hatch, Rourke nearly losing his balance as he impacted the roof of the train car, the engine dead ahead. Bullets whined through the roof of the car, Rourke realizing it would be grisly luck if one got through with sufficient remaining velocity to kill anyone, the roof of the train car dimpling with them, Rourke swept from his feet as he turned into the slipstream, to his knees. "Shit!" He was up, bending into the wind, his eyes squinted tight shut against it, the wind hammering him down again, to his knees, Rubenstein beside him, Han and the others clambering down from the J-7V as Rourke turned his face from the wind.

Despite the parka hood, the wind howled in his ears, deafening him. He crawled forward. As he looked up, Soviet personnel were clambering onto the roof from the car below, as soon as one would reach the roof, swept over by the wind, their assault rifles clattering away across the roof line, falling over the side. Rourke reached under his parka, one of the Scoremasters coming into his fist. He jacked back the

240

hammer and fired, killing the nearest of the Soviets, the body lurching forward despite the impact of the 185-grain jacketed hollow point. Another of the Soviet troopers— Rourke recognized the black uniform as KGB Elite Corps— was attempting to fire a pistol. Rourke fired first, twice at the man's chest and neck.

Michael was beside Rourke now as they neared the forward end of the car, Paul's six men led by the man named Wing who spoke English just behind them, Han and his men making the perilous jump to the next car back. As Rourke started to turn to face forward, he saw one of Han's men, caught up in a gust of wind, being hurtled to his death between the train cars. The noise of the wind which roared around him was too loud for Rourke to hear the scream.

They reached the forward end of the car now, a Soviet trooper pushing up to the level of the roof, Michael shooting him away with one of his Berettas. Rourke rolled over onto the access ladder, the roar of the wind suddenly all but abated. Rourke dropped to the platform level between the lead car and the engine, Michael down next, then Paul, Rourke jumping to the engine platform, then Michael following. The man named Wing was down, the others of Paul's group following. Paul gave John Rourke a thumbs up signal; blowing half a magazine for the Schmeisser into the front door of the car, two of Wing's men kicking it in, Paul and the man named Wing the first through, Paul's Schmeisser blazing from his right hand, the M-16 from the left, Wing with one of the Chinese caseless submachineguns in each hand.

Rourke turned to the entrance into the engine compartment, a massive door before him. He had inspected the door on the identical train they had ridden, knew where it hinged, had measured the height.

From one of the two musette bags that crisscrossed over his chest, beneath his parka, Rourke took a small block of the German equivalent of plastique, laying it into place on the outside of the door over where the upper hinge would be, Michael dropped into a crouch beside him, molding an identical brick of plastique over the location of the lower hinge; Rourke finished, then laid a third segment of plastique over the lock plate.

Gunfire ripped into the door and some of it penetrated, Rourke dodging to the side, Michael flanking the door opposite from him. For the most part the gunfire had simply dimpled the metal door.

Rourke leaned closer to the door again, inserting the detonator over the lock into the plastique. More gunfire through the door now, Rourke signalling Michael, his son nodding. Rourke tossed the detonator across the open space between them. Michael caught it, inserting the detonator into the plastique which was for the upper hinge. Michael set his own, the third detonator, into the lower hinge charge. Michael nodded, Rourke jumping back onto the adjoining platform, gunfire clattering from inside the first car through the open doorway, Michael jumping across. Michael drew back, Rourke upping the safety on the Scoremaster, thrusting it into his belt.

Rourke started out of his parka, the radio attached to his belt, throwing the parka into the slipstream. It was one of the German issue ones and replaceable enough. Michael did the same.

Waves from the turbulent surface of the Yellow Sea crashed within feet of them now as the train entered the narrowest portion of the forty mile strip.

John Rourke looked at Michael, then drew the Python.

They were small charges of plastique. But enough to do what was needed.

He stabbed the Python toward the upper hinge and double actioned a shot, turning his face, averting his eyes as the first charge blew, hearing the roar of Michael's .44 Magnum revolver dully as then Michael fired and the second charge blew. Rourke fired and blew the third charge, the one over the lock.

He looked at his son as he holstered the Python, one Scoremaster in Rourke's right fist, the fully loaded one in his left. His son looked at him, one Beretta in each of Michael's fists.

Rourke felt himself smile. His son smiled. John Rourke nodded, and together, they jumped the platform, Rourke's left foot and his son's right impacting the door at its center almost simultaneously, the door falling away on its hinges, inward, the engine compartment filled with KGB Elite Corps personnel.

As John Rourke and Michael Rourke stepped through the wide doorway, the KGB personnel started firing, and John and Michael Rourke started firing. The .45s bucked in Rourke's fists, the one in his right hand empty, stuffed into his trouser band. His right fist snatched one of the twin stainless Detonics .45s from the double Alessi rig, his right thumb jacking back the hammer, the little .45 bucking in his fist. The Scoremaster in his left hand was empty now, Rourke ramming it into his belt, the action still locked open, grabbing for the second little Detonics, ripping it from the leather, firing, men going down. Bullets ricocheted off the metal walls of the engine compartment, the cracking of Michael's Berettas, then suddenly the booming of his .44 Magnum revolver, Rourke's ears jarring with it. Rourke thrust the little Detonics from his right fist, empty, into his hip pocket, snatching the Python from the leather, emptying the cylinder into the last of the KGB Elite Corps personnel. Michael's .44 Magnum revolver boomed once more, almost in perfect unison with Rourke's .357.

There was always the roar of the wind, always the clacking sound of the train as it sped over the rails—but it was silent except for that.

By rough count, fifteen of the KGB Elite Corps personnel lay dead, scattered about the engine compartment.

A Chinese man, slight of build like Mr. Wing who now

accompanied Paul Rubenstein, but seemingly twice Wing's age, sixty or better, Rourke thought, emerged from behind the instrument bulkhead.

"Hi! Rourke grinned at the man. Michael started to laugh. As they started forward, both reloading their weapons as they walked, John Rourke said to his son, "How do you think you say 'Could you please stop the train?' in Chinese?"

Michael shrugged his shoulders, and reached for one of the switches and then pointed toward it and the Chinese engineer started nodding his head enthusiastically . . .

Paul Rubenstein and the slightly built Chinese agent with him, Wing Tse Chau, were running, only two of Wing's men left who weren't dead or wounded. They had cut through the first car and left some casualties but made no attempt to overpower the Soviet troops inside, Han and his men having caught the men in the first car in the crossfire with Paul and Wing and their smaller force. Over the second car, a battle raging beneath them between Russian troops and Han's Intelligence commandoes, then making the jump, Wing nearly going over the side as he lost his balance for an instant, Paul Rubenstein catching him and as the other two reached the boxcar and started over the top of it behind him, Paul realized that in the boxcar were the nuclear warheads. If whoever commanded the train were insane enough— He forced the thought from his mind and focused his violence against the wind which tried hammering him down. For each step he would take toward the rear of the car, he would fall forward, brace himself, then go ahead.

He reached the edge of the boxcar, the passenger car behind it, the second from last in the train, streaming smoke, small explosions coming from it now . . .

He had moved to the boxcar so as to personally guard the

warheads as soon as he had realized what was happening, ordering that his men fight to the death. Ivan Krakovski would write of their bravery, or immortalize them by making the warheads detonate.

Seven of his Elite KGB corps were with him. He thought of them as his own. They should have been his own.

If he detonated the warheads, they would not fall into enemy hands. And he knew the reason why the Hero Marshal wanted them. So the Hero Marshal could use them to get the American John Rourke and Major Natalia Tiemerovna. The woman who held off his best men in the second car from the rear of the train had to be Tiemerovna. And who else would have conceived such a daring foolish plan for stopping this train than the American Rourke whom the Hero Marshal so despised. And Krakovski knew that the Hero Marshal would full well destroy the planet if it took that to have his vengeance.

Krakovski decided.

He would give the Hero Marshal his vengeance. And, if somewhere some Soviet youth survived, then somewhere his courage would be sung

He began to open one of the containers in which the warheads were individually packed . . .

Natalia Anastasia Tiemerovna was out of ammunition for both the LMG and her two M-16s. She slung them back, empty, drawing the twin L-Frame Smiths from the holsters at her hips. There couldn't be too many more of the defenders at the front of the car. If only, despite the shot out windows, the smoke were not so thick.

Only amateurs thumb cocked double action revolvers except for the most precise shots. Precision would hardly be required here and she was no amateur. She made ready to stand and run forward, to win or die . . .

The engineer was saying something Rourke could not understand. And then he made what must have been a universal gesture. He pointed to the gunshot-riddled instrument panel, shook his head and drew his right index finger across his throat.

"The instruments are dead," Michael Rourke said.

John Rourke almost whispered. "He can't stop the train."

The engineer tugged at John Rourke's right hand and Rourke turned his eyes to follow the engineer's eyes. Over the control console was an illuminated map, showing the route; the engineer placed his finger over the map section Rourke mentally matched to the map Han had given him. There was a sharp curve approximately four-fifths of the way through the narrows where the train was now. The engineer was gesturing maddeningly toward it, then finally, gesturing to the engine cab around them. He quickly raised his hands and made a strange sound. Rourke shook his head. The engineer pointed to the map and then pointed away from the railbed and into the sea at a violent tangent.

"I think he said we'll derail—holy shit," Michael said softly.

John Rourke looked out through the window, toward the waves.

"Take the engineer with you. Get him to understand— we've gotta get everybody off the train. I don't care how you do it. I'm going for the boxcar. That's where whoever the leader here is and that's where the warheads are. Impact won't make them detonate. The water could because it will retard neutron emissions. But it might not. If the warheads are packed properly. Getting off the train may buy us ten seconds, or it could save our lives. But if somebody detonates one of the warheads—the German scientists say that—"

"I know," Michael Rourke told his father. "Maybe a dozen average yield weapons and—"

"Yeah," and John Rourke embraced his son, touching his lips to his son's cheek. And he broke into a run toward the blown open doorway . . .

Paul Rubenstein threw the full force of his body into the kick, the door into the rail car collapsing inward, Rubenstein thrusting himself through the door, his own SMG in his right fist, one of the Chinese submachineguns in his left, the smoke so thick he could barely see. He started firing at the shapes of men in black KGB Elite Corps uniforms, the shapes going down, the Chinese named Wing beside him then, the last two of Wing's men entering, Paul hearing the increased volume of firing.

"Cease fire!"

He shouted the command in English and Wing echoed it in Chinese.

The smoke was dense. But he could see another black shape, moving out of the smoke. He stabbed the Schmeisser toward it and his finger edged back to touch the trigger.

He didn't shoot. "Natalia!"

One of Wing's men started to fire and Paul knocked the submachinegun aside, a burst blowing into one of the seat backs, disintegrating it, Paul running forward into the smoke, the black shape gone from sight. He tripped over a body—it wasn't Natalia. "Natalia!"

And suddenly she was standing there. "I'm all right, Paul."

Paul hugged her against him.

There was apparently a public address system. Had there been one on the other train? He didn't remember.

The voice coming over it was either John's or Michael's voice. "The train will derail in less than five minutes, into the sea. Evacuate now. Evacuate now. Evacuate now."

Paul grabbed for the radio.

"John! I got Natalia—John! Come in, John!"

"Paul," the voice came back. "Do like Michael said on the PA—get out. I'm going after the warheads. Get out fast. You don't have to run. If the warheads go—Look—tell Natalia I love her, old friend. Rourke out."

"John! Come in, John! John! Damnit, John!"

No voice came back.

Paul Rubenstein looked at Natalia.

She was reloading her revolvers. "The boxcar up ahead?"

"Yes."

"Let's go, then."

Paul Rubenstein only nodded . . .

The wind seemed somehow stronger now and he was so cold his arms and legs barely responded, but getting rid of the coat was necessary. He had crossed the first car, jumped to the second and was half way across as he looked to his left, toward the sea. The curve that would precipitate the derailment couldn't be much further ahead now.

The wind buffeted him, throwing him forward, to his knees. He was up again, moving, the end of the car nearly in sight. There were small doors on each end of the boxcar, but whoever was inside it would expect attack from the front or rear of the car.

Falling again, he crawled the last few yards to the edge of the car, forcing himself to stand, the wind hammering at his back. He thought of the old Irish proverb about "May the wind be always at your back"; but was never meant like this.

He jumped, the wind actually making it easier to jump from one roof to another, but making it easier to fall as well — he hit the surface hard, starting to slip, the boxcar roof windslick, but he splayed his hands and arms out and held on. He started crawling, then got to his knees and then struggled to his feet, toward the center of the long boxcar's roof.

The wind was robbing him of breath and as at last he reached the center of the roof, collapsing to his knees, he had to cover his mouth against the wind so he could breathe.

The plastique in one of the musette bags.

He searched the bag and found the remaining segments.

Rourke placed them in a circle approximately six feet in diameter around him. There were not enough detonators.

He narrowed the hole's diameter to three feet, spacing the detonators one into every other segment, just barely getting them close enough together that he thought it would work. He had no idea of how many men might be below him inside the boxcar, but he told himself it couldn't be too many.

And what choice was there, he thought.

He crawled forward of the circle of charges, knowing that it would be easier to move rearward on the car when the time came because of the wind.

He flattened himself along the boxcar's roof and drew the Metalifed and Mag-na-Ported Colt Python. He levelled the revolver toward the furthest of the charges which contained a detonator. There were four detonators and eight charges all told.

He fired, shifted the muzzle, fired, the first explosion rocking him away, Rourke nearly losing his balance as he rolled right, catching himself, the second explosion coming, firing the Python, then again, the third and fourth explosions coming, the gaping hole in the roof of the boxcar visible now. He thrust the Python into the leather as he made it to his feet, running, vaulting up and dropping feet first through the hole into the interior of the boxcar. He crashed downward, onto crates, he realized—the warheads. He rolled clear, both Detonics Scoremasters coming into his hands, already cocked and locked, his thumbs sweeping down the ambidextrous safeties.

Black uniformed KGB Elite Corps personnel surrounded him and he fired, again and again, and again hearing a voice, "John! Take cover!"

Natalia's voice. He threw himself left and away from the crates of warheads, the roar of Paul's German MP-40 submachinegun, sharp reports of Natalia's matched .357s.

He was up to his knees. Seven bodies of KGB Elite Corps

personnel formed a ragged circle around him.

And he heard another voice. Russian accented, the voice a rich baritone. "I am Colonel Ivan Krakovski, Doctor Rourke." The man was average height, trim but not extraordinarily well built handsome featured. In his hands were two wires. "When I touch together these wires, one of the warheads will detonate and that will be enough to detonate them all. I am the man who will end the world. You should know that."

If Rourke fired, the wires could still touch as the madman died.

"John?" It was Paul's voice.

Krakovski's hands moved.

John Rourke hurtled the empty Scoremasters from his hands, his left hand moving to the sheath on the left side of his belt, his fingers popping the snap from the safety strap, his right hand tearing free the twelve-inch bladed Crain knife, his right hand coming down as the wires came together, the knife's primary edge finding flesh and bone and the Russian colonel's right hand severing, blood spurting everywhere as the Russian shrieked in agony, Rourke shouting, "Kill him!" as Rourke threw his body down, the Schmeisser, Natalia's .357s, the roar of gunfire momentarily deafening.

In the next second, Rourke told himself he was alive.

In the next second he was up. "Out the boxcar door—now!"

He was to the door, Paul to it in the same second, the door hasped and padlocked shut from the inside, Rourke sheathing the knife as he stepped back. Natalia gestured Paul away, the P-38 in her right fist discharged twice, then twice more, then the lock falling away, Rubenstein knocking it clear of the hasp, freeing the hasp with the butt of the Schmeisser. Rourke threw the sliding door open, grabbing Natalia to him, folding her into his arms.

Snow, beneath it rocks, he knew, beyond it the sea.

Hugging her body against him to protect her, he threw himself over, seeing a blur as Paul followed them, Rourke impacting the snow with his right shoulder and arms, rolling, losing Natalia, rolling, his legs scissoring outward, stopping the roll, Natalia rolling past him, Rourke reaching for her. Paul was several yards further ahead.

"Paul!"

He didn't know if the younger man could hear him over the roar of the train and the keening of the wind.

But Paul waved back. Rourke was to his knees, peering ahead through the swirling snow, He stood, Natalia suddenly beside him.

The train.

As John Rourke had worked his way toward the boxcar, he had seen everyone jumping clear, Michael among the last of them.

His eyes rivetted on the train. The curve. The train seemed to hesitate for an instant, as if somehow a living thing and determining its fate.

And then the engine jumped the track, tearing the two passenger cars, the boxcar loaded with Chinese warheads and dead maniacs, the two remaining passenger cars, tearing them from the track, vaulting over a rock ledge, lurching upward, the train seeming to jackknife over the leaping foam tipped waves, then collapsing as if all its energy were spent, into the sea.

If the warheads would go, they would go quickly.

He hadn't seen how they were packed.

He held Natalia close against him, his lips touching her hair.

The train disappeared beneath the surface.

The icy wind tore at him and he held her closer. He could see Paul Rubenstein limping toward them, looking behind him toward the submerged train.

They waited there, the cold something there was no time to feel.

251

And after a time, John Rourke kissed Natalia's mouth lightly and said to her and to Paul Rubenstein, "What do you say we go find ourselves some coats. And then what do you say we have a drink. But first," and he raised his face toward the sky, now still falling, filling his eyelashes. But he was alive to feel it. "Thank you," he said, then turned his eyes back to the earth.

JERRY AHERN

SURVIVALIST 14: The Terror

After everything, after the Night of the War, after the Great Conflagration and the Awakening, it had come down to this.

Revenge. One man on an utterly personal mission, ice cold in his grief.

And in spite of the Doomsday Machinery, the thermo-nuclear devices and the futuristic technology of war, the weaponry he selected for his man hunt in the desert was also very personal.

Trained by his CIA-trained weapons and survival expert father, John, Michael Rourke prepared himself with care. In the double shoulder harness were his twin Beretta 92-Fs. At his waist the modified Milt Sparks magazine four pack. And the knife.

Bowie-patterned, the blade was nine inches long, two inches wide, hand ground, sand blasted, the handle hollow, machined from a solid block of steel. Holes drilled in the double quillion style guard allowed it to be lashed to a pole, turned into a spear. This was a very particular, very lethal instrument of revenge.

Now he was ready for the hunt.

NEW ENGLISH LIBRARY

GEORGE G. GILMAN

Edge 55: Uneasy Riders

She was one of those Liberating Women.

Right now it was horses she was trying to liberate. Two of them, rightfully the property of the lawmen who'd just awakened the man called Edge and told him that *his* horse had been liberated by a night-time thief who'd been liberated from Nebraska's Carlsburg Penitentiary by his brothers-in-outlawry.

Altogether too much liberation going on.

Edge looked at the woman. She'd ambushed them like a man, handled a rifle like a man. Was dressed in a man's clothes — tho' she filled them just like a woman.

There and then he decided that this Woman's Movement had to be stopped in its tracks. Stopped dead if necessary.

NEW ENGLISH LIBRARY

GEORGE G. GILMAN

Steele 44: Code of the West

Maybe this was the new West. Adam Steele, elegant in cream suit and white satin shirt, a high gloss on his fancy boots, riding into town to consult with his banker.

Steele passing the work crew from the Telegraph Company, stringing the wire between the newly erected roadside poles, bringing the new age of instant communication.

But maybe the old West is still around. When a young girl's brutal rape can stampede an old-style lynch mob into action. When instant communication is replaced with sudden death. When not telegraph wire but an innocent man is set to be strung up.

NEW ENGLISH LIBRARY

MORE FICTION FROM
HODDER AND STOUGHTON PAPERBACKS

JERRY AHERN

GEORGE G. GILMAN
EDGE SERIES

STEELE SERIES

All these books are available at your local bookshop or newsagent, or can be ordered direct from the publisher. Just tick the titles you want and fill in the form below.

Prices and availability subject to change without notice.

Hodder and Stoughton Paperbacks, P.O. Box 11, Falmouth, Cornwall.

Please send a cheque or postal order, and allow the following for postage and packing:

UK: – 55p for one book, plus 22p for the second book, and 14p for each additional book ordered up to a £1.75 maximum.

B.F.P.O. and EIRE – 55p for the first book, plus 22p for the second book, and 14p per copy for the next 7 books, 8p per book thereafter.

OTHER OVERSEAS CUSTOMERS - £1.00 for the first book, plus 25p per copy for each additional book.

Name ....

Address ....

....